SHUNNED AGAIN

Shunned Again

JEANNETTE KRUPA

TATE PUBLISHING
AND **ENTERPRISES**, LLC

Published by Tate Publishing & Enterprises, LLC
127 E. Trade Center Terrace | Mustang, Oklahoma 73064 USA
1.888.361.9473 | www.tatepublishing.com

Tate Publishing is committed to excellence in the publishing industry. The company reflects the philosophy established by the founders, based on Psalm 68:11,
"The Lord gave the word and great was the company of those who published it."

Book design copyright © 2016 by Tate Publishing, LLC. All rights reserved.
Cover design by Dante Rey Redido
Interior design by Richell Balansag

Published in the United States of America

ISBN: 978-1-68301-557-4
1. Fiction / Amish & Mennonite
2. Fiction / Christian / Romance
16.01.25

I'd like to dedicate this book in loving memory of
my husband, Christopher Krupa,
who passed away on January 11th 2016,
and my dad, Owen Conely,
who passed away on November 25th 2015
They both will be greatly missed.
Heaven has received two big men in my life.

Contents

1

Shunned Again

Although Samuel was never the ideal husband for Katie in her mind, he was the one whom her parents had chosen for her to marry. Katie would talk with her friend Emily about the kind of husband she would want if the pick in was up to her. Never having the choice in the matter of how old or what kind of man she would marry, she would fantasize, while scrubbing the floors, about Robert Culbert, a young man who was not of the Amish faith. She had met him while sneaking away from her chores and taking a walk in the cornfield. Robert found a sudden attraction to Katie when he first met her, as did she to him. Katie had a smile that warmed the hearts of those around her, and that was one of the first things that Robert noticed about her.

As the two started to talk, he also took a liking to her shyness and the way she would tilt her head when talking with him. Robert being an outsider from the world that Katie was familiar to, she knew that she mustn't continue to talk of him or keep the feelings that she felt stirring inside her. But she was overcome by her feelings, and wanted to know everything about this young man, although it was forbidden for her to even converse with him. She told him that she was Amish and that she was a young woman of the Plain, and she was not allowed to talk with Englishmen. Robert, being a young man of seventeen, was not sure why he was not allowed to talk with Katie. What kind of religion would stop a fifteen-year-old girl from talking with a seventeen-year-old man?

While swinging on her porch at evening time with the lantern nearby to shine a light, Katie thought about her feelings which she had had when she first met Robert, the warm feelings she would get whenever she thought of him. Oh, she knew that she was never going to meet him again, but the very thought of him would burn deep into her very soul following the next several days.

"I haven't been able to let myself stop thinking about that boy I met in the corn the other day," Katie told Emily.

"Now, Katie Yoder, what has gotten into you? You know, as well as I, the teaching of the elders. We must never turn our backs against God and the elders," Emily scolded her.

"But isn't God a God who loves everyone, both the Amish and the English?" She insisted on getting some answers. "Why must they choose for us, Emily? I can't help my thinking. I do know that I have no feelings for Samuel, and I don't care to marry him."

"Katie, that is blasphemy to talk like that. You must marry him without any impure thoughts of him beforehand, not to mention anyone else. I'm not too sure if he would be willing to marry you if he knew that you were talking about him like this. If the bishop was to hear this come from you, then you could be shunned for the very talk of it all," she warned her.

"Then that would be all right by me," Katie said as she turned her back on her friend.

"If anyone was to get wind of this talk coming from you, Katie, I'm afraid that you would be shunned."

"Shunned." Katie turned to look at her friend.

"Yes, Katie, shunned. You know, as well as I, our teaching. I have seen where someone else was shunned for a whole lot less than the talk that you've been doing."

"Like who?" she asked, knowing well that the name cannot ever be mentioned again.

"Oh, Katie, you know we cannot speak their names."

"Then I will," she stammered.

"No, Katie, it is not right of you to do this." Emily looked around to see if anyone was in earshot of hearing what Katie was about to speak.

"I know Hezekiah is one that has left the teachings, as well as Micah." After she spoke the names of two Amish young men who have left the teachings of the Amish, Emily turned her back on Katie and ran away from her. "Emily, come back," Katie yelled. "I'm sorry. Please come back, Em." Katie, feeling so alone at the time, watched her friend run down the path that led to her home a mile down from hers. Katie stood still watching until she could no longer see Emily anymore.

"Now I have just lost the only best friend I have in all the world," she spoke to herself while walking back toward her home, which was up on a hill. Kicking up the dust with her left foot as she walked looking down on the ground, she did not notice someone walking in her path, coming toward her.

"Hi, I was wondering if I was ever going to see you again," a deep voice spoke.

Katie stopped dead in her tracks, just before her foot was about to kick him. "It's Robert, isn't it?" She had the smile that he remembered so well come across her face. Katie felt her heart begin to beat faster than she had ever felt before, knowing that he was the only person on her mind for the last couple of days.

"You remembered," he spoke with a big smile forming across his face. "I was hoping that we'd run into each other again."

"You were?" she asked, trying not to sound too excited to see him again.

"Yes, I had hoped every day since that first day meeting you. I was wondering why you said that it wasn't right for us to talk with each other. I tried making sense out of it, but I can't."

Katie looked around to see if there might be anyone in the near distance who would be able to see her talking with an outsider. After not seeing anyone near, she felt that she could answer his question. "I don't remember if I told you that day that we met, but I am Amish, and we—well, I am not allowed to associate with someone who is not Amish."

"Yes, you did tell me that you were. I kind of figured it by the way that you dress," he said as he lightly touched her white sunbonnet. "I think this gave you away the other day."

"Yes, I guess it would have," she spoke in a soft, gentle voice as she herself reached up and touched her own bonnet.

"So what do you think about you and I going somewhere where no one will see that we are talking with each other?"

Although Katie knew that what she was being asked from Robert was wrong, she just couldn't help what she was feeling. It stirred up inside her once again upon seeing him. It was like her smelling the roses as she would pass by the old mill on her way to Emily's place. It was there for the smelling for anyone who walked by them. Oftentimes, she felt like picking the flowers and making a bouquet out of them and bringing them home; but she knew if they were not hers, then smelling them as she walked by would just have to do.

"We can go to that old mill on the path over that a ways," she spoke, pointing toward where she was just coming from.

"Can you go there now so we can talk without you having to keep looking over your shoulder the whole time I'm talking with you?"

Katie knew that what she was about to say could cause her to be shunned from her people and her family. Everything that she had ever loved and cared for could be taken away from her. And what about her marriage to Samuel? Although she never wanted to marry him in the first place, it was in the order that she would become his bride at the age of sixteen. She was going to be sixteen in five months and seven days, and on that day, she would become Mrs. Samuel Hershberger.

"I have to go home now, but later at nightfall, I will be there."

"What time is that, Katie?" he asked when she started to walk away.

Turning back to face him—her mind swirling with the very thought of being alone with him but telling her to get out of there before she was to do something she might regret—she spoke what she wanted. "I'll meet you at sundown."

"Okay, at sundown." He looked at the watch he had on his wrist to see how much longer he would have to wait before seeing her again. It said half past twelve. He knew that in about six hours, he would get to see her again. He stood on the same spot from where she left him, watching her walk down a narrow path. He could see where the horse and buggies have gone down that same path many times over, where there was an imprint of the wheels on the ground. He couldn't understand why people who could drive a vehicle of some kind would choose to walk or ride horse and buggy all the time? He would admit riding a horse and buggy at times would be fun, but for it to be your only transportation, it could get boring real fast.

⁓

Katie went home and started on her afternoon chores. She didn't want anything to keep her from seeing Robert that evening. Her only hope was that whatever was causing her to be drawn to him, it would be worth her while. She just couldn't bear the thought of being shunned for something that she felt she had no control over. It was like a force being pulled inside her, making her want to be with him. She couldn't understand that kind of force. She had never had that happen to her before. She had thought when she was thirteen years old that she would later marry Jacob Miller, a young man she thought she would be promised to. But it just so happened that he was to marry Ruth Schrock, his second cousin. She would not have been against marring him if that was to be. She liked Jacob; he was more her own age. Samuel, being several years older than her, was married before to a woman by the name of Anna, who died giving birth to their child who also died at birth. The family thought it best that she marry Samuel and not Jacob.

Katie tried to put everything that she had been taught behind her so it wouldn't interfere with her and Robert later. She knew that the two of them came from two different worlds, and she didn't want to seem like she knew nothing of his world. She tried to rehearse what she would say to him, what kind of questions she would ask him, as well as what she thought that he might ask her. She would play over and over in her head things that she wanted to know about him, things that she wanted to know about his way of living compared to the Amish ways—just in case she was ever shunned, she would know what to expect in the outside world.

Katie was so busy working and thinking about what it would be like to be with Robert that she didn't realize it was almost time to meet him. When she heard the supper bell, which hung on the front porch, ringing, she knew that it was getting to be that time. Dropping everything in hand and running to the house so she could swallow down what was placed before her before heading to the mill, she nearly tripped over her own two feet trying to get there.

"Katie, what is your hurry? You must have worked up some appetite to run as you did," Katie's mother, Mary, stated.

"Yes, I did. I'm very hungry. I'd like to go for a walk after I eat, if I may."

Her mother looked her way, wondering the reason behind the sudden change of action of her daughter wanting to go for a walk in the evening time. This was not like Katie to go off when darkness was to set in. Mary didn't understand why she wanted to walk and not swing on the porch like she did most every evening.

"This is not like you, Katie girl, to go off in the night hours."

"No, Mama, it's not, but I wanted a small change from the porch swing. I thought if it be all right with you, I may go just for a little while. I promise not to be out late."

"Your father is not here right now, so I will speak in his place and say you may go."

"Oh, thank you, Mama. I won't be out late," she said as she shoved the last bite of bread in her mouth, and she was out the door.

As Katie ran down the long path to get to the mill to meet up with the young man whom she had spent every waking moment thinking about since the first day she met him days earlier, she had many thoughts coming in her mind. *Am I doing the right thing going against God and the teachings of the elders? I just can't marry Samuel. He's not the man that I dream about. Oh God, I hope that I don't get caught tonight with Robert.*

As she began to get closer to the mill, she slowed down so she wouldn't be out of breath before seeing him. Approaching slowly while looking around to make sure that no one was coming down the pathway of the mill, she edged her way into the open door on the side of the mill. She looked around as the dim light shined just enough to see if there was someone standing right in front of her. She called for Robert, but no one answered. She told herself that she would wait for just one more minute, and if he didn't show up, then she would go back home with the thoughts that he didn't want to get caught with a Plain girl.

She found an old bucket to sit down on while she waited for him. Then everything went dark. She woke up sometime later in the dark and did not know right away where she was until she gathered her wits. She remembered she was to meet Robert at the mill. Picking herself up off the dirty floor and looking around, feeling unclean and sore all over, she found that her lantern had been broken. She wondered what could have taken place to cause her to be on the dirty floor, asleep and feeling pain, as if she had been with a man for the first time. But how could she have? She had never known a man before to feel this way. She felt light-headed as she stood up, looking around for the door. She could see there was some light barely peeking through as she tried to walk out, holding on the sides of the doorframe. She could see that the sun was coming up.

How long have I been here? she asked herself. *What happened to me? Is anyone out looking for me and wondering where I might be?* Katie started to walk home, which seemed miles away from her now; but in all reality, it was just about a half mile away.

Walking slowly as to keep her balance up the hill, she tried not to fall. *Why did Robert not show up? Why did I pass out? I've never passed out before. My mother must be so worried for me. I better get home and get cleaned up before they see the likes of me. Maybe they haven't realized that I haven't been home all night*. Katie realized that it was the next morning when she saw the sun rising up from the east.

She knew that everyone at her home would be getting up soon, and she wanted to get home before that happened. She tried picking up her pace a little, but every time she did that, she would feel all sore, like something just was not right, so she would walk slower but steady.

As she now stood on top of the hill that led to her home, it looked to her as though she had gotten there before anyone else was up. She wasn't sure if anyone had noticed that she didn't come home last night, and she sure was not going to mention anything about it, not even to Emily. She wasn't even sure if she still had Emily as her friend, nor if she wanted her as a friend.

Katie quickly went out back to the washtub and began to scrub herself clean as a whistle. After she felt that she had gotten herself to look her best, she went into the back door and walked very quietly to her bedroom in hopes of no one hearing a sound from her.

She changed into clean clothes and took her dirty clothes to the washtub and began to scrub the bloodstains out of them to hang them before she was noticed. Unsure of the time, she finished without being seen. In a hurry, she climbed onto her bed as if nothing had ever taken place and stayed still until her mother came to wake her for her chores to begin.

"Get up, Katie girl. Morning awaits us."

"Okay, I'm getting up," she answered with a pretend stretching of her arms as if just to be waking up. *Mother must not know that I have not really been to bed at all. I sure hope that no one had seen me coming from that old mill.*

"How was your rest, Katie girl?"

"It was very good, Mama." Katie felt guilty for telling a lie, but she hoped that her ma wasn't asking because she knew that she was out all night.

"I'll be home again late tonight. Brother John and I will be taking a load of wheat over to the other side of town today," Katie's father, Isaac, interjected while Katie and her ma were talking.

After Isaac had walked out, Katie began to clean up the dishes and wash them. Her mother began to do the sweeping.

"Katie, we must wash the floor in the great room today. It has been undone far too long now."

"I thought that we just did it a week ago now."

Her mother stood still, as if thinking her daughter was right about the timing of washing the floor. "Yes, you are right, Katie, but I think that it might need it again, yuh?"

"Yes, Mama, I guess we can do that then. When are we going to start on a new rug? I've been saving all the old clothes for it."

"Maybe tomorrow we can ask some of the other women if they would want to help us."

"Ask who, Mama?" Katie wanted to know if one of them would be Emily. She was hoping not because she was very afraid that Emily just might mention about the talk they had. She felt that Em was mad as spitfire at her to the point where she would tell others of their talk.

"I thought that it might be nice if we ask the Troyer women if they would want to come and join us."

"I don't know if Emily would care to help us." As soon as those words fell out of her mouth, she regretted them.

"Oh, why is that, Katie? Did you and her have a falling-out?"

"No, we never had a falling-out. I just thought that she might be busy doing their own rug is all."

"Katie, I will start on washing the floor, and you go see the Troyers and ask them if they care to come join us."

Katie didn't want to go. She didn't want to pass by the old mill that was on its way. She had never felt that way before. It was really quite opposite of that. She had always liked walking by there and smelling the roses that was grown outside it. But now something was different, and she felt different about it, almost like in fear to pass by that place. She was unsure of what took place the night before, and even if she wanted to know why Robert never showed up, she had no way of ever finding out unless she was to see him again, which she felt she probably never would.

"Katie, you can go now," her mother scolded her, watching her just stand there.

"Okay."

Katie headed out the door and down the path toward Emily's house, walking very slow, keeping her eyes wide open in case she saw something that just was not right. As she began to get closer to the mill, she walked over to the far-left side of the path, almost putting herself into the field just so she could avoid walking by it. Looking over toward it, hoping that no one would come running out after her, she wasn't sure why she was so scared all of a sudden. All she knew was that something happened to her inside the mill, causing her to pass out and not remember anything. She stood on the front porch at Emily's house, trying to decide whether to knock or not. After standing there for what seemed to be a lifetime, Emily came to the door.

"Katie, what brings you here this morning?"

"My mother would like to know if you women of the house would like to come to our home tomorrow to help in the making of a rug."

"Come in, Katie. I'll go ask my ma."

Katie stood in the kitchen while Emily went into another room to ask her mother. Katie was hoping that they had other plans of their own.

"Hello, Katie, how are you this fine morning?"

"I'm fine, Mrs. Troyer." Katie never seemed to care for Emily's ma very much. The woman had always seemed to be much stricter than Katie's own ma—and that was pretty strict.

"So it seems to be that time of the year has come upon us once again for us womenfolk to be putting our hands to some good use braiding rugs, hey?"

"Yes, it seems to be." Although Katie could be a long talker at times, she sure wasn't going there with Mrs. Troyer. Short and sweet was Katie's model in life for the ones she didn't have a liking to.

"Is there something wrong, Katie? You appear to be in a quiet time now."

"I didn't get much rest the night of last."

"Why not? My Emily is made to go to bed just after sundown, so she may rise up early come morning. It will be hard for you, Katie girl, to be a proper wife to Samuel if you don't rise before him and have your wife duties going." The older woman was staring into Katie's deep blue eyes as if to see if she could find something wrong about her. "Tell your mother that we will be over come morning."

"Okay, I will. Bye." Katie was out the door and headed down the pathway going home. She wanted to get away from the stare she was getting from Mrs. Troyer. It had always seemed to her that the woman was just looking for something bad to find in her.

When she got home, she told her ma about the Troyer women coming to help come morning. Katie knew that she had clothes still out on the line, and she didn't want her ma to see them there, so she went outside to the line to check and see if they were dry. Squeezing them to see for any dampness that they might still have, Katie pulled them from the line and tucked them under her dress to take them in her bedroom. She figured a little dampness couldn't hurt much. She would just leave them out of her dresser for the time being.

Going back to the living room to help with the scrubbing of the floor, she listened as her ma talked about the making of the rug come morning. Katie knew that every year, the womenfolk came together and helped one another get a rug done. If only it could be some other ladies and not the Troyers. She knew that, come morning, she was going to do all her braiding at the opposite side of the room to keep her clear from Mrs. Troyer.

"Ma, to where will the rug we are set to make this year be going?"

"I thought since the one we made the year last was for this room, the one we start tomorrow will be for your room."

"Oh, thank you, Ma. I would really like that."

"Now, I remind you that you have your upcoming to Samuel, and that will be yours for the taking." She was smiling proudly about her daughter becoming a bride in just a few months.

Katie wanted the very thoughts of becoming Samuel's wife just to fade away. She knew that she had no choice in the matter, unless she was to run into Robert and ask him why he didn't show up at the mill then ask him to marry her and take her away from being told whom she is to marry.

Although she knew that rugs were nice to have under the feet, she hated to have to make them every year. She never understood, even with all her teaching, why her people didn't drive cars like everyone else. Even though there were some Amish who did that, she was not included in that group. Why make a rug when you can go to the store and buy one, like the English do? Whenever Katie was in town, she would look all around to try and see for herself what the Englishmen and women lived like. She would often dream of a life being able to do such things as driving a car or walking with her long brown hair flowing down her back without having to tie it up and cover it with a bonnet.

Katie wondered what it would be like to wear such clothes as pants and a T-shirt, like she had seen so many of the English women do. What was it like to go to their kind of school, to have electricity in their home, to have running water, even to take hot baths or shower whenever needed? If she were to marry Samuel, would he ever leave the teachings of the elders and become part of the English people for her? No, he would not!

"And I don't care to marry a man who wants to stay living in this kind of lifestyle. I won't. I just won't marry him," she told herself out loud. "I will make a plan so I won't have to marry him. But what? What can I do?" Katie went into making plans that would keep Samuel from wanting to be her husband. "But first, before I do that, I will have to work on the making of the rug today and get that out of the way. Then I can begin my plan."

Katie stood in the living room, hearing her ma welcoming in the others to begin the braiding of the rug. She listened as she overheard her ma telling Emily where she was.

"Hello, Katie girl. I trust that you have come to your senses by now and have that young Englishman out of your mind," Emily whispered as she walked up to Katie.

"Nah, I haven't quite been able to, but you are sounding more like your ma every time I see you."

"And you, Katie, sound more like the English every time I see you. Can we not talk if we can't be nice to each other?"

"Here are some clothes." Katie handed some over to her. Then she turned and walked away to sit at the other side of the room.

The women worked for eight hours that day on ripping up their old clothes into strips so they could braid them together. After it was all said and done, they had a finished rug with a nice length, with more colors of black and gray than any other.

2

A Time Past

Katie met a stranger in town when she went to watch the outsiders again. She was hoping to have a run-in with Robert, but she found herself talking with a man by the name of Roy. He was a tall man who had balding hair. Although young in age, he was quite attractive. Katie felt the attraction to him right away, yet she was ashamed to admit it. She came here to find Robert and to watch how the English lived. She felt that she needed to know everything there was to know, just in case she was to be shunned and would be made to eat at a separate table from the rest of the family, when she would tell her parents that she wished not to marry Samuel. Although her parents knew Katie's heart in the matter, they told her that love follows afterward. But no matter what they called love, she knew that she was completely in love with Robert and that the attraction she was having for this complete stranger was no more than him being an Englishman and Katie liking the English ways.

Walking away from the stranger, who felt like he wanted to know her more—and she did with him in many ways—she felt it sin against Robert, although she and Robert did not have ties that bound them together.

Sitting on a bench in front of the market store, Katie heard someone whispering about her; and turning her head to see who it could be, she noticed two small boys laughing at her. "Is there things that are funny to ya? I don't see them, but maybe you'd like to point them out to me, yuh?" she told them.

The boys took off running, as if she was going to chase them down and kill them. Katie knew that they must have not seen many of her people around for them to behave in such a way. It didn't really bother her. She would have liked to talk with them in hopes that they might know Robert. Maybe if she could have talked to them in a different manner, she could have found out what she was looking for.

Just as Katie was about to give up, she heard a voice that she had come to know—not in reality as much as she would have liked, but in her thoughts. "Robert," she called out.

Turning his head to see who called out to him and noticing it was Katie, he suddenly became frightened. Without saying a word, he headed in the opposite direction of her.

Katie, not understanding why he would do such a thing, ran after him. "Robert, did I do something that might have hurt you? Why did you not show up when we were to meet?"

Robert stopped dead in his tracks. "What are you talking about?" he asked her with a look of unbelief written all over his face.

"The last time that I talked with you, you said that we were going to meet. Don't you even remember what we talked about?"

Robert stood there almost like he was dumbfounded with what she was talking about. Then he found words to speak. "Yeah, sure, I remember now. Yeah, I couldn't make it. I had some things to do. But hey, it was nice to see you again, I got to go now. Bye." Without giving her a chance to say anything to him, he turned his back and was headed down the street, never looking back.

Katie couldn't believe what she had just witnessed for herself. She had spent every waking moment thinking about this young man, whom she thought she knew. Was she ever wrong at what she believed? Maybe her upbringing wasn't all that bad after all. *Look at how the Englishmen act*, she thought to herself. She had never known an Amish man doing that to someone they were supposed to care for. She walked back to her home with a heart that felt like it was just betrayed. She had thought that Robert shared her feelings. Now she could see that what she had been dreaming about for well over a month was just one-sided.

When Katie returned home, all she wanted to do was sleep. She felt so depressed about Robert not caring for her as she did him. All she thought about in her spare time when she was not working was how she wanted to be like the English. Now, after this and how her heart felt sick, she wasn't as sure as before. She would tell her ma that she was not feeling well and needed to lie down, in hopes that she would not be questioned.

Katie laid down thinking that it would be for just a few minutes like she told her ma, but those few minutes turned into hours, until her ma came to wake her.

"Katie girl, you have slept well into the day. It is time to come and eat. Your father and Samuel will be coming in to join us. Come, Katie, I expect Samuel will want you to join us." Mary stood there for a few moments before going on, waiting to see if Katie would respond; but after seeing no movement come from her daughter, she walked to her bedside and gave her a little shake. "Katie, come. It's time for our men to come home to eat."

Katie opened her eyes at the words she heard from her ma—*our men*. Ugh, how she hated to hear Samuel being called her man. "I'm up, Ma. I'll be right down."

"I don't know what has happened with you lately, Katie, but I expect it must be with your upcoming marriage to Samuel that has got you so worn out with all the planning and such."

Katie sat up, looking at her ma as she was closing the bedroom door. *My marriage to a man whom I don't even like, let alone being married to him*, she thought. Standing up and walking to the mirror to make herself presentable before going downstairs, Katie felt discomfort in her belly as she walked. Placing her hand on her stomach, she wondered why she was having a discomfort that she had never felt before. Ignoring it, she fussed with her bonnet and tucked the few strands of hair that came out of it while she slept back into it. She walked downstairs to help with what she could to have the meal set for the men.

"Katie," her ma asked.

"Yes, Ma, what is it?" she asked, facing her ma.

"Is there something that I should be told by you?"

"No, Ma. Why do you ask?" Katie asked.

"You look pale, my Katie girl. Are you sure that you are not holding something from me?" She looked at her daughter with pleading in her eyes. "Please, Katie, it would be for my ears only."

Katie, shocked by what she had just heard her ma say, looked at her. "What?"

"If there is anything you wish to tell me, it would be for my ears only. I would not say a word to another."

Katie heard her ma the first time, but she knew that it was unlike her ma to have said that to her. It was not for the Amish women to ever withhold anything in secret from their husband. Oh, how Katie wanted to open up and tell her ma that she had no desire in her heart for Samuel and she wished not to marry him. But how could she? It was not her choice. Just as she was ready to open her mouth and tell her ma something that should never be mentioned to another, Samuel and her father walked into the house. Her ma gave her an eye that said, *We will talk later.* Mary turned around, placing the last bowl on the table before sitting down to join the men.

As the family took a hold of one another's hands to bless the food, Samuel gave Katie's a light squeeze, which made her pull back her hand from his, causing the rest of the sitters to look at her behavior.

"Katie, is there a reason for your behavior?" her father asked with his eyes staring deep into her very soul.

"No, Da. I was just stunned. I'm sorry, Samuel. I didn't mean any harm to ya." She looked at him for just a moment then turned her eyes down to her bowl.

"Oh, that's quite all right. I like to see the woman whom I am to marry not willing just to let a touch go on before marriage." He gave her a smile.

After the eating was finished, Samuel asked Katie if she cared to walk outside to have a talk. She was reluctant at first, but seeing that her father was watching her very closely, she chose to walk out with him.

"What is it, Samuel?"

"Katie, I know that we are to marry here in just a few months, so I thought that we might want to know each other in words beforehand. I know that you are young, Katie, and this is all new for you. I would rather you talk to me about something that is on your mind about the marriage than to wait afterward."

Shocked again by what she was hearing, she said, "Really?"

"Yes, I am not like all those others, Katie, that we know. I am willing for us to talk beforehand if you feel like you need to. I've been watching you, and I know that you have not always liked the way of the Amish. Am I telling the truth?"

Unsure of just what he was implying, she wanted to know more before opening up on her feeling of things. "I'm not quite sure of what you are saying."

"Katie, do you want to marry me, or is there someone else you have in mind whom you would rather marry?"

"Oh, Samuel, must we speak of these things now?" Katie said as she knew well that marrying Samuel was not the one she had in mind. But how would she tell him that? What about her folks and what the elders had planned for her?

"I feel that between us, Katie, we can have this talk. I know that it's not something that we are to talk of or mention beforehand, but I don't always agree with all the teachings and customs of the Amish."

Katie was very unsure if she was being tested by this man who was to be her husband if her father had his way. Or was he being sincere about really wanting to talk with her about her feelings? Being unsure of his real intentions, she kept silent at first.

"Do you not want to have this talk with me? Am I so much older than thou that you don't seem to want to communicate with me? Or is it just me altogether, Katie?"

"Samuel, I am unsure of what you are asking of me. I have never known any man who will have a talk with the one they are to marry like this before."

Samuel put his head down, like he was in thought. "Katie, I told thee once that I don't always agree with all the teaching. There are some things that I believe should be allowed between two people."

After seeing the way he was behaving, she felt as though she could trust that he really wanted to talk. So she figured it was time to open up and have a talk with him. "I believe that two people who are to marry should talk beforehand also. What is it that you would like for us to talk about?" she asked, still feeling a little afraid to fully open up.

"I would like for you to tell me what your thoughts are of marrying me, Katie."

Surprised by his bluntness, she stumbled on her words. "Er...awe...well, to be quite honest, Samuel, I have always thought that when I would marry, it would be to someone I love, and—"

Before she finished, he interjected. "It's all right to speak your mind, Katie. I know that many women want to know love before marrying someone. This is where I feel that we are wrong with our teachings, among some of the others."

"Like what others?" she asked, surprised to hear him talk like this.

Samuel looked around to make sure they were not in hearing range of another before going on, "Can I just be honest with you, Katie, and it not go any further than us right here?"

"Yes, please do, Samuel." Katie's eyes widened. She wanted to know just how this man she was to marry really felt. She wanted to know if he was anything like her thoughts of a husband ought to be.

"I want to hear music, Katie." Before going on with anything more, he looked at her to see what her reactions were. Much to his surprise, it was what he was hoping for.

"Me too. I go into town at times just to hear the music coming from the stores." After she said that, she wondered if she spoke too much.

"I would also like to have indoor plumbing, but I just can't see how that is going to happen when we have menfolk and women come over to see that we are following the teaching of the Amish."

Katie was unsure of what to think at this time. All she knew was that her Samuel was not the man she had always thought him to be. There was so much more to him. So much of what he expressed was what Katie had always thought she wanted in life. Now she was left sitting on the porch swing, wondering if he would ever leave the teachings of the Amish ways. Would he ever walk away from what he had always known to truly be happy elsewhere?

"If we were to be allowed plumbing on the inside, that truly would be much more of a blessing, yuh?"

35

"Yes, it would, but this must not go any further than us, Katie."

"I won't reveal it, Samuel, but I should say that much of what you are saying, I have dreamt it to be for me. I don't agree with all the teaching either and often wonder just how as a wife and mother I will be someday."

"You don't see being a wife and mother with our teachings, Katie?"

"You said it yourself, Samuel, that you don't agree with it all. All I say is how I feel. I want to be able to marry with love and happiness and someday have a family. But, Samuel, when I look at how hard everything is to make a happy life, I have a hard time wanting that for my family."

"If you were to marry me, Katie, would you ever leave the Amish and become what we see the English ways are?"

Katie was in shock of what she was hearing. Never before has she ever heard of this talk with the Amish before. Yes, she had thought on the very same thing for at least two years now, but to have the one whom she is to marry just three months away make such an offer would be a dream of hers. But what about her ma and her da? She would never be able to see them again. Thinking about all these things were all right, but could she really walk away from it all when it came down to it?

"I have thought of this for a long time now, Samuel. I would love to dress like the English and have plumbing in my house, but what about my ma and da? You know, as well as I, the teachings."

"Yes, Katie, but I too would be walking away from what I have always known. This is why I felt the need to have this talk with you beforehand, Katie. I am hoping that you would walk away with me after marrying and begin a new life. This is my plan, Katie. I have thought long and hard about this."

"What would you do for a living, Samuel? Where would we live? And if this is something that you really want, then why marry me when there would be so much more to choose from among the English?"

"It is you that I have set my heart on, Katie. Oh, I know that your heart doesn't care for me in the same manner. But it will take some time. I am a patient man, Katie. That will come after marriage, if not beforehand. I can wait for it. I know that you are young, yah?" He looked at her.

For the first time, she saw something in his eyes that she had never seen before. She saw a man whom she could truly love and marry. For the first time since Robert, she saw a man who was saying all the right things that made her heart melt. Right now, at this very moment, all she wanted to do was kiss him and tell him that she was all his. But how could she? That was something that would have to wait until after marriage.

"That is nice of you to say, Samuel."

"I know that the hour is getting late, Katie. Can I call on you the morrow and we go for a walk in the cornfield or down the road for a talk?"

"Yes, Samuel, that would be nice." Katie gave him a smile that drew her to him even more than he already was. And without thinking beforehand, he reached out and touched her cheek with a light rub before walking away.

Katie felt chills of excitement run all through her veins. She stood on the porch as she watched this man whom she had misread for as long as she could remember walk away with, remembering all the time she wasted on a man who seemed to care at one time, then just walk away from her in town, she could have been getting to know the man whom she is to marry in just three months. While at one time she regretted the very thought of marrying him, now she was wishing that time would fly by so she could be all his. She went to bed with a new feeling of excitement for the morrow to come. She lay in bed dreaming of what life would be like living in the English world.

"Katie girl, it's time to rise and start your day," her mother was calling for her at the bottom of the stairs.

"Time to start my day?" Katie asked herself, looking toward the window and noticing that the light was beginning to shine through. "I must have fallen to sleep." She thought for a moment. "Oh, that's what I was thinking before falling to sleep—*Samuel*," she spoke just above a whisper with a smile crossing her face. Jumping out of her bed, she got ready to start her day. Remembering that she was to go for a walk with Samuel that evening gave her day of work a new meaning.

"You must have been very tired. I thought that you might not be feeling the best today, Katie girl."

"I feel fine, Ma. I was just tired," she said as she gave her ma the same sweet smile she gave to all the others.

"You appear to be in a good mood today. Are you ready to start your day of work?"

"Yes, ma'am, I am. I will go care for the chickens. Then I'll get some milk from old Betsy."

Her ma looked at her in complete amazement. Mary knew her daughter, and she knew that it was unlike her to give her work attention as quickly as she did today. What was it that made her so different today? Why the sudden change? She watched Katie as she put on her boots to head out to her chores. Standing next to the window, she watched as Katie skipped her way to the chicken coop.

"Here, chickie chick, come and get it," Katie called as she tossed the corn kernels on the ground for the chickens. After she fed the chicks, she went after old Betsy's milk to go with her morning breakfast. Today she felt different from the day before. It was a new day, and the things she had thought before about Samuel being a stick in the mud no longer was an issue for her. She now felt his heart, about how he was raised to believe and think, as much as hers.

Now she knew that if she was to marry him, she could feel free to leave the world she was accustomed to since birth and move to the English ways that she desired.

3

A Walk to Remember

The evening came for Katie to take her walk with Samuel. She wondered what she would say to her ma and da about the walk. She knew that it was not something her religion was accustomed to do before marriage.

"Ma, can I speak with you about Samuel and me?"

"Yah, Katie girl, speak your mind."

"Samuel and I talked with each other in the evening of last, and he thought that before marriage, we might want to have a walk and talk."

"Katie, do you know what you're asking?"

"Ma, it's not the same as it was before. Things change, Ma. Why can't we have a walk before marriage? How will we know if we like each other if we aren't permitted to talk?"

"Katie, that is blasphemy to speak of this. You musn't talk of such things before you are joined as one."

"Please, Ma, we must talk with each other."

"If your father was to hear of such talk, he might have you and Samuel go before the council. Now I will hear no more of this. You know the teachings as well as I."

Katie stood there with her arms now folded in the other, upset that her ma of all people wouldn't allow her to speak freely. She had thought that her ma would understand where she was coming from. Now how would she take her walk with the man she was to marry without her parents being aware of it? Would Samuel go along with her folks, or would he find a way to meet with Katie without her being found out? She tried to figure a way to get around it so she would not be caught by any members.

Katie planned a way to go on her walk as she cleaned inside the house. She could hardly wait to see Samuel when evening came. She never thought of Robert today, but maybe once he crossed her mind briefly—as quickly as he entered, he left. She was excited with the thought of marrying Samuel now more then ever. If only she gave him a chance before, she would never have wasted her time on wanting Robert, the man she thought wanted her as much as she wanted him.

Samuel showed up with her da to eat with the family. Much to Katie's surprise, it was her father who told her about the walk that Samuel wanted to take with her that evening.

"Samuel spoke with me about a walk he would like to take with you this evening. I told him that I give him and you permission to go."

"Thank you, Da," Katie said as she looked toward her ma. She couldn't believe that her freedom with Samuel was coming from her father and not her ma. As she looked at her ma, she could see the surprise look from her also.

"Shall we go on a stroll?" Samuel asked Katie as he held the door open for her after they ate.

"I won't be late," she told her folks as she disappeared behind the closed door of her home. "I'm very much surprised that my da allowed us the walk, Samuel. Did you have a talk with him before coming back to the house?"

"Yah, I asked him for the walk, telling him we needed to before getting married. And he agreed with me. I think partly because I was married before and you are young, Katie," he said as he took her hand to hold it when out of sight from her folks' home.

Katie didn't pull back this time when he touched her like she did the last time. She had a better understanding where things were between the two of them. She noticed that they were headed in the same direction as the old mill. When she looked ahead and saw the mill, chills ran down her spine to the point where she wanted to take a different way to walk, but she stayed on the same path as Samuel while still holding on to his hand. Although she was unsure of what took place the evening she was to meet Robert back over a month ago at the mill, she knew that whatever transpired there left her in fear of the place where, at one time, she loved to come and smell the flowers that surrounded it. How she wanted to tell Samuel of that evening and of her desire to live as the English did. She wanted to tell Samuel so much that she had fallen for an Englishman who had promised to meet her at the old mill and when he never showed as she waited for him, something bad took place to where she was left unconscious and bleeding when she woke up. Somehow she was afraid that Samuel might not understand and then he would no longer care to marry her and take her away from the life she had always wanted to walk away from.

"You seem to be in deep thought, Katie," he said as he looked into her eyes. Seeing that she quickly glanced his way then turned again, looking down the path they were walking on, he went on to talk more, "Have you given any thought to what you want us to do once we marry?"

"Are you referring to if we should leave the ways of the Amish?"

"Yah, Katie, I'd like to know what you feel. Are you able to leave the Amish ways and live as the English do?"

Katie looked at Samuel. Seeing that he was sincere in his asking, she nodded her head.

"If that is a yes, Katie, are you saying that when we marry in a few months, we, together, will leave what we have been taught and have always known to become like the English?"

"Yah, Samuel, I will do as you will."

Samuel was so pleased to hear that she was willing to live what they both have always known and to start a new life outside the Amish ways. "I promise you, Katie, that you will not ever regret it. I am going to be a fine husband for you, one whom you can be truly pleased with. And if your ma and your da ever feel that they can forgive us for leaving the Amish, they will be welcomed by us. Now that I know that when we marry we will leave the Amish and become like the English, I will get started right away on getting some plumbing for our home."

"Oh, Samuel, do you really believe that once we leave here, we will ever see them again?" she asked with sadness written all over her face.

"Come now, Katie. This is what we have talked about together. Do you feel that after we marry, you will not be able to make the move that we have discussed?"

"It's not that, Samuel. It's about the hearts of my folks. They will never be able to mention my name again. We will forever be shunned. I don't know that feeling yet." Even though she could hear her voice speak, those words of being shunned by her folks, inside she never really believed would happen. She felt that their love for her was much too deep for them to ever forget about her.

"But we will be happy, Katie. I will make you happy, and we will be able to have us a fine family and raise them to be English," he said as he drew her in his arms to give her a light kiss.

Katie responded to his kiss as if she had been kissed before, but the truth was, this was her first time ever to be kissed.

He stepped back at first when she responded with a kiss and looked at her. "It doesn't seem to me that this was your first kiss with a man, Katie."

"Yah, Samuel, it is my first."

"You sure you're not telling me a lie?" he asked with a half smile.

"I'm sure. There has been no one," she answered back.

"Okay, I trust that you are being upfront with me. Then I will have to say, you are going to please me after we are married, Katie."

Katie turned her face from him when she could feel that it became warm with the words that Samuel chose to use. She just knew that it must have shown red as she put her face down. Even though with the darkness closing in, it would be hard to see it. She was not used to any man talking this way about her or any other.

"Come now," Samuel said as he lightly picked her face up to look into her eyes. "If we are to marry and become like the English, then we must act like them or we will be out of place once we live as they do."

Katie knew that Samuel was right, but she also knew that it was going to take time to become one of them. Samuel continued to talk while she thought if her ma and her da would still want her to marry him if they were ever to find out about Samuel and his persuasion. Somehow she felt that they would never approve. The more she listened to him talk, the more she was forgetting all about Robert and focusing on her upcoming marriage to Samuel.

"Katie, you look to me as if you are in another world. Have you heard anything that I have been saying to you?"

"I'm truly sorry, Samuel. I was just thinking about what it would be like for us to be married and leave what we have known all our lives. Would my ma be so hurt that she would no longer be able to speak my name?"

"Yah, she will be very upset with me for taking you away. I hope that you won't wind up hating me for taking you away from our teaching, Katie. I don't believe that I could go on with my wife hating me. That's why I need for you to really think long and hard about what we have been talking about. You really have to make sure that this is something you will be able to do."

"I know that this is a big step, but it is something that I have dreamt about for as long as I can remember. I only wish that my ma and my da would come along. I have come to appreciate my ma and her wisdom, which she has given to me over the last few years. Don't get me wrong, Samuel. I love my da too, but it's my ma who has taught me what a wife must do for her husband. I will truly miss her, but I will go with you where you choose for us to go when we are married."

Samuel was pleased when he heard her response to his request. He took her by the hand, which just a few minutes ago he held tight as if to never let it go. "Katie, I want to speak of love to you, but I feel you may turn from me. I only wish to let you know what my thoughts of you have been over the past few months."

"I will let you speak your heart to me, but I have to let you know, I have never had another talk with me in this manner. I too have come to care for you, Samuel, and I look forward to that day when I will become your wife."

Samuel held on to her and began to kiss her slowly. It was like he used to kiss his wife when she was alive. Katie had never known this kind of kiss before, but the more he kissed her, the more she liked to be kissed. Her response to him was making him feel like she wanted more, so without another word spoken between the two of them, he walked her over to the hayfield that had fresh hay lying all about the field.

Katie followed close behind him with her heart beating faster. He laid her down on the ground. Without trying to walk away from him, she lay down on the mound of hay and allowed him to kiss not only her lips but also her neck. She lay there unsure of what she was to do and how she should respond to him. Before she even realized, she opened up her eyes, which had been closed ever since he began to kiss her neck, and saw that the darkness was settling down on them even more. Samuel took it a step further and began to lift up her dress. Katie began to breathe heavy, with her heart beating so fast that she thought it would come right out of her chest. Sitting up faster than Samuel could even move to the side of her, she just about knocked him on to his backside.

"I'm sorry, Samuel, I can't do this."

"It's quite all right, Katie. I am truly sorry. This is no way for a man to act to the one he loves. I was just allowing myself to be like if we were married. Can you ever forgive me, Katie?"

"Yes, I do forgive you. It's just that I have never been with a man before, and I'm unlearned in this way. I don't want to disappoint you in any way."

"You could never disappoint me. I only wish that we were already married so we could do what a man and a wife do together."

Katie sat on the mound of hay speechless, as if in shock of what she was hearing. Before he could say another word to her, she spoke with the most shocking words he would have ever guessed coming from her. "Samuel, would you like to have me?" she asked while lying back down on the hay.

"Katie, this is something that I wish to happen between the two of us, but I don't want you to hate me, for not wanting us to wait."

"I won't hate you, Samuel. I too want to be with you. I just don't want to disappoint you. I know that you have been with a woman before. On the other hand, it is I who have never been with someone."

Samuel began to kiss her once again. Then he was careful how he was with her for their first time. He never wanted to hurt her any, so he was as gentle as a man could be with a woman.

"Katie, are you angry with me for allowing us to contaminate our love before we are married?"

"No, Samuel, I'm not in any manner. I only hope that I pleased you like a wife ought to please her husband."

"You were everything that a wife is to be for her husband. I pray that I wasn't too rough on you. What I mean to say is, I hope that I didn't hurt you any."

"No, not really, maybe just a little at first. Samuel, the darkness has closed in on us for quite sometime. I hate to see my da come looking for us and finding me in the hayfield. Maybe we should gather our wits and head back." Feeling ashamed in some way, she tried to change the subject.

"Are you sure that things are good between us, Katie? You seem to be in a hurry to head back home now." Samuel knew that what the two of them just did was overstepping their boundaries. Now he was worried if she were to change her mind about marrying him.

She put her hand on top of his hand and gave it a light squeeze. "It's fine, Samuel. I don't want my da coming to look for us. We will come together again soon, but please, can we head back? I don't want to explain our whereabouts to my ma and my da. I have never been out past dark like this before, and I don't want them to worry none."

"Come." He stood up on his feet and took her by the hand to help her get herself together. "We will start back now. I'm sorry for keeping you out so late. If you would like, I will have a talk with your da and explain that we took a long walk."

Katie looked at him in disbelief of what she was hearing coming from the man she was to marry. The more she learned of his ways, the more she knew that she really didn't know him at all. Somehow she never would have guessed that he was the type to like the ways of the English, let alone pursue her in the manner that he had already done. Now to withhold truth from her da about their walk was more of a surprise altogether. Although she liked the thoughts of leaving the Amish ways and becoming like the English, she questioned now within herself just what kind of a man Samuel truly is. Was he an honorable man, one to whom she could put her full trust into?

"Katie, although I can barely see you look at me right now because of the darkness before us, I should say that you have something going on in thy head that concerns me. Do I need to worry about us, Katie?"

"No, Samuel, no need to worry." *Now, look at who is lying*, she told herself.

"I'm sorry, Katie, for acting with you as if we were married together already. I know that it was not right before the eyes of God. A man should never do what I just did to a woman before she becomes his wife. I have no excuse. I was overcome with you as we took the course of kissing before marriage. Can you ever forgive me for the actions that I took toward you?"

She looked at him, and although she couldn't see the look of his face very well, she could hear that what he said came from his heart.

"Yes, of course, I forgive you, Samuel. I don't want for you to feel bad when I too wanted you."

4

The Touch

Katie was helping her ma scrub the great room floors when she began to feel a movement in her belly that she had never felt before. Without paying any attention to her ma working beside her, she put her hand on her stomach when she first felt the movement begin. Right away, her ma caught sight of what her daughter did. She knew that something was not right for Katie to do that to her belly so fast, for she herself had done the same thing when she was carrying Katie.

"Katie girl, tell me it's not true that you and Samuel came together in love before your vows?"

Not expecting to hear her ma ask her a question that was so blunt, it startled her to the point of falling back onto her butt. If truth be told, she herself had thoughts that she might be with child. But how would she tell her ma that she and Samuel had slept together several times, with the first time being three months ago when her da gave them permission to go for their walk?

"Katie, I expect an answer from you now." Her ma was now raising her voice higher than usual. It frightened Katie so because it was very unusual for her ma to raise her voice. Without waiting for her to answer, her ma continued, "How can you betray your faith like this when you are so close to marrying Samuel?"

"Ma, I don't know what to say," she answered, putting her head down in shame.

"You just did, Katie. How could you?"

Katie began to cry. "I'm sorry, Ma. I didn't know that this was going to happen. I didn't plan for this to happen. It just sort of happened."

"Your father will not care for Samuel after this, and you will be shunned."

"Shunned?" she asked with a look of shock written all over her face. She never expected to hear that word until after she and Samuel would leave the Amish ways. It put fear into her heart to where she almost felt like she was going to faint, but nonetheless, her ma continued.

"Your da may ask the two of you to go before the coucil and ask for forgiveness. If the brothers feel to forgive, then you may have to marry before your sixteenth birthday, so do not shame yourselves any further."

"Oh, Ma, I truly am so sorry, but couldn't I and Samuel marry now so this will not be revealed?"

"I don't know how to look at you anymore until I talk with your da," she said, turning her head from her daughter.

"Ma, please." Katie reached out to her ma while her ma turned away from her. Then she stood up and walked into another room.

She sat on the floor watching as her ma walked away from her. Her heart ached, knowing that she has brought shame unto her and Samuel. Now she had the back of her ma facing her. She wondered what Samuel would do when he came back to the house with her da when the day of work was over. Would he take the responsibility and own up for the wrong doings that they have done and ask to marry her right away? How would her da react to the both of them when he was to come home and find out about her being with child? Katie had many unanswered questions popping into mind, and she felt so terrified of what her da would be like to her and Samuel when her ma would share with him the finding of today. Katie continued to scrub the floor alone now, with tears falling down her cheeks and sobs following right behind them.

With every sob, Mary's heart was feeling for Katie, but although that may be true for a mother to feel that way, she knew the teachings of the Amish, and she knew that the Amish must not behave like so many of the Englishmen do. All she really wanted was to take her young daughter into her arms and tell her that everything was going to be all right, but how could she go against everything that she'd been taught and do what her heart felt like doing? If she was to go behind her teachings and reach out to her daughter who did wrong, she herself could be shunned for going against the council.

Katie finished up the floor and picked up the bucket of the leftover water to carry outside to dump it. When she walked out to the edge of the porch to throw out the leftover water, she noticed her da and Samuel coming up the pathway with the buggy. Her heart began to beat faster and faster to where her hands that once held the bucket lost grip of it, and it fell to the ground. Quickly bending down over the porch, she grabbed ahold of the bucket and brought it back into the house. Going to her bedroom and waiting to hear what her da would do after talking with her ma, she sat on the edge of her bed with her heart pounding as if to pop out of her chest. Then she heard her da begin to yell for her. Without a second to waste, she quickly responded to his calling.

"Yes, da."

"You and Samuel will leave my home at this very time. I never should have allowed you to go off for walks if I had only known that you would do this against us, Katie. You are no longer welcome in this home. You will go now." After he spoke his mind, he turned his back on her as her ma did earlier.

Katie didn't know what to say. She stood there in shock, looking at Samuel, who was holding out his hand toward her. "Come, Katie. We will go as they wish." Then focusing on her ma and her da, he said his last words to them before exiting the home, "I am truly sorry for disgracing you and Katie and myself. I only wish that you would not bring blame to her. It was I who proceeded to go after her."

"No, Samuel. I will not allow you to take fault in this alone. It was I too." She looked at her parents, who had their backs turned against her. With her heart feeling sick now from the outcome with her da, she took ahold of Samuel's hand. "Come, Samuel. We will leave as they wish."

After walking out of the home, Samuel put his arms around Katie and gave her a kiss on the cheek. "I'm sorry, Katie, that I have brought shame upon you. Will you ever be able to forgive me?"

"It was I too who fell into temptation. We are both at fault here, Samuel, but I need to know—what shall we do?"

"We will do what we planned on doing before this came out."

"What is that, Samuel? Do you mean, leave the Amish ways?"

"Yes, Katie. That is, if you are still willing for us to go."

"I think that is all we can do now. I just never expected it to happen like this. Where will we live, Samuel? Who shall marry us?"

"We shall go to the justice of the peace."

Katie looked at him, not knowing to whom he was referring. "I don't believe I know who that is."

"It is a man who will marry us outside of town," he answered.

"How do you know of such a man?" she inquired.

"I have heard of him from a man who was at the mill when I took in a load of corn. He was telling another who was standing by him that he and his girl went there and got married. So I feel that it would be the same for us. That is, if you are still willing to marry me after I brought shame to you?"

"Yes, I will marry you. We were to be husband and wife in just less than a month away anyway. I hurt deep in my heart 'cause of the shame I brought on my ma and my da. I will not be able to see them again, Samuel, and they will not know our child."

"How long have you known about the child?" he asked, looking at her as they walked down the path toward his home.

"I was unsure until my ma confirmed it to me."

"What happened there, Katie?"

"Me and my ma were scrubbing floors when I felt a movement in my belly. Without thinking much on it, I grabbed ahold of my belly. My ma took notice right away and asked me if we have lain together. I had no answer to give to her, Samuel. I was just so surprised she had known it."

"When do you believe to expect it to come?"

"I think I must be about three months along. I'm unsure of when it happened."

"We will go to be married tomorrow after a night of sleep at the house. Then we will no longer have to feel the shame that we have on us now."

"As you see fit," she said while approaching his farm home.

"Katie, I have gotten for us indoor plumbing, and I will have the lighting of the English come here too. I will not expect my wife to do as the Amish ways. I believe the ways of the English in many ways."

"Thank you, Samuel. That is what we talked of before. If you can kindly show me where I am to lay my head. I think that I'd like to sleep. I feel sick with everything that took place today."

"You can share my bed with me."

"If you wouldn't mind, Samuel, I feel shame like no other. Can we wait until we are married before sleeping the night together?"

"Sure. If you would like, come this way. I have a second room over here."

Without a word, Katie followed close behind him. Seeing a single bed in the room where she was to sleep, she sat on the edge of it. Sorrow overcame her very soul when Samuel walked out to leave her alone. She began to weep until her small-framed body began to tremble when she cried. Samuel was unsure if he should come back in the room when he heard her cry, but after what seemed to be a long time of crying, he tapped back on the door before opening it up.

"Come, Katie. Let me hold you for the night. I'm so very sorry that I have done this terrible thing to you. I have brought much shame to you, all because of my own selfishness. Please, Katie, forgive me. I was unfair to you when I talked you into bedding down with me before marriage."

"It was I too who sinned. Do you think that God will ever forgive us for what we have done?"

"Yes, I do. He is a God of love and kindness, and that is one of the reasons I was willing to turn my back on the Amish ways. They never seem to feel that we can enjoy the things that God has given us."

Katie looked at him as if he had plumb lost his mind. *He can't be meaning that God gave us the desire to bed with each other before we married, could he?* She questioned him with her eyes and not speaking a word.

"What I mean by that is we both feel that God gave us music, and yet the Amish say it is not allowed. Why can we hear it within ourselves and it be so wrong? Even in the teachings of the Bible, we read where David played the harp, and it brought peace to King Saul. Then he danced to music, and we read other places in the Bible about music. So how can that be wrong? Yet we are raised to believe that it is wrong. Now I have heard of some of the young will listen to that music that you can't even hear what they are even saying. I can't believe that God likes that when He wouldn't understand what it says Himself."

"Are we going to buy something that will allow us to hear some nice music, the kind that we hear when we go into stores?" she asked.

"After we marry, we'll go into a department store and buy us a stereo. I have been in love with you, Katie, for sometime now, and I believe that now you and I will be married, we will have what we've both been wanting."

"I feel so ashamed of what we have done. We brought shame to my ma and my da, not to mention ourselves. I only pray that one day they will forgive me for what I have done against them," she carried on.

"But don't you see what you are saying here, Katie? You are saying what you have done against them, but not what we have done against God. Katie, it is God whom we failed. He is the one who will have to forgive us."

"I understand that, Samuel, but I hurt my folks by going against the teaching. I knew that what I was doing was wrong, but I have always been a little rebellious ever since I was very young."

"Like how, Katie? I can't imagine you ever being that way really."

"Yes, I was. Like whenever we went into town, I would sit around listening to the music of the English as much as I could. I have always liked it no matter what my folks said to me about it."

"I was the same way ever since I was a very young lad. My folks also told me different, but in my heart, I have loved to listen, and I would dream of a day when I myself would have it in my home."

"So why now, Samuel, when we are to be married and not when you were married before?"

"She never wanted to go against the teachings, so I respected her desire and we lived as the Amish do."

"I'm very tried, Samuel, and would like to lie down and get some sleep, if you don't mind." She wanted to stop the conversation that they were having. Somehow talking of his dead wife was not a subject she cared to have.

"You can lie with me the night and I will hold you, or you may take the bedroom that you are in already. I promise to only hold you in my arms and nothing more."

Katie looked at his face as he pled with her about lying next to him. "Okay, I will lie next to you for the night."

5

The Marriage

After the two were married the following day, they headed to a store to where they could pick up a stereo just like Samuel had promised her.

"How would you like this one in our home, Katie?" he asked, pointing out one that was a duel cassette player and CD player. Now to find music of their liking to go with it. The two listened to the music before buying to make sure it was something they would listen to and that God would understand it also.

"How about us going over to where they sell their clothes and buy us some of what the English wear?" he asked, taking her by the arm gently.

"Okay, I wonder if I may try them on first so we know if they fit us?"

"We will ask someone over here," he stated, walking by the clothes.

"How does this look, Samuel?"" she asked, holding up a colorful dress.

"I thought the purpose of us looking like the English is to wear what they do, like that woman right there." He pointed at a woman about the age of twenty walking by in a pair of blue jeans and a tank top.

Katie watched her as she walked by. "Really! Like that, huh? Okay then, I must look over here then," she said as she found the pants folded up on a shelf. "I wonder what size I am to wear?"

"Ma'am?" Samuel asked a lady who worked at the store.

She stopped dead in her tracks, noticing that it was an Amish man calling for her. "How may I help you?"

"My wife would very much like some clothing like these here, but we don't know the size she would wear. Can you pick something out that she could wear and look like the English do?"

The lady looked at Katie, trying to see what size she would wear. As she moved Katie's dress close to her waist, Katie moved backward quickly. "It's okay. I'm just trying to see your size so we can find the right size of these pants for you," the lady said.

Looking over at Samuel and seeing that he nodded his head to say, *Let her find your size*, Katie then moved her arms out to the side so the lady could find her size. "Sorry, I'm not used to this," Katie apologized.

"That's quite all right. It's not every day that we get the Amish in here needing to find their size. You look like you would wear this size here." She pulled out a size 4 in blue jeans. "You can go into this room here and try them on if you would like. I will wait out here with your husband if you would like."

"Oh yes, please," she said while taking the pants from the store lady and going into the changing room. She then opened up the door and showed Samuel the pants on her while she held up her dress. "What do you think? Is this me, Samuel?"

Samuel looked closely at her to see if he liked what he was looking at. "Yuh, Katie. How you like them on you?"

"I like how they look, but the feel of them is kind of uncomfortable. Maybe I need to get used to them," she said, giving her husband a smile, which he loved. "But I will have to have a top to go with it. I don't think you wear a dress with this."

"Yuh, a shirt for you is what we need." He looked over at the lady. "What kind of shirt goes with her bottoms?"

The lady looked around close to where they were standing. Then grabbing a top that would go with Katie's pants, the lady handed it to Katie to try on.

"Samuel, how do I look?" Katie asked after trying on her shirt and looking just like the English do.

"Yuh, Katie, you look like one of them."

"Do you like it, Samuel, or is it to much?"

"No, I like what I see you in, Katie. We will buy it and more, and we will need shoes too."

"Would you like my help, or do you think that you can take care of it from here?" the store lady asked.

"If you wouldn't mind, I'd like your help still," Samuel said.

"Sure. What is it that you're still in need of?"

"We are unsure of how to tell the size that we are. We are Amish, and we make our clothes."

"Oh, I see. Here, I will show you what it is that your wife has already tried on. Do you see the tags here?" She showed him what was on the top and inside the pants.

"Yuh."

"This is the size she wears, so if you take a look at these tops over here, they show you your size. Now, you are welcome to try anything on before buying them just to make sure that they fit."

"Thank you."

"You are very welcome." She walked away, leaving her two customers to fend for themselves.

Samuel and Katie were like two kids who were let loose to go shopping for themselves for the first time. Never before having clothes besides what she or her mom made, Katie wasn't quite sure how to fold up the clothes that she unfolded after looking at them. She had her own way of folding clothes, and it was not the same as the store's ways. She and Samuel must have tried on half the store, never putting anything back to where it belonged. After trying on all that they wanted to, they had several outfits picked out for each of them. When all was said and done, they looked like the rest of the English.

"That cost you a lot of money, Samuel, for what we got."

"Yes, it cost more than I thought that it was going to, but now we are who we want to be. If an Amish was to see us look like this, I'm sure that they would not recognize us. Now we will go to a nice place to eat."

"Are you sure that you can afford it after we got all these clothes?"

"Yes, we can. I have plenty of money for us to eat somewhere. You don't have to worry your sweet, pretty little self about that. We Amish—"

As soon as he said the words *Amish* and *we* in the same sentence, he stopped himself. "What I meant to say is, the Amish have always learned to make money and hold on to it."

"What will you do now for work?"

"I have my own land, which I will continue to work just like I have for several years. It's my land, and just because we walked away from the ways of the Amish, it don't mean my farm goes with them." He looked at her, not quite understanding why she would ask him something like that.

"I'm sorry, Samuel. I wasn't being myself. I know that your land belongs to you and they have no rights to it. I guess I just wasn't thinking very clear is all. This is something new for me, and with us now becoming like the English, it may take me a while to get used to is all."

"Aww, that's okay, Katie. Many times I say one thing when I mean something entirely different. So how does it feel to be a married woman?" he asked, looking at her with a big grin, hoping to get a big smile as well as a good word back from her, but he never got either.

Katie was unsure of what to say at the time of his asking. If truth be told, she felt scared half to death. She, being so young, was so unsure of many things. Was she going to be the wife whom he had hoped for? Was she going to be a good mother to her child?

"I don't know what to say to you, Samuel. I just pray that I will be a good wife and mother to our child."

"Oh, Katie, I'm sure that you will be the perfect wife and mother. You yourself had a great role model. Your mother was strict but a good mother, don't you think?"

She listened as he talked, all the while thinking about the place she used to call home and from which she was now shunned. It felt like a deep pain within her heart as he talked about her ma. Looking at him while he talked, she was only hearing part of what he was saying.

"So what do you think, Katie?" he continued.

"Yes, Samuel, I had a very loving ma, and I believe that I will miss her and my da greatly."

He looked at her as he was pulling his buggy up his drive. "I'm sure that in time they will come around, Katie. Although they are Amish, they truly love you. You are their only child, Katie. Sometimes in life, one has to go without knowing what they have, and I believe that they will come around and miss you and want to see you and our child."

Although he sounded so sure of himself, she just didn't feel the same way. She would love for Samuel to be right about his feelings on this subject, but she still could hear it ringing in her ears—what her folks said to her as she was banned from them.

"I wish that I could feel the same as you, Samuel, with my ma and my da wanting to see me in the near future. But somehow I don't feel that I will ever get to be part of their life again." She turned her face from him with tears forming in her eyes.

"We shall see, Katie," he stated as he helped her down from the buggy. Handing her a couple of bags as she was firm on the ground, he smiled at her, seeing the sadness written on her face as the talk of her folks brought back painful memories.

Taking the bags from him and walking toward the house, Katie noticed John, Caleb, Annie, and Eva Stolzfus riding by their place in the family buggy looking their way. Although she was friends with the family at one time and hung out with Annie, Katie seemed to feel ashamed when she saw them look her way. Quickly turning her head from seeing them stare at her, she hurried along into her home, which she now shared with her husband.

She talked to herself just above a whisper, "At least I have the love of a man, so you can just stop staring at me as you pass my home."

"What did you say, Katie?" Samuel asked, thinking that she was saying something to him.

"It's nothing, Samuel. I was talking to myself."

"Oh, is this something that you do often?" he asked in a teasing manner, taking her in his arms and hugging her.

"No, not really, only when I see others looking at me as if I carry some kind of a plague."

"I saw the Stolzfus family coming by and giving you and me a look that was not out of kindness. Is that what you are referring to?"

"Yuh, I used to be so close to Annie sometime back ago. Now it seems to be as if we are strangers to each other."

"I hope that you won't let their way bother you none, Katie. We just need to stay focused on our home and life now. I'd like it if we could find a place of worship, and there we will find friends who I hope won't judge us for who we are. Would you like that, Katie?"

"Yes, very much, Samuel. I will need someone to be friends with. You are gone so much of the time working your land."

"*Our* land," he interrupted.

"Our land," she continued. "I just don't want to be alone here all the time. I was used to having my ma and friends to talk to. Now I have—"

She stopped right there, looking at Samuel.

"I know, Katie, and I understand. You are very young and need someone to talk to. We all do. So today, when I go into town with a load of corn to take to the mill, I will ask where there is a good place of worship."

"Oh, thank you, Samuel. I do want to worship God in music and singing." Katie looked around the home to find a good place to put the new stereo they bought in town. Finding that they had an end table next to the couch that held only a book, she decided it to be the proper place for the stereo.

Samuel turned the stereo on and took ahold of his wife, moving her slowly to the music. She laughed at the little circle he was going in. "Oh, you don't care for my dancing, huh?" he asked her while giving a light chuckle.

"Yuh, I love it. This is something that I have wanted to do all my life. I love it, Samuel, but I must say you have done this before."

"Nuh, my first time. But I have wanted this too most all my life."

"I'm not quite sure if God would call this wicked of us. What do you think?" she asked.

"Now, Katie, have we not already had this talk before?" he said, giving her a sigh.

"I didn't mean anything by that, Samuel. I just know that this is not the way of our teaching. Forgive me, Samuel. I really didn't mean anything by it."

"Oh, Katie, I know that you didn't. It's just that I want the two of us to become like the English are, and I don't want the way we were taught to stand in the way of our happiness."

"Okay, Samuel, I won't let it bother me again," she said as she took her husband by the waist and gave a little sway to the music.

Samuel decided to take ahold of his wife and move around the whole room with her. Before they knew it, they were laughing and dancing all around their home, until Katie felt so tired that she motioned for Samuel to stop so she could sit.

"To much for you, Katie?" he asked.

"I have to admit, it's a whole lot of fun. But with the baby and all"—she held her belly—"I seem to tire much faster then you."

"I understand, and so sorry for not thinking about that, Katie."

"That's quite all right. I believe that we both are learning together. I must say that when this baby comes, I will be happy. Then we can dance for much longer." Right after saying those words, Katie grew quiet, to where Samuel took notice of her sudden change.

"What, what is it, Katie? You were happy, but now you carry a frown on your face. What is going on inside that pretty little head of yours?"

"It's nothing really. I was just thinking about ma is all. Will she even want to see her only grandchild when it's born?"

"Maybe not right away, maybe she might in time. We will pray for it to happen."

Katie looked at him as she talked. "Pray for what to happen?" she asked.

"For your ma to want to see you and the baby. I just can't imagine not wanting to see your own grandchild."

"Samuel, would you mind terrible if I was to go to bed now? I really feel quite tired."

"Would you like to eat something first?"

"Oh, Samuel, I am so sorry not thinking about my wifely duties. I will go fix you something before I go lie down."

"That's okay. You go a head and rest for the night if you want. I don't mind. I will fix me a sandwich and come join you for the night. We ate not that long ago while in town."

"If you're fine with that, then I will be going to bed now. Good night."

"I'll be in to join you in just a minute."

Katie walked into the bedroom feeling sad about the birth of her baby coming soon and her not having her ma there for her when she would have her baby. She had always thought that when the time came for her to have a baby, her ma would be at her side. Even though she had always dreamed about becoming English when she was grown up, little did she stop to think about what it would cost her to become like them and walk away from the teachings of the elders. Now with regret of mistakes made, she knew that she had been shunned from the only family she had until Samuel. Katie would never think about shunning someone dear to her, nor treat them differently because they might do something that they were not taught.

She looked toward the bedroom door as she undressed, wondering if Samuel might walk in the bedroom while she was trying to put her nightgown on. Although she had become his wife and the two were about to become parents together, she still felt uncomfortable when standing without clothes in front of him. She wondered if that was how all wives felt around their husbands, or was it just her? Nonetheless, she tried to pull her gown over her head as fast as she could before Samuel would walk in. Slipping under the sheet and finding a comfortable position to lie on, she closed her eyes just as he opened the door and entered.

"Are you asleep?" he asked as he entered.

Not wanting to talk at this time, she never answered him. She could hear as he undressed to get in his pajama bottoms and slip under the covers. Then right when she was about to fall asleep, she was startled by the clearing of his throat. Slightly jumping then getting a grip of what he just did, she kept silent so he would not begin talking to her. Right when she thought that all the clearing of his throat was done to where she could go to sleep, it started again. Not knowing what to think about it or if she should say anything, she lay there wondering if this was something that he made a habit of doing just before falling asleep.

"Sorry," he spoke out loud just in case he had woken her up.

Once again, she acted as though she was fast asleep. Lying there with her back turned against him, she had mixed feelings crowding her mind. *What if I have a baby girl and not a boy like Samuel wants? Will he be disappointed? Will he think bad of me and want to try again right away? Will my ma and da ever be able to forgive me for what I've done?*

The next thing she remembered was waking up and Samuel being gone. She sat up on the edge of her bed, trying to wake up enough to walk outside to the outhouse. She began to wonder when she was going to get her bathroom inside her home like Samuel had promised her. She was praying for it to be done before winter set in. Although she loved the winter for a short period of time, just enough to go sledding for a couple of times, she wanted the warm weather back. Having a bathroom in her very own home was more than she had ever had before but had always dreamt about having.

6

The Birth

Time came and went, and still Katie was unable to patch things up with her folks. She was close to giving birth, and she wanted the support of her ma, but she was nowhere around. At least she had the love of a husband and friends from the church the two have been attending for four months now. Katie was cleaning her floors with a mop, which Samuel had purchased for her when the two went shopping for things that the English used in their home. As she swiped back and forth with her mop, she thought about the time that she helped her ma scrub the floors the hard way. The way of the Amish was so much harder than Katie had it now.

Although things were much easier for her to clean—and even for Samuel when it came time to do his chores out in the fields since he bought a tractor he could ride—after everything was said and done, she still thought about the ways of the Amish and missed some of those times and wished she could go back to it. But she knew in her heart that there was no going back. How could she ever ask Samuel to go back to something that he hated in many ways, not to mention the work was so much harder? How could she give up her music, which was part of both her and Samuel's lives now, and not to mention the church to which both of them enjoyed going?

As she was just about finished with mopping her floors, she felt a sharp pain in the bottom of her belly. Dropping the mop to the floor and putting her hands on her belly, she cried out, "God, help me." Finding a seat to sit in and reaching for the phone she now had, she called Samuel on his cell phone, asking him to hurry home to help her.

"I'm here, Katie," he said as he rushed through the door to her side. "What is it, Katie girl? Are you ready to have the baby?"

"I don't know for sure, but what I feel is not right. You better take me to the hospital so they can see what it is."

Samuel began to pick her up without thinking about anything else. He loved his wife, and he knew that if she felt something wasn't quite right, then he needed to get her some help. Although he helped deliver calves when some of his cows had trouble giving birth and everything turned out all right with them, he wasn't about to take a chance with his wife and child. Samuel carried her out to his truck, which he now owned for three months, and drove her to the hospital.

"I hurt really bad, Samuel. Something's wrong, I just know it," she cried.

"I called up Pastor Mike for prayer for you. He told me that he will call others to be praying for you too. I'm praying too, honey. I believe you will be just fine."

As Samuel was telling Katie that everything was going to be fine, he had some doubts running through his mind. He knew that a few years back, he lost his wife while she was giving birth to their baby, as well as the baby. This time, he wasn't taking any chances. He was driving just about as fast as his old truck would take him, all the while praying for his wife and unborn child.

"Samuel, I don't think that I'm going to make it…I…"

Just as she was talking, her body went into lifeless mode.

"Katie, Katie." He began to shake her while driving as fast as he could now. "Oh please, God, help my wife," he screamed out in panic.

Pulling into the parking lot of the emergency room, he began to blow his horn, not knowing just what he should do. He saw those close by walking stare at him like he was nuts while he kept hitting his horn. Finally, after seeing that no one was coming out of the doors of the hospital, he jumped out and ran into the building, screaming, "Help! Please, someone help me, my wife. My wife needs your help."

All of a sudden, two nurses came out of a room to see what all the commotion was about.

"Can we help you, sir?" one of them asked.

"It's my wife. She's out in my truck, and she's having a baby, but something is wrong," he said as he headed back outside to Katie.

One of the nurses grabbed a gurney and began to follow close behind. When they reached the truck, they could see that there was no movement coming from her. They picked up her unconscious body as fast as they could and rushed her down to the emergency room, calling stat.

"Please wait out here. I'll get someone just as soon as I can to come have a talk with you."

Samuel called up Pastor Mike to let him know what was going on and to ask for more prayers. Samuel waited for just a minute or so when a nurse came out, asking him to sign some paperwork for treatment. He couldn't understand what he was signing, but he knew that he needed to do whatever it took to get help for his wife. A different nurse came out and asked him all kinds of questions about his wife's health. For the most part, he didn't even now how to answer.

"Is my wife going to be all right?"

"Yes, she has lost some blood, and she is very weak, but she is awake now, and we are getting ready for a little baby to be born. Would you like to come back with me and be there for her as she gives birth?"

"Oh yes, ma'am, I surely would." He walked behind the nurse, and seeing Katie with her legs put up in those things he had never seen before made him a little uncomfortable. But he walked over to her side and held her hand.

"It's time to push now," the doctor told Katie. "Come on, the baby is ready to see the world. Give it a big push."

"I'm trying," Katie said as she pushed with a loud scream. "Is it out?" she asked.

"Not yet. Give it another big push to get the body out," the doc asked.

Katie gave another big push with a loud cry, and this time, she could feel her baby give a light little cry. But something inside her told her that something was wrong. "Is my baby all right?" she asked, trying to pick her head up to look at it.

Samuel didn't say a word but watched what the doctor and the nurses were doing.

"You have a boy. We are just checking to make sure that everything is good. We do this to all our new babies. It's just standard."

"You have a healthy baby boy, and he is very alert for being just a couple minutes old."

The nurse took the baby over to Katie and placed him in her arms. "Here is your son."

Samuel had an ear-to-ear smile come across his face. "He sure is handsome, just like his mama."

"Did you hear what your pa just said? He said you're handsome, and he called me handsome."

Samuel looked at his wife while she was talking to her baby. "Sorry, I meant nothing by that. You are beautiful to me, but you know what I meant by that, didn't you?"

"Yes, I did. I was just teasing you a little bit. I sure am glad that this little guy is bright and healthy. What do we call him?" she asked, looking at Samuel.

"I think that Hezekiah is a big name."

"I thought that we were going to be like the English are, and I've never heard that name among them, have you?"

"No, you're right. Why don't you come up with a name for him then."

Katie sat there looking at the baby, trying to think of a good name to match his looks. "Well, I think that Michael is a good name. What do you think?"

"Is that common among the English? Have you heard it before?"

"Sure, I have," she stated, looking down at the baby, "haven't I? Michael, do you like your name?"

"I guess Michael is his name then—big, strong Michael," Samuel said while the baby held his finger with a tight grip.

The time came and went, and Katie was leaving the hospital and going home. She was so excited to get him home to his new room, which she and Samuel had painted a neutral color. Although the two have decided to be like the English, they still had so much of the way they were raised stuck in them. Like when it came time to paint the baby's room, it should have been a bright color of some kind; but now walking in the room, Katie could see it looking too dark for her baby, and she wasn't happy with it. "Samuel, I hate the color of gray we painted the baby's room with. Why did we decide on this dark color anyway?"

Samuel stood there looking at all the four walls of the room. "Hmm, I don't know for sure what we were thinking. Maybe it comes from what we are used to."

"I think we need to paint it all over again," Katie stated, looking at Samuel.

"Okay, but we have the baby home now with us. What would you like me to do? What could we do at this time?"

"Can you go back into town and buy another thing of paint? I really hate this color. This is just about all I've seen growing up, and"—she paused for a moment before going on—"well, I hate the color. Can you please go get a nice, bright color for a boy?"

"Your wish is my command. What color shall I get?" he spoke with a light laughter following close behind.

"Where did you pick up that cute little saying 'Your wish is my command'?"

"Oh, I heard a gentleman in town say that to his wife when she stopped over to the cider mill the other day. I just thought that it was quite cute is all. Did it bother you by me saying that?"

"No, not at all. I liked it. It sounded very much English," she stated and, quickly changing the subject, added, "Can you pick up some paint? And I will paint his room tomorrow. I guess he will be able to stay in here tonight."

"Okay, I will go, but what color do you think will look good in here for him?"

"How about a light green? I like that, the thought of a light-green room for the baby."

"Okay, honey, I will go back into town. Is there anything else that you can think of that you might want while I'm there?"

"I can't think of anything at this time. I think the paint will do just fine. Samuel, do you think that we can get the indoor bathroom put in soon now that we have some plumbing put in?"

"Yes, honey, I will look into doing that very soon. Will you and the baby be all right while I'm gone?"

"We will be fine. What are you going to do come morning when you have to leave for work? Take us with you?" she asked, teasing him.

"I know that I'm being overbearing just a bit, but this is all new to me. I have wanted to be a father for a very long time. It might take me some time, but I won't crowd you for too long."

"You're not crowding me, Samuel. I just know that a man has his work to do, and us women have our work."

"Okay, I'm leaving to go get the paint." With those words, he was out the door and off in his old truck to pick up paint.

"Well, baby Michael, it's just you and me, your mama. I am so happy to have you in my life." She walked over to the rocking chair to sit down and feed him. "It's time for your feeding. Are you hungry? Here, look at what I have here for you," she said to the bright-eyed little baby as she tried to get him to eat.

Katie began telling him all about her upbringing as she fed him. "I really wish that you could meet your grandma and grandpa, but they have shunned me because I made some mistakes they feel can't be forgiven. But I want to tell you something very important. No matter what you do in life, I will always love you. No matter if you go to a different church than I do when you're grown, I will still love you."

Just as she was talking to him, she heard a knock on her door.

"I have to put you down for just a minute and see who's at the door." Placing the baby in his crib, she walked to the door in her kitchen. She didn't expect the visitor who was standing on her porch. "Mama," she said as she looked for her da.

"It's just me here. Yer da don't know I come on over here. Katie, I had to come. It's been months, and I wanted to see you and my baby grandchild. I heard some of the ladies talking about you having your baby."

"Yuh, Ma, I did, a beautiful baby boy two days ago."

"May I come in, Katie? I don't want to be seen standing here by anyone."

"I'm sorry, Ma, come in. Would you like to meet your grandson?" She was unsure of what to say at this time.

"I would like that very much," Mary said as she walked in the door.

Katie noticed that her ma was standing there looking around at everything in her home. Katie could see the look of disappoinment in her ma's face when she saw that she had running water in her kitchen. Looking at all Katie had, Mary then made a statement that brought Katie to tears.

"I should go. This was a mistake coming."

"No, don't go, Mama. Please stay and meet Michael." Right after she said the baby's name, she knew that her ma would give her a disappointed look. "I'm still your daughter, Ma, and didn't you raise me to believe that God is a good God? Then if you and Da can't forgive me, then what do you believe in God for?"

"Katie, that is blasphemy. You know better than to talk of God in a careless manner."

"Mama, God forgives me and Samuel for doing what we did before we got married. He's a loving God. Why can't you and Da forgive me?"

"Katie, where have you learned this talk of the English ways? It's lies. I don't know who you are anymore. You had such promise to look forward to for both you and your husband. Now both of you are lost, Katie."

"No, Mama, we're not lost. Jesus forgave us, Mama."

"Jesus, Katie, that is blasphemy," she went on. Right then, they heard the baby cry.

"Come meet my son, your grandson," Katie said as she led her ma into the baby's bedroom. "Michael, it's Mama," she said as she bent over the side of the crib, picking him up. "Ma, this here is Michael, your grandson."

Mary stood there looking at her grandson. Then without a word, she ran for the door, never to hold the baby. Flinging the door wide open, she ran off the porch and headed for the path that led to her home.

"Ma, ma!" Katie called out to her while she stood holding her baby close to her heart, with tears of sadness falling down her face. "I will never do that to you, Michael, never—I promise."

Katie watched her ma run down the path until she was no longer seen. Walking back into her home and closing the door behind her, Katie wished that Samuel was home so she could tell him what took place.

Sitting down to finish feeding her baby, she heard Samuel's truck pull into the driveway. "Papa's home, Michael, with a new color for your bedroom."

She could hardly wait to get started on Michael's bedroom, but with the hour of the day closing in, she thought that she would start first thing in the morning after Samuel left for work. She went over to the living-room window and watched Samuel take the paint out of the back of his truck. She wanted to tell him about the visitor who had shown up unexpectedly and left so quickly after coming in their home and seeing things that were like that of the English. Katie never did quite understand why anyone would want to work harder at everything when there was an easier way to go about it and get the same results.

"I'm home," Samuel said as he walked through the doorway. "I hope this color is too your liking."

Katie looked at the color spot they put on the cover and saw that it was indeed a light-green color like she had specified for it to be. "If what's in the can looks like this color here,'" she said as she pointed to the circle spot on the lid, "then it's what I was hoping for."

"Good, it took the man three times to get the shade that I thought you were asking for."

"Who knew that mixing paint was so hard to do." He laughed slightly after saying that in a silly way.

"Samuel, we must have a talk."

"What's going on? By the look on your face, something tells me that you're unhappy."

"Mama showed up here to see me today." She looked at him before going on to see if the look on his face would be a look of shock. And it was just what she thought that it would be—complete shock.

"Really, so how did that go?" he asked.

"Not good at all. She came in when I invited her in, and she stood in the kitchen just staring at everything. She didn't even get a chance to hold our son. She was so disappointed by the kind of things we have. And when I named our son, she said she made a mistake by coming and ran out the door."

"I'm so sorry, honey, but what was it that disappointed her so much?" he asked, looking around the kitchen to see what could possibly have made her ma act like that to her, especially after coming all this way—and he was sure that she came behind her husband's back.

"Well, for one thing, it was the running water in our home that upset her. Ma and Da have the pump outside that we got our water from."

"Is that all? Or is there more to it than that?"

"I'm not sure if she took notice of the coffeemaker and all of our things that use electric. You know that the Amish never drink coffee. Ma and Da have never tried coffee before, and here we are with a new coffeepot on our counter."

"Yes, honey, but we have made a choice to separate ourselves from what we have always known and be like a Christian couple without all the rules of what they call good. God said to follow him, and he never said we have to work harder than we need to, to make it to heaven. That is just religion, nothing more, and God hates religion. He wants our heart."

"I know that you're right, and I want to follow God and his word. And it does make life so much easier having the thing that we have. I just hate that my ma and da act the way that they do toward me. When I was at home and thought about leaving the Amish ways, I guess I never really thought that if I ever did, my folks would disown me like they have. It makes me question the whole Amish ways like I never did before. If you truly love your child, then how can you walk away from them like they never even existed before? I know one thing is for sure—I will never do that to Michael no matter what."

Samuel walked over to his wife and put his strong arms around her. "Honey, we knew that by walking away from the ways of our teaching, we would be shunned. We talked about it before we left or did anything to cause us to be shunned."

"Yes, you are right, but just watching her run down the path toward the home was just wrong after her coming all this way to see her grandchild, then to just leave before holding him."

"All we can do is pray and ask God to speak to their heart and to give them a love for you and Michael like God loves you. I don't know what's harder, to have parents who will have nothing to do with you or not to have any parents at all, like me."

"I don't know how to comment on that really, but if your folks were Amish—which I'm sure that they were—wouldn't they have shunned you too when you became like the English?"

"I'm sure you are right. After all, that is what they too have been taught. Disown the ones you love because they don't act and do everything that you want them to. But I do know that in some places, there are some Amish whom you would never even know to be Amish because of the things that they do."

"Like what?" she asked, waiting for him to stop kissing the baby's foot to answer.

"Well, I'm not sure who they are, but I do know that they are Amish. They drive trucks, shoot guns, get in fights, curse and swear, and they even have wild parties. Now, if they were ever to get caught doing those things, then I'm sure they would be shunned as well."

"Where did you ever hear of such a story?" she asked with a look of disbelief that there could be those who still call themselves Amish and live that way. If that is true, then why not walk away from the Amish and be called English?"

"I was talking to a couple of men at the mill when I took the corn in, and they were telling me about a show on television that they watch, and it's all about the Amish and them breaking their laws."

"Wow, where are they? Not around here, I hope."

"No, they're in Ohio, but that don't mean that it's not at some places around here too. I think that they're getting tired of not ever being able to do anything."

"Are you saying that you think that it's okay to act like that?"

"No, of course not. It's wrong, but I do think that if they want to do things, then they need to conduct themselves in a right manner. Not everything is sin the way we've been taught all our lives, but they need to find themselves in a godly way like we did. I know that we made our share of mistakes, and if it wasn't for the church that we are now going to and being taught by Pastor Mike, I might have felt like we were going to hell in a fireball, just as soon as God got around to sending us there.

"But we now have been taught that God forgives us from our sin and he loves us even though we fall short from time to time. I would love to be able to talk with these Amish men and women and let them know that they don't have to act out in a crazy way but conduct themselves as Jesus would have them be. And if they choose to leave the

Amish way and become English, then our door is open to help them."

"Okay, well, maybe you will get that chance to meet them," she told him before sitting down to rock her crying baby.

7

The Marketplace

"Hey you," a man's harsh voice yelled out to Samuel while he was getting ready to pay for his supplies. Turning his head to see who was doing the yelling, Samuel noticed a tall gentleman walking up close behind him as if he wanted to fight right there in the store.

"Do I know you from somewhere?" Samuel asked the angry man.

"Well, you should. You and your bunch of freaks tried to rob me the other night when I came out of the bar."

"You have me confused with someone else, I wasn't out any night. I was home with my wife and son."

Without saying another word to Samuel, the man gave him a shove on his shoulder. "I don't think so. You look just like the man that I'm talking about. I've been wondering when we were going to run into each other, and what do you know, here we are."

"Please don't put your hand on me again, sir. I already told you that you have me mixed up with someone else. I have no need to take from someone when I have my own way of living."

"I take it you think that you can take me on. Well let's see just what you are made of," the man said, trying to get on Samuel's last nerve.

"I'm not sure just what you're asking from me, nor do I really care. But I will be going back home to take this food to my wife, which she has asked me to pick up for her. Now, if you would kindly move out of my way so I may pass." Samuel was now looking straight into the man's eyes to show him that he was not afraid of him.

"Oh, so you think that you're so tough? Well, put your money where your mouth is and fight like a man."

"I am not looking for any trouble, nor do I want to fight. I told you already that you have me confused with someone other than me. Now, I won't ask you again to please move so I can go my own way," he said as he looked at all the spectators standing by.

The store manager came out from the back room to find out what all the commotion was about. "Is there something that I can help the two of you with?" he asked, looking at the men.

"This man here has me confused with someone other than myself. I'm trying to leave, but he wants to fight me for what another has done to him," Samuel stated, looking at the man.

"Well, I will not be having anyone fight in my store, so if you would kindly allow this gentleman to leave," the manager said as he stood to make sure that Samuel would be allowed to leave without any more coming from the tall man.

"I'll be seeing you around," the tall man spoke, giving Samuel a shove as he passed by him walking toward the door.

Now, Samuel, coming from a background where he worked much harder than the normal man, wasn't about to take much more from a man who felt like it was okay for him to put his hands on him. "I told you, mister, not to put your hands on me again. Now, for the last time, I did not take anything of yours. You have me confused with someone else. But if you still feel like you want to fight and you feel like you can hurt me by your cruel words, then let's go outside and take care of this right now."

The man stood there. He saw that Samuel, although shorter than he was, was not going to take what he was dishing out. The tall man looked at him. "You sure look like one of the men who came by my place and stole from me."

"Really now? You were telling me that it was when you came out of the bar. Now, which one is it? Coming out of the bar or at your home?"

Now the man was confused with just what he was talking about. He was unsure himself. "Sorry, man, I think I have you confused with another," he spoke as he looked around and saw people standing there looking at him. Without saying another word, he brushed past Samuel and some of the others who were standing close by and walked out the door.

Samuel, unsure of what to think, gathered his wits and walked out the same door the man had just exited. Getting into his truck and looking down the sidewalk, he could see the man walking slowly like he was all mixed up, unsure of what he was doing. Samuel said a prayer for him, "Lord, only you know why that man acted the way that he did. Please help him find his way, in Jesus's name, amen."

Samuel headed home after buying what he was sent into town to buy, wondering within his heart if his actions were inappropriate to others in the store. He knew that he was a Christian man, and he was unsure if his actions were unpleasing to God. Could he have done something else or talked in a better way to the man who had accused him of stealing? Something deep inside Samuel's heart made him feel ashamed of his actions.

God, please show me what I should have said or done. I feel that I was wrong the way I handled myself.

He went home feeling down about his trip into town but didn't want to bring it home to his wife. Trying to get his mind off what happened before going into his home, he put his mind on something else, like what Katie was going to fix for supper.

"I'm home, Katie girl."

Katie came out from the living room to join her husband in the kitchen. "I'm glad that you're home. Were you able to get everything that I need from the store?"

"I did," he said as he began to take the food out of their bags. "This is everything that you asked for, isn't it?"

Looking at what was on the counter, she commented, "Yeah."

"What are we having to eat for supper?"

"These ribs, and I thought baked potatoes and corn would be good. Does that sound pleasing to you?"

"Oh yes, quite pleasing. I know that you are an excellent cook, Katie. Your ma had taught you well," he said as he put his arms around her, trying to forget what took place in town.

Katie felt like something was wrong just by the way he has hugging her and leaning his head on the back of her. "Samuel, is there anything wrong?"

"Nah, why you ask?"

"You have hugged me a good many times from behind, and never have you laid your head upon my back like this. I feel that something is not right."

Samuel didn't want to tell her what took place, but how would he avoid the truth from her without it being a lie? "I had a slight run-in with a man in town today is all." He was trying to make it sound like it was really nothing.

"I don't know what you are talking about. You had a run-in? What does that mean, Samuel?"

"There was a man in the grocery store that I went into today who got me confused with a different person." He was hoping that was enough to satisfy her to where he would not have to go into the whole long story of what really took place. If the truth be told, all he wanted was to forget what happened, partially because he was upset at himself for not handling it the way he should have, and another was because he should have reached out and tried to help the man who was so confused.

"Is that all? It just seems to me that there is more to it than that. Is there something that you don't want me to know?" she asked.

"I guess you can say that. At first he wanted to fight me, thinking that I was someone else. But it didn't come to that. I let him know that I wasn't whoever he thought that I was." Without going into any more detail yet telling the truth of the matter, he moved on to a different subject. "So how is Michael? Has he been eating good?"

"Yes, he has. He must be going to be a very big strong boy. He has a huge appetite. He wants to eat every hour, like nothing I have ever seen before."

"Must take after me, I guess, because you eat like a little mouse. You barely eat enough to keep a bird alive," he continued.

"Oh, come on now. I eat a lot more than that. I have to eat more just so I can produce more milk for him."

"Do you need any help out here in the kitchen, or can I go spend some time with our boy?"

"This is woman's work. You have your own work to do, and I don't go help you. So you can go spend time with Michael. I'll call you when supper is done." She began to shoo him out of the kitchen.

Samuel rocked his son with such pride of being a father for the first time. This was something he had always wanted since the first time he was married, and there was a time after his first wife died that he wondered if he was ever going to marry again, let a lone be a father. Now he sat rocking his son and singing a child's song to him.

"You are my miracle boy that Jesus gave to me. He sent you from heaven above with a sweet melody. The love that I feel for you is never compared to God's love. His love is more than I can give, but I will try to father you just as he would have me be."

Samuel was unaware that he had someone listening to him other than Michael, staring at him as he sang. Little did he know that when Katie was cooking, she listened as well. She rarely heard him sing in church. His voice stayed at a low tone so others could not hear him. Now she heard that this man whom she married had such an amazing baritone voice. She didn't dare interrupt him as she cooked, but she felt as though she could cook all night just to hear him sing. Like all things when they come to an end, her cooking was done, and she was ready to serve it to her husband.

"Come eat now, Samuel, while it's hot."

"Something sure does smell good." said Samuel.

"I was going to make ribs and baked potatoes and corn but decided on something differrent. This is a recipe that I got from Judy Smith, the lady at church. She said it's one of her husband's favorite dishes. It's called Lady Mar's goulash, and according to her, it's the very best. I hope that it's as good as she says it is."

"Well, shall we say the blessings? And then we will see."

The two held each other's hand, and Samuel pronounced a blessing on the cook, as well as the food. He took his fork and gave his wife a wink as he picked up some of the goulash to taste it. She watched as if she had cooked him poison of some sort.

"Wow, I do believe she just might be right. This is simply wonderful."

"Oh, good," Katie said as she then took a bite to taste it for herself. "Hmm, this is really good. I think I just might have found a new favorite of mine, and it's so easy to make."

"You can let Judy know that I think this has become my favorite dish as well."

"I'm sure that she will be pleased with that." She looked at him then decided to tell him what she thought of his singing. "I heard you singing to Michael, and I must say that you should join the choir at the church. You have a voice like an angel. As I cooked, I listened, and it was just beautiful."

"You could hear me above the cooking?" he asked, giving her a shy look.

"Oh, trust me. There is nothing to fear about me hearing you sing. I really loved hearing you. When we are at church, I can barely hear you. You're so quiet. So this was quite a treat for me today, to cook a new meal and hear the best singer in all the world."

The next morning, when Katie woke up, she saw that Samuel had already left for the fields, so she did what she had been doing come every morning when waking up, and that was put a pot of coffee on. This was something that her friend Judy introduced her to when she started to go to the church she and Samuel had been going to for nearly a year now. Ever since she had a taste of the coffee, she found that she loved it so much that she felt like she had acquired the taste for it.

8

The Arrest

Samuel did what he did every morning when he got up, and that was to say a prayer before going into the fields to put a day's work in. Little did he know that this day was going to be one that he would not soon forget. Riding on his tractor plowing up the field so it would be ready to plant, he noticed two men wearing police uniforms walking out to meet him on the field. Stopping his tractor and jumping down, he walked up to where they were.

"Can I help you, officers?"

"Are you Samuel Hershberger?" asked one of the officers.

"That would be me. How can I help you?"

"I am here to place you under arrest for the murder of Kenneth North."

Surprised by what he was hearing from the officers, he stepped back quickly. "What are you saying? I don't even know who that is. I have never met any Kenneth North. Who is he? Murder? And how did he die?"

"Sir, would you kindly come with me? I have a witness putting you at the scene where it took place."

"Where what took place? I'm here working my fields from sunup to sun down most every day. You can ask my wife. I don't know who this man is that you are talking about." Samuel pleaded with them to believe him, but they didn't want to hear what he had to say.

"You claim to not know this man, but I heard from another source that you and him got into a fight at the market just the other day," one of the officer said as he placed the hand cuffs on Samuel and put him into the back of the police car.

"A fight?" Samuel stated. "So that's who you're talking about? We never got into a fight. The man had me mistaken for someone else whom he thought had robbed him coming out of the bar one evening."

"So did you?" asked the officer.

"Did I what? Rob him?"

"Yes, it seems to me that there was something going on there for him to think that you did."

"I have never stolen anything in all of my life. I have my own. I have no right to ever want someone else's belongings."

"I agree. You should never want another man's things. So why don't you cut through the chase and give it to me straight. What happened between you and this man?"

"Nothing. I'm telling you the truth of the matter."

"Something happened. Otherwise, this man would still be alive. There's something that you're not telling me, and we will get the truth from you one way or another."

"Do I get a phone call?" he asked as he entered the jailhouse.

"You can have one phone call. I hope it's to your lawyer because you're going to need it," one of the officers said to him as he handed him a phone.

Samuel could not believe what was happening to him, murder of all things to be accused of. He must make a call home to let Katie know where he was at and what was going on. "Katie, it's me, honey, Samuel. I need some help. I've been arrested, and I'm down here at the jailhouse."

"Arrested? For what, Samuel? What is this all about?"

"They think that I killed a man, the same man I told you about, the one whom I ran into at the store. Please call up Pastor Mike."

"It's going to be all right. I'm calling him right now."

Samuel was led to a holding cell until he was to be seen by a lawyer or appear in court. As he sat there, he began to question his faith. "Lord, is this some sort of punishment for me lying with Katie before we wed? Are you angry with me for something that I did or didn't do?"

As soon as he spoke those words to God, he remembered the thought that came to him when he was watching the man who was now murdered walk down the street. Samuel had felt within himself to go talk to the man. But instead, he got into his truck and prayed and headed back home to his wife.

"Lord, are you angry with me for not speaking to the man as I should have? Are you mad because I walked away from the Amish faith and became Christian?" He couldn't understanding why this happened to him.

All the while he was talking out loud to God and himself, he had no idea that he was being heard by another, much like when he sang to his son. But he indeed had a listener. It was one of the officers who brought him in. In fact, it was the same one who told him that he needed a lawyer, basically because he thought that Samuel was guilty. But now he listened closely to every word that Samuel prayed to God, and he was questioning now if he was the killer.

"Lord," Samuel continued on, "please help me, Lord, to be able to go home to my wife and son. I didn't even know that man, Lord, and I don't know who killed him or why they killed him. And, Lord, please help the officers to find the real person who did this terrible thing to that man."

"Samuel, your lawyer is here to see you. You will have to come here with me so you can have a talk with him."

"My lawyer, who is that?" he asked, not knowing whom the officer was referring to. He knew that he never had a reason before to have a lawyer, so where did one come from? Was this something they provided for the people they arrest?

"I'm not sure who he is, but no matter who he is, one is better than none," the officer answered him.

Samuel didn't say a word. He just followed the officer into a room where he was to meet his lawyer for the first time—at least, it was the first time meeting him as his lawyer. "Hey, Brother Josh, what are you doing here? Did my wife call you up?" asked Samuel.

"She called up my father, and he called me. What a surprise to hear that you have been arrested for the brutal murder of Kenneth North. Can you tell me anything that would give the officers reason to believe that you have committed murder?"

"Are you my lawyer that they told me about?"

"Yes, I am. Is that fine with you?"

"It's more than fine. I had no idea who they were even talking about. And as far as the man who was killed, I only had one encounter with him."

"And when was that? And what did it have to do with—I'll put it to you straight. They say they have an eyewitness who can put you at the scene of the time that it happened. I need anything that can prove to the court that you did not do this. Just for the record, I believe that you did not do this crime. Did you?"

"No, I never even knew the man. Like I said, I only saw him the one time I was at the grocery store picking up some food that my wife had asked me to get for supper. As I was ready to leave and come home, this man, whom I have never seen before, shoved me."

"He shoved you?" Josh asked, surprised that a complete stranger would just come up to someone and start to shove them.

"Then what did you do?" he asked.

"At first I didn't know what to think, and I asked him what he did that for. He started to shout at me and say that I robbed him coming out of the bar. Now, Brother Josh, I'm a farmer. I have to get up so early every morning to work my fields in this season. I'm never out late. I'm always home with my wife and son."

"I believe ya, brother. What else took place that day?"

"I told the man that he had me confused with someone else." Samuel told all that he could remember to his friend and lawyer Josh. After it was all said and done, Josh told him that he was going to be talking with the store manager and find out who else was in the store who might have seen what took place between Samuel and Kenneth.

The two men shook hands and said their good-byes. After having a talk to his lawyer, Samuel felt much better about things but still was concerned about Katie and the baby. Oh, how he wished that he could just go home and talk to his baby boy and hold his wife in his arms. He sat back on his bed, feeling so lonely for his family and questioned why this had to happen to him. He wondered if he knew who the real killer was. Was he being set up by someone who knew that he used to be Amish and they didn't like the Amish? Somehow, deep in his heart, he felt like he was being set up by the real killer, and it wasn't just by mistake. But how could he prove that to the court? He was locked up like a common criminal. He would pray and ask God to send someone to find the truth so he could return home to his wife and son.

Lord Jesus, please help the real person who killed that man to be found. Lord, you know that I'm not the one who did that terrible thing. So I ask you this in Jesus's name, amen.

Samuel was finally able to shut his mind off enough to sleep after praying. He woke up with a whole new thought coming to him after talking with his lawyer about the case.

"Samuel, I wanted to stop here and talk with you before we head over to the courthouse. I stopped by the market and had a talk with the manager about what took place there when you had a run-in with Kenneth."

"Did he tell you the same story that I did? Did he back up my story?" he asked, feeling anxious about court.

"Yes, he did, and there is more. He told me that he heard the same man who started a fight with you do the same thing to another man the following day."

"Did he say if he knew who the other man is?"

"He said the man was a younger man, about eighteen years old. His name is..." Josh pulled out the folder he had on him with all the information written on it. "Here it is right here. His name is Robert Culbert. Do you know anyone by that name at all?" he asked, looking at him.

"No, it don't ring a bell to me. Of course, I see young and old at the mill whenever I take in a load of corn or wheat.

Unless it is one of them who work there, I wouldn't know who he is."

"I'm going to have you make a plea of not guilty today in court and ask for a bail be made so you can go home to your wife and son."

"Oh, that would be wonderful. I don't know how anyone would ever want to break the law to where it would put them in this place. I didn't get much sleep. I kept thinking about Katie and Michael. Do you think that the judge will allow me to return home to my family?"

"Yes, I do. You have never been in any sort of trouble before. And I have enough evidence here for him to believe that this really was a setup from someone else, and that someone else is the real person who did this. Now I'm going over there and file some papers. An officer will bring you over to the court in a few minutes."

"Okay," Samuel said as he watched Josh walk out of the room. "God, please help me to be able to go home to my family. I need to get my crops put in before it's too late."

One of the officers who placed him under arrest came to his cell to take him over to the courthouse. Trying to be nice to Samuel after hearing him talk to God about him being innocent when at first he thought he was guilty, the officer said, "I hope whoever did this to Kenneth will be found so you can go home to your family."

Shocked by the man's words, Samuel in turn thanked him for believing in his innocence. "Thank you. I hope they find whoever did this too so I can go back home. This has devastated my wife. She is young with our little baby boy all alone at home, not knowing what is going to happen to me. At this time, I don't know what to say to her."

"I have to confess something to you." The officer looked in his rearview mirror as he talked to Samuel. "I heard you praying yesterday. You were talking to God about being innocent. I heard you say, 'God, please help them find whoever did this terrible thing.'"

Samuel listened closely as the officer talked, wondering what this was all about.

"Until then, I must confess I thought that we had the right man. Most everyone who comes to jail is guilty of something, and when we arrested you for the murder of Kenneth, I thought you did it. But after hearing you pray, I don't believe that now anymore. I prayed last night that the guilty will be found."

"Are you a man of God? I mean, if my prayer touched you, then you must be."

"Yes, I am, and I now know that you are also. Well, here we are," he said as he parked his police car. "As much as I believe in your innocence, I still have to do my job and take you to the courtroom and stay in there with you."

"I understand. I must say I had you all wrong too. When you arrested me, I didn't care for you even thinking that I could have done something like that. I'm glad to know that you believe in me now."

Samuel got out of the car and began to walk with handcuffs on alongside the officer. As he was approaching the door of the courthouse, his heart felt like it was about to explode. He prayed silently, *Oh Lord, please help me today. Calm my nerves down. Help me be able to go home to my wife.* Just as he finished up praying, he saw his wife and son standing in the hallway of the courthouse waiting for him.

"Samuel," Katie called out. "It's going to be all right. I'm here for you, Samuel, me and your son. I've been praying, honey."

"Thank you, Katie. I sure miss the both of you."

Katie stood there watching as the officer led her husband in the courtroom. She followed close behind them then, taking a seat in the room, tried to keep her mind in a positive place. She played with the baby so she would not let her mind go wild. Waiting to see what would happen next, she prayed again silently, *Please, dear Jesus, help him today. You know that he never did this wicked thing.*

Samuel tried to keep himself calm while waiting for the judge to enter the courtroom. Then it happened, where everyone had to stand up when he walked in.

"This is the honorable Judge Ryan Davis presiding. All, stand," a man in the courtroom stated.

Samuel watched as the judge sat down and began to speak, "Today is September 11, 2013. My first case I call is Samuel Hershberger."

Samuel stood up with his lawyer and walked up to where he was to stand to talk with the judge.

"Are you Samuel Hersheberger?" asked the judge.

"Yes, Your Honor."

"I see here," he stated, looking at the papers in front of him, "that you are here today because on September 10, you were placed under arrest for the murder of Kenneth North."

"Yes, sir, Your Honor."

"Your Honor, I am Joshua Perish. Samuel is my client, and I will be representing him. Your Honor, I have proof that Samuel was nowhere around Kenneth North at the time of his murder."

"Proof? So let me hear what you have for proof," the judge asked.

"Your Honor, on the day in question, Samuel was at home with his wife and son. She is here also to verify this as true."

The judge looked back at Katie sitting there with the baby. "I'm sure that she will. Tell me in your own words what took place on the day in question."

Samuel was unsure of what to say. All he knew was that he did not do the crime. "Your Honor, I'm not quite sure of where to begin at. All I know is that I was at home with my wife, and I would never do what I am being accused of doing."

"Young man," replied the judge, "what I am asking you is to tell me what you all did on the day in question."

"I have farmland that I work at this time of year. I got up at five in the morning, and I worked until suppertime, about six in the evening. Then I went back to work until around nine. I came back in and played with my son for a little while before going to bed." After stating what he did, he felt tired explaining his whereabouts.

"Your Honor, my client has never been involved in anything that would have been considered a crime before. Up until a year ago, my client has been part of the Amish community. He has always been an exceptional man, a man of honor with a caring family. We believe we know that man who really did this, Your Honor. The sheriff department is looking into it as we speak. There is a witness who came forth and told them that this man was fighting with Kenneth on the night in question."

"Is this all true?" the judge asked the officer who brought Samuel into court.

"Yes, it is, Your Honor," the officer confirmed.

"Your Honor, in light of this information, we are asking that the court allow my client to return home with his family." Josh asked.

"After hearing and taking it all in, I am going to throw this case out for lack of evidence. I want to see this man in question picked up, and I want to see him before me. Sir, I have never done this before—and I'm not quite sure of why I am right now—but you are free to go home." He hit his gavel and said, "Dismissed."

After Samuel heard those words fall from the judge's mouth, he shook his lawyer's hand and walked over to his wife and gave her a big kiss.

"I know why he dismissed it. It was because God had him do that, and he don't even understand why," Samuel declared.

"Well, brother," said Josh, "we know why he did that, but I must say I have never seen that happen before. God was in this place today. He set you free to go home to your family."

"Thank you so much, Josh. I owe you so much. By the way how much do I owe you?" Samuel asked.

"Every once in a while, I have a case I do pro bono, and this is one of them times. I'm just so glad to know that we serve a God who hears our prayers and answers them as well." Josh shook hands again and was gone out the door, leaving Samuel and Katie standing there, feeling very happy that Samuel was able to return home.

9

The Meeting

Samuel was happy to be home with his wife and son after facing charges of murder. He knew deep in his heart that God would answer his prayer and let him go home to his family. He admitted to Katie that for a while he felt scared. Then when he prayed, he could feel peace fall on him. Now holding his son and talking to him all about facing the judge and God being present in the courtroom, Samuel was telling him about how someone had set him up to face charges of murder.

"You know, Michael, if it had not been for God hearing your mom and my prayers, I could have been taken away from you for a very long time. But you see, we serve a very big God, one whom we can always trust and believe in."

Katie was cooking while secretly listening in on him talking to their son again. She loved to hear Samuel sing and talk to the baby and to see the way little Michael looked at his dad whenever he would talk to him. The meal was ready to be served, but she failed to call for Samuel to come and eat. She hated to interrupt him while talking, but after a few minutes of thinking that she wanted it to be hot when she served it, she knew it best to call for him.

"Samuel, would you care to join me in eating?"

"Well, Michael, it looks like I will have to put you in your bed for a while. Mama has my supper ready for me," Samuel stated as he put the baby back in his bed.

"Is the baby asleep?"

"No, but I think he's getting tired. As I was talking with him, I could see his eyes close then open again. My guess is that he will be asleep before we are done eating."

"That would be nice. I'd kind of like to have some time with you by myself. I missed you when you were being detained for a couple of days." After saying that, she felt bad because it was like she was letting light of him sitting in jail when she really hated the very thought of what happened to him.

"Are you having fun on my expense?"

"No, not at all. I really didn't mean for it to come out like that. I really did cry when you were locked up like a criminal. Please believe me when I say I hated it for you to go to that terrible place."

"I do believe you, honey. I'm just playing with you is all." He gave her a big teasing smile that warmed her heart.

"I love you, you know. And I am so glad to have you home with me. I will not take us for granted anymore."

"You took us for granted?" he gave her a look of surprise from her comment.

"Sometimes couples take each other for granted, like we think that they will always be there for each other no matter what. We don't stop to think that in any given minute, it could all be taken from us."

"I know what you're saying. When I was locked up, I thought about how I always thought that I'd be there for you and Michael, but when I was locked up, I saw how I wasn't, and it hurt me so bad. All I could do was pray that God would take care of the both of you because I couldn't. I hope that whoever this Robert Culbert is will be caught."

After hearing the name *Robert Culbert*, Katie nearly spit up the drink she was just ready to swallow. Seeing her begin to cough, trying to catch her breath, Samuel jumped up to help her. He raised her arms straight up above her head and allowed her to catch her second wind. She swallowed deep.

"I'm sorry about that, Samuel, but that name Robert Culbert—I know him, Samuel." Right after she admitted knowing him, she wished she would have said nothing of the sort.

"How do you know an Englishman, Katie girl?"

"I thought that we are now one of the English people too, Samuel."

"Yes, we are now, but have you known him for long now?"

"I met him while walking down the path of my ma and da's home before we married."

"Did he seem to you that he was an upstanding guy? Or was he one of these guys who belong behind the jail bars?"

Katie listened as Samuel spoke about Robert, remembering how she felt about him when she first met him. But how could she ever tell her husband that? He could never understand that she loved another, or was it really love that she felt? After all, she was to meet up with him at the mill one evening, and he never showed up—just to find herself waking up from a dirty floor, all filthy and bleeding as if she had been touched by a man for the first time. Never understanding what took place that evening and never telling another what happened, she just learned to bury that deep inside until now.

"Katie, are you listening to me? I asked you something."

"I'm sorry, Samuel. I was thinking about that man, if I think that he is the type that needs to be behind bars. Well, I didn't know him that well at all. Maybe he is."

"Some people seem to think that he's the guy who killed that man Kenneth and set me up for it."

"Why would he do that, and why set you up for it? Do you know who he is?" she asked.

"No, I've never met him before. But it makes no sense to me that someone I've never met before wants to blame murder on me. What would be the purpose in doing that?"

"I don't know."

Though she didn't know why anyone would do that, she wondered if Robert had purpose behind it, if indeed it was

Robert. But why him of all people? It couldn't be because of her. Why would it be? After all, he didn't want anything to do with her. Not only did he not show up at the mill like he said he would, but when she saw him in town and tried to talk with him, he went the other way, not wanting to pay any mind to her at all.

"If it was this Robert who did this terrible thing, I sure hope he gets caught and arrested for it."

"Yes, I do too."

"Well, just maybe, we will hear more about it sometime tomorrow. Whatever the case may be, I am cleared of doing the crime."

Katie and Samuel spent much of the night together after feeding the baby and putting him back to bed for the night. They danced, holding each other tight in each other's arms, as if never to let go. They were determined to never take each other for granted again.

Morning came, and it was the start of a new promise to each other, the start of a new beginning. They could hardly wait to get back to their routine of working the farm and attending church with their friends and praising God Almighty for everything he had done in their life. Samuel could hardly wait to get back on his tractor. He missed two days of working his field, and he knew that it would set him back for a little while. But he was free to work it as he pleased, and that he would never forget or take for granted ever again.

10

The Catch

It was three weeks after Samuel was found not guilty that Robert was picked up trying to go across the border of Mexico. Katie got a phone call from Samuel's lawyer, Josh, telling her that Robert was picked up trying to escape the warrant that was out for his arrest. He was wondering if she and Samuel might want to come to his court appointment. He promised to keep them informed on when Robert would go to trial.

"I will let Samuel know when he comes in from the field. I'm sure that he will want to come to the courthouse at the time of Robert's hearing," Katie told him.

"Okay, that sounds very good. I'll keep you posted when it will be."

Katie could hardly wait until Samuel was to come in for supper. She knew that he was not coming in for any lunch. He had told her not to make anything up for him because he wanted to get caught up on where he left off when he was arrested. She went about her household chores, cleaning and scrubbing until it felt like her hands would fall off her. She hadn't worked so hard since living at home with her folks. There she was used to working hard, but since getting married, Samuel made work so much easier for her, just like he had promised to do. Now, instead of working until she felt like she would drop on most of her days, she still had energy to dance and watch some television with Samuel when he came in when the darkness fell outside.

Samuel came walking into the house some hours later, hungry as a bear. "Good evening, Katie girl, how has your day been? How is Michael today? Giving you any trouble? Is there anything to eat? I'm starved!"

"To answer all your questions, my day has been a busy day of cleaning and cooking. The baby has been awake for most of the day, watching me as I cleaned. He has not given me any trouble at all. And supper is all done and waiting for you to come in to eat."

"That sounds great. I sure missed you and the baby while I was out in the fields. I thought of you all day long, and thank God for a wonderful wife and the mother of my son."

"Aww, Samuel, that is so sweet of you to say that. I missed you and thought of you a lot through my day as well. I got a phone call earlier from Josh Perish, your lawyer."

"Oh, what did he have to say?" he asked, looking at Katie with wide eyes.

"He said that the police have arrested Robert Culbert at the border of Mexico. It sounds like he was trying to leave the country so he wouldn't face charges of murder."

"When is he going to court, do you know?"

"Josh said that he will let us know so we can attend if we want to."

"Oh, of course, I will be there for sure. I need to know why this man would try and set me up for what he did. It makes no sense to me for a perfect stranger to do something like that. It seems like there would be some kind of reason for someone to do that. But I have never met the man for him to have a vendetta against me."

"Here, honey. Come sit down and try to relax and enjoy your meal, okay?"

She wanted to get her mind off Robert. After what she had recently found out about him, she thanked God that the two of them never did get together. Samuel was a much better choice for her—even though in the past, when she would dream of Robert, Samuel was far from her mind. What she couldn't understand was why Robert had it out for Samuel. It made no sense to her at all. She was hoping that in court at his trial, she and him would never come up. She didn't know how to explain it all to Samuel. After all, it was just a crush and nothing more, and the crush was just something that was one-sided. It was clear to her that Robert had not the same thoughts or feelings.

"Katie, you have really outdone yourself with this meal. It is wonderful." Right when he was telling her how much he loved her cooking, they heard what sounded like the baby choking from the baby monitor. "What is that?" he asked as the two ran to the baby's room.

Katie reached down, picking the baby up out of his bed. "Michael, Michael," she yelled, patting his back, trying to get him to stop choking.

"Here, lift up his hands above his head," Samuel said as he lifted up Michael's hands. "I wonder what that was all about. Had he ever done that before?"

"No, that is the first time that has ever happened. Look at his face. It looks so red. Do you think that he will be all right?"

"It might be red like that because of him coughing like he was. Bring him out here with us as we eat, and we will keep an eye on him. I want to make sure that he is all right."

"Yes, me too. I think that I will bring his little swing out in the room with us and put him in it for a while. I want to make sure whatever it was that brought it on isn't going to happen again."

"You carry him, and I will bring the swing," Samuel told her.

"Okay." She gathered up a rattle for the baby and a pacifier for him to suck while she and Samuel finished eating. "No more coughing like that, honey. You scared me and your dad," she said, waiting to put him on the swing.

"You're not kidding. That is scary to hear that come from him. Look at his face. It's still very red. You would think that it wouldn't be this red still."

Katie began to feel Michael's face to see if it felt hot or flushed. Though to her he felt like he would be just fine, his face was much too red for being fine. "Samuel, I think that we should take him to the doctor's. Something is just not right. A baby don't get a red face for nothing."

Without saying anything, he took Michael from Katie and wrapped a blanket around him and began to walk toward the door. Turning his head to see if Katie was following close behind him, he motioned for her with his head, telling her, "Come on, let's go."

Grabbing her purse and following her husband and son, she was out the door, getting into his truck. "Samuel, you're scaring me. You're not saying anything to me."

"I'm sorry. I just don't know what to make of him being red like this and not running a fever. I'm just praying and asking God to heal him. I need you to be praying also and not be scared, okay?"

"Okay." Although she agreed with Samuel, she sat looking at her son's face, which did not look normal, and it brought fear to her. In her mind, she knew that fear was not of God, and she asked him to help her to not fear but have faith that all is well.

"Samuel, Samuel," she cried out. "Hurry, hurry, get him to the hospital. He has white foam coming from his mouth."

Samuel looked her way and, seeing what she said was true, stepped on the gas, going just about as fast as his old truck could go. "God, help my boy! Please, God, help him."

Katie could tell by his voice that he was also allowing fear to take ahold of him, and she knew that it was not doing either of them any good to be in fear. "Okay, Samuel, we know what God's word tells us about fear. We both need to get a grip of ourselves and pray, believing that God will take care of our son."

"Let's pray again, but this time, with faith, huh?"

"Dear Lord Jesus, you are the Creator of all things. We ask you right now to heal our baby in Jesus's name, amen."

They pulled into the parking lot of the hospital. This time around, Samuel knew what to do, not like when he brought Katie in when she was having the baby. "It's this way, honey," he said as he opened the door to the emergency room. "Help, someone, please help me with my boy."

A nurse came running up to them, seeing he was carrying the baby.

"I don't know what's wrong with him. At first he was choking, then he got all red, now he's got white stuff coming out of his mouth."

"Okay, let's put him in this room over here," the nurse said, leading him into a room. "I need a doctor now," she said to another nurse. "I need you folks to stand back."

Katie and Samuel watched as the nurse cut the baby's shirt off him and placed black tabs all over his chest, hooking them up to a monitor.

"What's happening to my baby?" Katie asked the nurse. "What's wrong with him?"

"Please, let me do my job. I don't know what it is. I need to check everything."

The doctor came into the room, asking the nurse what she had done so far. Then as he worked on the baby, he asked questions to the parents. "Can you tell me when this all began?"

"He was fine a couple of hours ago. I came in from work for supper, and my wife and I were sitting at the table eating when we heard him choking. We ran into his room and picked him up. After he seemed to be settled down, we put him in his swing. But his face seemed to stay red, and he wasn't hot or anything. So we decided to bring him in to see what is wrong with him, and on our way, he began to have white foamy stuff come from his mouth."

"You never noticed anything different with him today?" the doctor asked.

Samuel looked over at Katie, knowing that he was in the field for most of the day.

"No, not at all. I cleaned the house while he was on his blanket, watching me as I worked. I fed him like I always do. He seemed to be happy all day, until this. What do you think that it could be?"

"I'm not sure yet. I will have to run some tests on him, but I'm leaning toward kidney complications. One thing that I am sure of, that white foam coming from his mouth, he was having a seizure, his little body was going into shock."

"Kidney?" Samuel said, looking at Katie.

Katie took ahold of his hand and gave it a light squeeze. "Remember our prayer. Don't lose hope."

"I know, honey, but his kidneys."

"God made his kidneys, and he will be just fine."

The doctor interjected, "I need to run some more tests on him. I need to ask for the two of you to go out into the hallway or go down into the waiting room. I will have someone come to get you in just a while."

After the doctor sent them out of the room, they walked down to the cafeteria to get some coffee.

"Try not to worry, honey," Samuel commented, looking at Katie rubbing her hands together as if to rub them raw.

"I'm trying not to, Samuel. I'm really trying to have faith that he is in God's hands. I just don't understand it. How can something like this happen to a perfectly healthy little baby?"

"I don't know, honey, and really, we don't know what is wrong. It could be nothing at all to worry about."

After they had what seemed to be several cups of coffee, with their heart racing faster than normal—they weren't sure if it was the coffee or what happened to Michael—the nurse came in to get them. "The doctor would like to talk with the both of you. Please follow me."

The two looked at each other with their heart racing within their chests—what was it? Could he have found the problem? They couldn't get down the hallway fast enough to hear what the doctor had to say.

"Do you know what it is that made my baby choke?" asked Katie.

"Your son has a bad kidney. He will need to have a kidney transplant."

"Kidney transplant!" yelled Katie.

"Oh my gosh, I can't believe what I'm hearing," commented Samuel. "What can we do?"

"How is your health?" the doctor asked, looking at the both of them.

"Mine is fine, why?" asked Katie.

"Mine too," Samuel spoke.

"The case we have here is that we need to see if your blood is a match for your son, if you are willing."

"Yes, of course, we are willing," stated Katie then looked at Samuel for his reply.

"Yes, what do we need to do?"

"First of all, we need to send you down to the lab room where we will have your blood checked to see if you're a match. Then we will do whatever it takes to get your son well."

"What if we're not a match?" asked Katie.

"Then he will go on a waiting list. We have some time, but the sooner he gets a transplant—assuming we find a donor—the better off he will be. Most likely, one of you will be a match. There usually is one parent that is a match."

"What about how young he is? Will that matter?" asked Samuel.

"It could be a little more difficult, but he has a very good chance at a complete recovery," the doctor commented.

"Just lead the way," Samuel said as he took Katie by the hand, and they followed close behind the same nurse who came to get them just moments before.

The two sat down, waiting to have their blood checked to see if it was a match for their little baby.

"Jesus, please help my little baby," Katie prayed out loud while she watched a man in the lab room take two tubes of blood from Samuel.

"Okay, ma'am, if you can sit over here, I'll get some blood from you now," the man in the long white jacket asked.

She sat down, pulling up her sleeve so he could put the band on her arm and draw the blood. She watched Samuel as the blood filled up the tubes. For just a moment, she squinted her eyes as the tube was being changed from one to the other, lightly pushing the needle back in.

"Okay, we are done here. I will get this checked right away to see who's the match. If you would like, you can go back down to your son, and I will let the doctor know what the outcome is as soon as I can."

The two walked back to their son's room with high hopes that a match would come back so their son would get a new kidney and live a normal life.

It felt like life was barely hanging on to Katie as she watched her son lying on a bed that was not of his own. What could have went wrong for this sort of thing to happen in one's life? She hurt so deep inside that it felt as if her heart would just stop at any given time. *God*, she cried on the inside so as not to let those around her hear her prayer, *please help my baby. I just can't go on without him.*

Samuel noticed that she had sobs coming from her and was trying to hold them back. "It's going to be okay, honey. I just know that it is."

"I just have a very sick feeling that something is not right. I can't do anything about it."

"You can pray," Samuel commented.

Katie looked at him with a disappointed look. "Do you think that I haven't been praying?" she snapped at him.

Taken by surprise at the tone of her voice, he looked at her in shock. "I didn't mean to offend you, honey. I know that you're praying. I was just merely answering your comment is all."

Katie quickly realized how she must have sounded to him. Taking ahold of his hand, she gave it a light squeeze. "I'm so sorry how I acted toward you. You must know that I did't mean it at all."

"I know that. It's all right, honey."

Just then, the doctor came back in the room. He had a look on his face that showed uncertainty.

"What's wrong?" Samuel asked before the doctor was able to speak.

"Is your son adopted by any chance?"

"No, why?" Katie spoke up, standing to her feet and grabbing Samuel tight by the hand.

"I'm really quite surprised by the outcome of these blood tests," said the doctor.

"Like how?"

"Your little boy does not have either of your blood type."

Katie and Samuel both looked at each other. "That has to be a mistake. I birthed him. I know I did." She looked at Samuel, who was looking confused as she was. "Is there any way that our baby could have gotten switched with another baby?" Katie asked, completely shocked that neither her nor Samuel had the blood type of their baby.

"I will check both of your blood for a DNA testing on the baby."

"How long will that take?" asked Samuel.

"It shouldn't take long for that at all. I'll get some samples from both you and the baby and have them checked."

The nurse took samples of everyone to find out if there was any way that a mix-up with the babies that was born on the same day at the same hospital could have happened. After the test came back, it was handed to the doctor. Looking at the paper the nurse handed him, the doctor gave Katie, then Samuel, a strange look. "Do I speak frankly with both of you?"

"Yes, of course. What is it?" Samuel asked.

"According to this test"—he stopped and looked at Katie again before going on—"according to this test, there is no possible way that this baby can be your child, Samuel." He looked at both of them.

"What!" Samuel shouted, looking at Katie.

"And me, Doctor? What about me? He's not our son—are you sure?" Katie asked.

"Katie, the baby is your son, but he's not Samuel's."

"What!" It was her turn to get loud. "But how can that be? I have never been with another—never." She looked at Samuel standing there in shock at the news about him not being the father. "Samuel, never have I been with another."

"My wife would never deceive me. Check it again," Samuel asked the doctor.

"I'm sorry to say this to you. I know what a shock it must bring to you. But I had the lab check it three times just to be sure, and every time, it came back the same. There is just no way that he can be your son." The doctor looked at Katie, not knowing what to say any further.

"Katie, how could you have deceived me like this?" Samuel turned his back on her.

"It's got to be a big mistake, Doctor. I know that it is. You see, Samuel is the only man that I have ever been with. We used to be Amish, and I was never with a man before him." As soon as she said those words, she remembered the one night that she was to meet up with Robert at the old mill, and he never showed up—or so she thought until now. "Doctor, do you think that the test can be a mistake?"

"No, Katie. It shows me here on this paper that it was checked three times, and every time, it came out the same. There is just no way that Samuel could be the father of your baby."

"Samuel." Katie grabbed his hand to talk with him. "Please, Samuel, I think I might know how this could have happened."

"Oh, are you suddenly remembering you being with another before you were ever with me?" he asked in a hurtful way.

"Can we talk alone, please, Samuel?"

"You lied to me about everything. How could have done this to me? It's no wonder this has happened to Michael. It's because of your sin, Katie," he shouted at her then ran out the door, leaving her standing there, not knowing what to think.

"I'm sorry to give you this bad news, but is there any way that you can get ahold of his father and see if he would be a match for him?" the doctor said.

"I was telling you the truth when I said that I have not been with another man, at least not that I have known."

"But how can that be? This test is complete and true."

"Can I ask you a question?" she asked.

"Sure."

"Before I was ever with Samuel, there was a young man that I have talked with from time to time. You see, when I was with my ma and my da, I was raised Amish, where I was never to have anything to do with the English. I met this guy, and one night he asked me to meet him at the old mill by where I used to live. I went to the mill and waited for this young man to show up, but the thing is, I never saw him show at all. I woke up on the dirt floor the next morning, and I was bleeding as if I had been with a man. I was unsure of what happened to me, so I never told another of this until now. Do you think that I could have conceived at that time? I swear to you, that is the only time that I could have ever been with another and not have known about it." She could hardly believe that she was breaking her silence of that night, to a doctor, and not her husband who has now gone out the door.

"If what you are telling me is true, then I would say that the young man you speak of took advantage of you and raped you. Would you know how to find this guy?"

"Yes, he is sitting in jail right now."

"Jail…I'd say that you go down to the jail and tell them what has happened up to now and ask them to allow me to take a blood test on him to see if he is the father of your baby."

"He's got to be. There is no other way that this could have happened."

"There is another."

"You don't believe me, do you?" she asked.

"What I meant by another way is that there could be that slight chance that it wasn't him who showed up. It could have been another."

"I'm going down to the jailhouse right now. Can I please get a piece of paper from you asking for this testing of him so I can show the police officers?"

"Yes, of course." Katie stood there in complete shock of this news she had just found out. She watched the doctor as he got on his computer, typing up words then printing it out.

"This should do it. Take this and see what comes of it."

Katie took the paper and was out the door after bending down and giving her baby a kiss. "I'll be back as soon as I can. I love you, Michael."

She thought about Samuel and the pain in his heart from what was found out today. How could all this even be? Did she have a home to go to? Would he love her even though he was not the father of the baby? Or would she be shunned again? All these questions came to mind as she waited for a reply from the jailhouse.

"I will have an officer bring Robert right over to the hospital. Are you going to file charges on him for rape?" the officer asked her.

"If it comes out that he is my baby's father, then I will have no other choice, will I?"

"No, not really. He is coming right now. You might want to get back over to the hospital to let them know that he is on his way."

Katie saw Robert come into sight with an officer standing at his side, handcuffs on his ankles and his wrist. She quickly turned her back and ran out the door when she noticed that Robert gave her a mean look. She was unsure why he gave her the nasty look because it was not anything that she could have done wrong. After all, she at one time felt like she wanted to spend her whole life with him. Now her past was catching up with her. She must confess everything to Samuel, although she was unsure of what to confess. To her, she had never been with another.

133

It had only been Samuel, but now she knew that there had been another.

Dear God, please help Robert to be the one who did this to me. I don't know anyone else who it could be. And, dear God, my little baby needs help, so please, please, help it to be Robert who did this terrible thing to me.

She noticed how insane she sounded, asking God to help this man—who was headed to prison for murder—be the father of her baby. She felt so desperate to have someone be the father so he could possibly save her child.

"They are bringing him right over so you can check to see if he is the man who fathered my baby. I need to know. How long will it take?" As she asked the doctor, she saw the officer bring Robert in.

"Please follow the nurse down the hallway to the lab so we can get some blood from this man."

The officer gave Robert a light tap at his shoulder to nudge him to follow the nurse. Katie watched as he followed the nurse. She only wished that he could walk faster to the lab, but with chains on his ankles, he was moving very slow. She sat next to her baby and sang to him, praying inside that Robert would be the father.

11

The Results

The test came back with Robert being the one who fathered Michael. Katie was relieved to know that she found out the truth about what happened to her that one night where she didn't know how she wound up on the floor all dirty and sore. But even more importantly, she needed to know if he was a match and would be willing to save her son by giving him one of his kidneys.

She knew that she was on her own at this time after sitting next to Michael's bedside feeling lonely and left all alone. Seeing Samuel had not come back to the hospital, she was indeed shunned again and left to take care of everything on her own. Her heart felt pain cut deep within her very soul as she tried to keep her mind focused on Michael at this time. Although she understood what Samuel must be thinking from finding out that he was not her son's father, she had to stay focused on what needed to be done to save her baby.

She would have a talk with Robert. She must know if he was willing to save her son, save his own son. Even if they had not planned to be parents together, Michael was still his son. She would go back to the jailhouse and speak to Robert, the man who had indeed raped her and fathered her son. How would she ever explain this to Samuel—how, after Robert's name had been mentioned several times and she never mentioned to have ever known him in that way before, even though she herself did not know the truth of it until now? She must not focus on Samuel right now. She must think about getting a kidney for her baby. She gathered her wits and walked back to the jail to talk with Robert. Sitting down in the waiting room while she waited for the officer to bring him in to talk with her, she tried to think of just what she would say to him.

"Well, now, Katie this is a surprise seeing you here. What can I do for you? Did you come here about your husband and why I killed someone?" Robert asked her while she tried to hold back the tears from the thought of their son lying at the hospital slowly dying.

"No, that is no concern to me right now. I came here because of my son."

"What's that got anything to do with me?" he asked, all puzzled.

"You don't know?"

"Know what? That you are married and have a son now?"

"I know that it was you who raped me. Samuel is not the father of my son"—she paused a minute—"you are."

"What are you talking about? Not only am I getting railroad for killing someone, but now I'm being accused of raping you and fathering your son? You have got to be kidding me. Where is this all coming from? I don't see you for god only knows how long—then suddenly I see you out of no where telling me this load of crap."

"Robert, I don't have time to waste on what you did or didn't do. The fact is the blood test that you took came back showing me that it was you who fathered my son, our son. He has a very bad kidney, and I am not a match for him." She took in a deep breath. "I was wondering if you would ever get checked to see if you are a match and give him one of your kidneys?"

"Wow, I'm in here for murder, and I'll be going to prison for years, girl, and all you can say is give your son a kidney?"

"You raped me, Robert!" she shouted loudly. "And he is your son too." She began to cry, her tears falling to the floor.

"And if I were to see if I am a match, since you say I am the father, then you must know that it was me who took advantage of you that one night. What are you going to do for me?"

Katie didn't know what he was asking of her. What would she do for him? What could she do was the question. "I don't know what you mean."

"Oh, come now, Katie. I can clearly see that you are no longer living in the dark ages as you were when I first met you." After seeing that she still had no comment to give back to him, he finished with what he had in mind. "If I were to give him one of my kidneys, would you be willing to tell the court that it was mutual between us when you got pregnant? The last thing I need is to have a rape charge against me too."

Katie was always known to tell the truth when it came down to it. She was a whole lot of things like disobeying her folks and God, but now he was asking her to tell the court a complete lie, where she would not only look bad in the eyes of her husband but to all of her church friends.

"You are already going away for murder, so how does rape really make a difference?"

"First of all, I just didn't kill for no reason. It was to protect myself, and I might be able to walk after I go back to trial. So do we have a deal?" he asked.

"I don't know what you mean to protect yourself, but that is no concern for me right now. I have to stay focused on Michael." She thought for a minute. Then she told him that they had a deal. At this time in her life, she would do just about anything to save her son if she could.

"Okay, I will get checked to see if I am a match. I don't know why I should even care since I will be going away for many years anyway if I don't beat this thing. But I don't want my son, as you say that he is, I don't want him to think that I never cared to save him."

Katie didn't care what reason he had. All she cared about was her son and giving him a chance at life. What would she tell Samuel? How would she ever get him to believe in her ever again? First things first, finding out if Robert was a match.

"I'm going to see the doctor and tell him to let the officers know that you have decided to get checked out." She pushed her chair back to walk out the door. "Thank you, Robert."

It was the following day, and Katie had not heard what the test results for Robert was yet. She had seen Samuel a couple of different times stop by to see the baby and to drop off some clothes for her and money so she could eat while staying at the hospital. She tried to approach him on each occasion, but he was still unwilling to hear anything that she had to say to him. Her heart ached deep within her spirit because she was being rejected by the man who had promised to love her and be there for her. But now he was walking away from her just like her folks had done one year ago. She was glad to know that he must still love Michael because he would stop by and check on him; and deep inside, he must still love her or at least still cared enough for her because he brought her clothes and money. That gave her a little hope, and hope and prayer were all she had now.

"Katie." A friend from the church by the name of Brenda had just walked in the door to Michael's room. "How are you doing, honey? How is Michael?"

"Oh, thank you for coming. I am still waiting to find a match for him." Katie was unsure how much Brenda knew about her situation and about Samuel not being the father of the baby.

"Can I be open with you, honey?" Brenda asked in a low voice so anyone near the door on the outside could not hear what was being said.

"Sure," answered Katie.

"Samuel came by my house and had a talk with Ralph and me last night. Now I am not here to pass judgment on anyone, and I want you to know that. He told us that he is not the baby's father and how hurt he is to find out that you have been lying to him this whole time. Now, honey, I don't know what happened up to this point. All I know is what I hear, and I will say that I just can't believe this to be true at all. I felt like I had got to know you with all of our talks and what have ya." She stopped and waited for some kind of reply.

"What Samuel has said about him not being the father of Michael is true." Before going on, she noticed Brenda's eyes widen. "But I myself had just found that out when he did."

"But how can that be? Are you saying that you really believed that he was the father this whole time? I never thought that the Amish well just forget that." She stopped and looked at Katie, hoping that she would just forget what she was about to say.

"First of all, just because someone may be Amish, it don't make them with no desires of the fleshly things. The Amish are people just like you and me—well, how I am now. They just are different in their beliefs. I think confused in some of it is all. I will say that just until the other day, I have always thought that Samuel was the only man I had ever been with. I had not known another in that way."

"Katie, do you even hear what you are saying? You must know that when the test came out that he was not the father, that meant that there was someone else?" Brenda looked at Katie as if she was saying that she still believed Michael to be Samuel's.

"Brenda, up until two days ago, I had always believed that Samuel was the only man I had been with. Now I found out that I was raped." She paused. "You see, something happened to me before I was ever with Samuel, and I just never knew."

Katie proceeded to tell Brenda of the night where she was to meet up with Robert at the old mill, when she never thought that he even showed up.

"Now can you understand what this is all about. I wasn't even going to say anything to anyone because I told Robert that I would not say in court that it was rape so he would give Michael one of his kidneys if he is a match. I was to tell the court that it was something that we had between the two of us."

"You do know that is called lying, don't you?" At that time Brenda wished that she would have not said that, knowing that Katie was already going through so much.

"Of course, I know that. Don't you see what this is doing to my marriage? I have to do everything that I can to save my son. I know that Samuel thinks that I lied to him about everything, but I can't worry about that right now. I have to think about my little boy, who needs a kidney, or he will die."

"Honey, have you been praying for him at all or just worrying about him? I'm sorry for saying that. It was not right of me to say that to you. I am sorry for what has happened with you and the rape. But, honey, I just hate to see a marriage break up over a complete lie."

"To answer your question—yes, of course, I have prayed and prayed, but he still is lying here dying as we speak. If God wants to heal him, then he will. I did all that I could do. Now the rest is up to Robert and God."

"Katie, do you even hear what you are saying? You have to believe in what God's word says, not just know what it says. The Bible tells us that we are healed, not that maybe if God wants us to be healed, then we are. He said we are healed, then we are. Stop doubting his word. You must believe in what he had said. If you want your baby to go home with you, then you must believe that he is healed."

Katie listened to her friend, and what she had to say was true. Katie was just tired and scared of losing her baby. She knew that God was a good God and he did not tell lies, but how did she get to where she was now? Why did he even allow her baby to get sick in the first place? She had all these questions coming to mind ever since this happened with Michael. She must stop worrying and doubting but believe just like her friend said and what God's word said.

"Brenda, will you please pray with me? I just can't keep going on like this."

Right when she had asked for prayer from her friend, her pastor came walking in. Pastor Mike Perish was a very tall, slim man in size and very soft-spoken.

"It looks like I have gotten here just in time for praying for some healing power to come in this place in this young child of God." He held his hand out toward the baby lying on the bed. "God, right now, my sisters in Christ and I reach out to you for the healing for this little baby. Lord, you are the Healer of all mankind. We, first of all, want to thank you for dying that we might live. We ask that this baby will live and be made whole, complete, in Jesus's mighty name. And, dear Lord, I pray for my sister Katie, God, that you will bring peace in her spirit, that you will bring forgiveness to her family for whatever things are going on in her life right now. Touch the whole family, Jesus, and we give you all the glory and praise right now, amen."

The two women opened their eyes and looked at him.

"Thank you, Pastor," Katie said then looked down at her baby lying on the bed next to where she was standing.

"Thank Jesus, Katie. He is the Great Physician. He is the Great Healer. Oh, I know that the doctors have their job to do too—and I thank God for them, I really do—but when it comes time for me to ever need healing for anything, I go to God because I know that he created me and no one knows me like he does. So I lean on to him for all my needs, and I just believe that your boy won't need a new kidney from any other than our God." He looked down at the baby then laid a hand on him. "Heal him now, Lord. Restore a brand-new kidney in this child, and we thank you for it. Just believe for him, Katie. I bet you when the doctor comes back in here that the baby is going to be feeling a whole lot better. I just feel that in my spirit."

Katie wanted the faith that she could hear coming from her pastor. She wanted to believe with all her heart that her boy would be feeling much better and not have to ask for Robert's kidney. She hated the very thought of getting a kidney from him, but she was willing to do whatever it took to bring health to her son. She kept hearing inside her, *Believe what God has promised in his word.* Then out of nowhere, she shouted, "I believe," scaring Brenda. "I believe that my baby is healed. I believe that he won't have to have a kidney transplant. Pastor, you are right when you said that God is the Creator, so who knows more about us than he? He knows what my baby is in need of. He knew before I knew or the doctors knew. I believe that this all happened because then I could know the truth about that one terrible night that I was raped, and now Robert can be charged with rape as well as murder."

The pastor was lost with Katie's rambling, but he was all for her understanding that God is the Great Healer.

"Honey, I don't know what that is all about, but I do believe that your son is moving quite well right now," he said as he watched Katie pick her baby up after seeing him move around as if there was never anything wrong with him.

"I knew it, I knew it," she said with excitement. "When you said that no one knows us like God knows us because he created us, I just knew that he was going to heal Michael. Look at him. He is healed." Katie began to shout so loud and praising God that two nurses came running into the room.

They flung the door wide open and rushed in the room. "Is everything all right in here?" asked a nurse, looking at Katie holding her baby. "What's going on? What happened?"

"Jesus is what happened." Katie looked at the two nurses standing there as if they were looking at a ghost. "Jesus healed my baby. He gave him a brand-new kidney. Just look, he's all right."

Katie was very excited holding on to her baby. The pastor and Brenda began to praise God right there in the room. The two nurses ran out, yelling for the doctor to come quickly.

"What's going on?" the doctor asked.

"I don't know, but the baby, the baby!" The nurse pointed toward the room. "He's up."

"What do you mean he's up?" he asked as he pushed past the two standing in the hallway. Walking into the room and seeing Katie crying and thanking God for healing her baby, he asked to see the child. "Can I please take a look at the baby, Katie?"

"Yes, you can, but you won't find anything wrong with him." Katie watched as the doctor laid the baby back down on the bed and began to look over him well.

"I'm not sure what is going on, but I'd like to run some tests on him. I just can't believe what I am seeing."

'Go ahead, run your test, but you won't find anything wrong. You see, God gave him a brand-new kidney," Katie repeated herself to him, but she didn't care. All she cared about right at the moment was that her baby was healed. She had no reason to go to court and lie to the judge. Her son was healed, and she wanted to find Samuel somehow to let him know all about the past up until now.

"I need to find Samuel. I need to tell him about Michael and tell him the truth about Robert. I want my family back the way God wants it."

"Katie, you stay here. I'll go find Samuel, and I will tell him if you would like," Brenda offered.

"Can you please go tell him that I'd like to see him and talk to him? I feel that I should be the one to tell him about Robert, but you may tell him about God healing Michael."

"Okay, I will try and get him to come here." Brenda was out the door, leaving the pastor and Katie waiting to hear what the doctor had to say.

The doctor came back sometime later. "It's a miracle. I can't explain what has happened to this little baby. All I know is that there is no sign of a bad kidney. We took every test that we could to see about his kidney, and every test came back normal. I just can hardly believe it. I have never seen anything like this in all my years of practice."

"Just know that if God can put the whole world together in six days—and that includes making man—don't you think that he is able to heal us when we are in need of healing?" Katie spoke with such joy for her son having been given a brand-new kidney from God. "I know one thing, I will never doubt what God can do ever again. So when can I take him home?"

Right after she asked the question, she thought, *Take him home? What home am I talking about? Where would home be for me and Michael? Would I be homeless?* All these thoughts began to come to mind. Then she remembered the miracle that had just been given to her son. If God was willing to heal him, then he would be willing to save her marriage and bring Samuel back to the hospital to pick up his family.

"Maybe you might want to let him stay another day here with us, just so we can keep an eye on him, in case something goes wrong," the doctor said to Katie with a puzzled look on his face.

"But you said yourself that there is nothing wrong with him, but if you feel it necessary to keep him one more day, then that will be fine with me. We will stay until tomorrow, but I know that he is healed." The only reason she agreed with letting him stay another day at the hospital was because she was unsure of what Samuel was going to do about letting her come back home. She was trying to find time to talk to him and explain everything.

Samuel decided to come up to the hospital to hear Katie's side of the story after the talk he had with Brenda. "Hi, Katie," he said as he walked through the door, seeing her sitting on a chair next to the bed where Michael slept in. "Brenda said that you wanted to talk with me? Is that the truth?"

"Yes, I need to explain everything to you. Can you come sit on this chair here so I can talk to you?" she asked, pointing at a chair next to her.

He walked over, turning the chair so he could face her as she talked to him. "Okay, I'm listening. By the way, I am so thankful that Michael will be okay."

"First of all, I want you to know that I have never lied to you about anything."

"What are you talking about? You're lying to me right now by saying that. I know that Michael is not my son, so that makes you a liar," he scolded as he interrupted her.

"If you will please let me tell you everything—I never thought for one minute that Michael was not your son. I never knew that he wasn't!"

"I don't believe what I am hearing. You told me that I was the only man you have ever known," he spoke with an angry tone in his voice.

"Samuel, I was raped!" she shouted, louder than normal. It was unlike Katie to talk loud and in an angry voice, but he wasn't giving her much of a chance to speak what needed to be said.

Samuel sat there without saying a word for just a moment while staring at her. "What! You were raped? How? Why didn't you ever tell me about that before?" he asked with accusing eyes.

"It's true, Samuel. I never knew it myself. I knew that something had happened to me one night but never knew what it was because I was knocked out. And when I woke up, I was a dirty mess and bleeding. It wasn't until all the test was taken on Michael that I realized what really happened to me that one night."

Before saying a word, he looked into her eyes and could see that she was telling the truth. "I never knew…I mean, I should have let you tell me. Katie, I am so sorry for the pain that I have caused you. Can you ever forgive me for the way that I have acted toward you? I am so ashamed for the way that I treated you, and without cause. I sure wasn't being the husband that I thought that I was, nor the man of God that I thought I was either."

"Then does this mean that you still love me?" she asked with tears of joy falling down her cheeks.

Samuel pulled his wife close to his side. "Please, honey, forgive me for everything? I am so sorry."

"Samuel, I do forgive you, but there are some things that I need to explain about Robert Culbert. I never told you everything mainly because I never really thought that it made any difference if I knew him before or not." She watched the way Samuel looked at her as she began to tell him of the first time she and Robert met. He listened as she talked without interrupting her one time. After she was done telling from the very beginning, all he could do was hold her close to his heart.

"I understand why you never wanted to talk about him. I would have probably felt the same way. But now that we know that he is the reason for you getting pregnant in the first place, how do you feel about him now?"

"I have to forgive him for whatever he did to me, but I don't want anything to do with him. I will go to court and let them know what kind of person he really is. He had no right to ever do that to me, let alone kill a man—and somehow it was you that got blamed for it."

Just as they were talking, the doctor came back in the room with a nurse walking in behind him, holding the baby.

"I have run several tests on Michael, and to my surprise, there is nothing wrong with him. He is one healthy little boy. I can't say why the sudden change in his condition, but I can say that there definitely is a very big change. And it was all for the better. He can go home tonight. I will not need him to stay here any longer."

"I can tell you right now that it was God who healed my baby. If that don't make a believer out of you, then nothing will," spoke Katie as she took her baby from the nurse who was handing him over to her.

"I do believe that there is a higher power working in this situation. I haven't seen anything like this happen before. That's not saying that I haven't heard of some strange things happen for other doctors before. I have some colleagues who have told me about some strange events that have taken place in their practice before. Now you take him home, and if anything changes, please bring him back."

Although Katie knew that it wasn't anything the doctor did that brought healing to Michael and that it was an act of God, she still did not let what the doctor did for Michael go unnoticed. "Thank you, Doctor, for everything."

She and Samuel walked out of the hospital, with his arm wrapped tight behind his wife.

"Katie, I need to ask you to forgive me for acting the way that I have the last couple of days."

"Samuel, I have forgiven you. It is I who needs to ask you for forgiveness for not telling you more of Robert."

"I want us to start over now that we know the truth about what happened to you, and I want you to know that I will never look at Michael not being my son. To me—and I hope to you—we will always look at me being his father."

"I wouldn't have it any other way. You are his father, and he will always know you as that."

12

A New Beginning

Samuel and Katie began their new life knowing the truth about what happened to her that one dreadful. The two had promised to start their life over without all the past lingering on, and when Robert went before the judge, Katie stood before the judge and confessed what he had done to her. Robert had gone to prison for the murder of a man, and rape charges were added on. Although Katie had told the truth about Robert in court, she knew that she had to forgive him for what he had done to her. She decided to go to the prison and see him to tell him that she had forgiven him.

Taking the phone on the other side of the glass, he picked it up to talk with Katie. "I thought that when I saw you in court, I'd seen the last of you," Robert spoke, giving her a nasty look. He had a roughness about him that she had never seen before now. She wondered what it was that made her feel the way she did before. But now looking at this man on the other side of glass, she felt sorry for him. She knew that he would be spending many years behind bars for making wrong choices in life.

"I came here to tell you that Jesus healed Michael. He no longer needs a kidney."

"Healed? Are you telling me that you believe in all that junk? Well, at least I know why you lied to me about what you told the judge."

"I never lied. What I told you is if you give Michael a kidney, I would not tell the judge what happened between us, but you never gave a kidney because God healed him. I felt that I needed to tell the truth about that night. That's not why I came here to see you. And yes, I do believe that Jesus heals, and I can honestly say that my little boy is healed. He is no longer in need of a kidney. He has a brand-new one."

"Why did you come here? I know it's not because you care anything about me."

"I came to tell you that I forgive you for what you did to me. I don't now why you did what you did, but I forgive you. I also want you to know that Samuel is all the father that Michael needs. I don't plan on telling him anything about you. I wouldn't want him to think that this is how he got here, through an act of violence. I do pray, Robert, that one day you will ask Jesus to forgive you for everything that you have done in life that was not pleasing to him. I will keep you in my prayers." She was just about to hang up the phone when he began to say something to her.

"How can you say that you forgive me for what I had done to you?"

"It's easy for me. I have learned in life that we all do things that bring us to shame. Some are greater than others, but still sin. When I asked Jesus in my heart, I decided then that I, as a Christian, must be like Jesus as much as I can. He forgives me when I do wrong—and one sin is as another—so I, as his child, need to forgive too." She smiled at him as she talked about Jesus. She really did hope that Robert would ask Jesus to be Lord of his life. She knew that God was willing to forgive him for what he had done.

Katie felt like she did what she was supposed to do by talking to Robert. She knew she would tell Samuel all about her conversation with him when she got home. When leaving the place that would hold Robert for many years to come, something inside her felt like this would be the last time she would ever see him again.

"Hello," said Samuel as she walked into the house. "How was your visit?"

"I feel that I said all that needed to be said, so it was good." She looked at the way Samuel was staring at her as she talked. "I told him that I hope he will ask Jesus to forgive him for all that he did wrong so he will make it to heaven. How is my big boy doing?" changing the subject, she asked as she reached down to take Michael out of Samuel's arms as he was sitting on the rocking chair.

"He has been very good. I've been watching him close, and he is very good."

"That is what I like to hear. Hey, baby boy, how are you doing, hun? Mama loves you, baby."

"Are you hungry? I made supper for us."

"Hmmm, what did you make? It sure smells good," she replied.

"I made chili, and it's not to spicy for you. I know how you don't care for all that spice."

"Thank you, Samuel. I think that I will have a bowl right now."

"Just sit here. I will get it for you. Are you planning on going to see Robert again?" he asked, raising his eyebrows.

"No, there is no need to anymore. I did what I felt like I needed to do, and now the rest is up to him and God. I do hope that he will ask Jesus into his life before it's too late. You can never tell how life will be for you when your life is being held behind bars. Who knows if he will ever get out. He has so many years there."

"It sure don't pay to live a life of sin. You can give the devil an inch, and before long, he is right there to take a mile. Then before you know it, you have wasted your life on nothing good, and it cost you everything."

"I may not have the love of my ma and da anymore, but I have the love of a husband and my little angel right here, and the love of God that no man can take from me. What else do I need?" she said as she kissed her baby boy on his chubby little cheeks.

"Here you are, honey. Sit down and eat. Tell me if you like it or not. Let me take Michael while you sit and eat. And I feel the same way about having you, the baby, and God. I am such a foolish man to have done what I did to you, leaving you to care for everything on your own at the hospital, all because I had too much pride to talk things out with you." He looked at Katie with a sadness in his eyes as he told her how he felt.

"I came so close to losing you and Michael, and I want you to forgive me for being so foolish. I love you, Katie girl, with all of my heart, and the very thought that I turned on you must have made you feel like you were shunned again. Am I right? Did you feel like I shunned you again like your parents did to you?" He knelt down at the side of her while she tried to eat. "Please, Katie, forgive me for being so wrong about everything."

"You answered your question. Yes, when you left me at the hospital, I hurt all over because I couldn't understand why the test came out saying that you weren't the father to Michael. I did feel that you turned your back right when I needed you the most. I also felt like I had been shunned again, and I hurt deep inside. But I knew that if I had a chance to talk with you, then you would be able to understand everything as well as I did, and now you do. I do forgive you for what had happened, and I want us to be very happy and put the past behind us," she said as she touched his cheek with a gentle rub of her hand. "I love you, Samuel."

Without saying a word, he could feel her love through her touch, and he laid his head on her lap while holding the baby on his as she sat eating the chili.

"Samuel, this is very good chili. I think that I like it more than I like my own."

Right when the two were talking, there came a knock on the door.

"You sit and eat. I'll get the door," he said then stood up, still holding the baby as he went to the door. To his surprise before opening the door, he could see a couple that he never thought would ever darken his doorsteps.

"Yah," he said, talking like the Amish once again.

Although she didn't know who was at the door, Katie knew it had to be someone from the Amish family. Listening as she finished up her bowl of chili, she thought that she heard her da's voice. Standing up and just about running into the kitchen to see if it was his voice she was hearing, she came around the corner of the wall that parted her kitchen from her dinning room where she was eating.

"Da, Mom, what are you doing here? I mean, what brings you here? Oh, this is not coming out right at all. Is something wrong? Are you okay?" she had so many questions, being surprised by their visit.

"Will you both come in, please?" Samuel asked while holding the door open.

Katie noticed both of them looking at the baby in Samuel's arms. They stepped inside the door but stood so close to it as though they were to run out of it at any moment, like her ma did a couple of months back ago.

"Please come and sit awhile. There is something on your mind that brought you here today. Please come." Katie motioned for the two of them to come into the living room to sit.

"Can I get the two of you something to drink?" Samuel asked.

"Nah, we came to see how our girl is doing. I know that we ought not to have come, but we heard that the baby was not doing so good and had come to the point of death. But what I see here, he looks like it might be well, no?"

"Da, Ma our baby was at the point of death. We had just brought him home from the hospital after Jesus healed our Michael."

"You speak of blasphemy so open now, do you?"

"Da, it's not blasphemy to speak of Jesus when doing it in the way of giving him thanks. You see, the baby was dying and in need of a kidney, and we believed in healing when we prayed and asked Jesus to heal him. He gave Michael a brand-new kidney. Now he no longer needs to have one from someone else."

"You have changed so much Katie. I don't know you any longer," her dad spoke with much anger in his voice.

"Can't you love me like the Bible tells us to love each other? Can't you forgive me like the Bible tells us to forgive each other? Da, the Bible tells us we have all fallen short from the glory of God."

"I don't know this that you talk about. This is not the way of the Amish."

"I know that it's not, and Samuel and I have come so far from that old way and have learned so much that God himself speaks of. Da, don't you care to know the truth? The way of the teaching is not correct, Da. It teaches unforgiveness, and that is not what we must do to get into heaven. God said that we must forgive those who have done wrong to us, love them even though they do wrong, show mercy and kindness." As she was talking, she noticed that her da was no longer interrupting her but sat there until she was done with what she was saying. This was hard for her to believe, for she knew her da as a man of sternness in what he believed in and the way he had taught her to believe.

"What you are saying is that your ma and I ought to forgive you for what you have done when you brought shame on us?"

"Yes, Da, that is what I am saying. But you must not only forgive me, you must forgive Samuel and me both. We both have sinned against God, and he has forgiven us. He loves us. That is why he sent Jesus to pay the price for us on the cross. It's for our sins. God knew that we as humans are going to make mistakes in life, so he sent his son without sin to die for us."

"This, I know, but you speak against the teaching of the elders. We have been taught a way that we know, and we must teach our young the same."

"No, Da we must not, if it's not the truth. Samuel and I no longer believe that way, Da. We believe in the way that God teaches us in his word. The Bible said that it is sin to take away from his word or to add to it. Da, the Amish take away, and then they add what they want. That is sin, and we no longer will be part of it."

It was several hours that Katie's folks stayed and talked with her and Samuel about the things of God. They even went as far as to play with their little grandson, whom they had just met for the very first time. They promised to come back for a visit, even if the teachings were against it. That night, when Katie lay down to sleep, she dreamt that her da and her ma were coming to the same church that she and Samuel went to. She never said anything to Samuel about her dream, but it was one dream she would talk to God about and wait for it to come to pass.

13

The Letter

Katie and Robert wrote letters back and forth with permission from Samuel. Her husband told her that it would be all right to write him and share the Bible with him. He had a love for Jesus that was greater than worrying about her writing the man who raped her. He had learned to forgive him for what he had done, trying to set him up for the killing of a man, as well as forgive him for what he had done to Katie. He himself wrote some things in a letter that Katie was writing to let him know that he also forgave him. After the letters were sent back and forth, with each one talking about Jesus and his love and forgiveness, they stopped coming in after the last one was sent, saying that Robert had asked Jesus in his heart. He told them of how, while he was in prison, he would be telling others about the love of Jesus.

Katie didn't understand why he no longer wrote to her and Samuel about what he was doing about sharing the good news of God. Then after two months went by, she received a letter from a prisoner, telling her that Robert was killed telling some men about Jesus. He stated in his letter that he was one of the guys whom Robert was sharing Jesus with and how, because of Robert, he had asked Jesus to come into his heart and be Lord of his life. But it was with regret that he told her that the others didn't like Robert talking about Jesus with them, and they took him into the bathroom where they knifed him until his death. The prisoner stated that the last words Robert said were, "Jimmy, I will see you in heaven." Then Robert died.

Katie's heart felt sick knowing that someone killed Robert. Then after looking at the address and the name on the envelope, she saw that the name was Jim Cartwright. "Oh dear Jesus, please help me with this," she prayed, holding the letter to her chest. Then all of a sudden, she had a peace flooding in her soul. She knew that Robert was with the Lord in heaven now, and he no longer would have to sit in a prison for years to come for a crime that God had forgiven him for. She knew that he was well deserving of prison for what he had done, but she also knew that he was in a much better place with Jesus than any place here on earth. She felt that she would write Jim Cartwright back and let him know to be strong in Jesus just as Robert was in his death.

"Dear Jim," she would start out to right. "It grieved me to receive your letter, letting me know what happened to

Robert. Then as I was crying, I had a peace cover me. He is now with our Lord Jesus. I am happy to know that you have received Jesus as your Savior, and I pray that you will continue to do what Robert was doing, telling others about Jesus. I know that being in prison—where some will want to hear about God, and others can die because of their relationship of knowing him—it must be hard to know what to do at times. I'm sure that Robert must have felt like that at times, not knowing what others might do. But we as Christians must share the word of God to others. That is what a Christian will do. I will be praying for you daily that you will continue to live for Jesus and share him with others. Feel free to write me at any time, and I will write back to you. Thank you for letting me know about Robert. God bless you and keep you in his loving arms. Katie."

After writing the letter, Katie was saddened at the death of Robert, knowing that her son's birth father had died in such a terrible way. Then she thought about the words that she had read several times in the holy scripture, that the wages of sin is death. It's true. Even though Robert had repented, he still had to go to prison for what sin he had committed. Not every person who kills someone will die, but in this case, Robert did. He chose to take a life, and his was taken from him. *No sin is worth what a person will face for committing that sin*, Katie thought to herself.

Holding the letter close to her heart, she prayed before going to send it out. "Dear Lord God, I ask you that you will keep your hand on Jim. Help others to be blessed as he tells others about you. Help him to stand firm in your word and not be dismayed with what others may say to him. I ask you, dear Lord, that you will keep him safe. Please don't let the same thing that happened to Robert happen to Jim. Keep him safe to where he can continue to tell others about you, in Jesus's name, amen."

Katie did what she thought that needed to be done and mailed the letter to Jim Cartwright. She could hardly wait for Samuel to come in from the fields so she could tell him what she had just found out about Robert. She wondered if, deep down inside, he might somehow feel happy knowing that Robert would no longer be in their lives or in Michael's life. She hoped that he would feel some remorse, as she did, but would understand if he felt differently than her. Nonetheless, she knew all in all that he was a man of God, and she knew that he would not be ill with words of unkindness toward the passing of Robert, for she knew that he himself said that he forgave Robert for what he had done.

Supper was ready and waiting for Samuel. In the meantime, Katie was feeding Michael and singing to him while he ate. Michael never knew what kind of thoughts were going on inside his mom's mind. He just opened up his mouth and trusted that what she was giving to him would be good.

"I sure hope your dad gets in here soon, buddy, before his supper gets cold," she said in a soft voice.

What seemed like hours went by before Samuel arrived home. Michael was already in his pajamas and ready for bed when Samuel finally walked through the door. Looking to see where Katie was as he took off his boots, he said, "Sorry, honey, I'm so late tonight. It seemed like I was never going to finish in the left field." Seeing the look on her face, he decided to stop what he was talking about to find out what was wrong. "Is something wrong? By the look on your face, there is something wrong. What is it?"

"I received a letter in the mail today. It was from a man by the name of Jim Cartwright. He is a man who was in prison with Robert."

"What? Is the man out now?"

"No, that's not it. He wrote me a letter, telling me that Robert was sharing the gospel with some men who didn't want to hear about it, and they killed him."

"What! No way, you're kidding me. Wow, that is to bad that it happened right after he asked Jesus in his heart." Looking at the way she was listening to him while he talked, he embraced her in his arms. "Tell me, how does this make you feel?"

"At first it grieved me quite badly knowing that he was finally on the right track in life—then for something like this to happen. Then I felt the Lord give me great peace about it. I believe God did not want me to grieve his death in any way. He gave me peace knowing that Robert did change his ways before something happened to him."

"So you're all right then?"

"Yes, I'm fine," she said, looking at Michael lying on the floor. "You know, even though he did change his ways, which is a very good thing, I still look at you as being Michael's only father."

"Thank you for saying that, honey. Did you hear anything about what they're going to do about a funeral?"

"No, I haven't heard anything about that at all. This Jim guy never mentioned it to me at all. I really didn't know much about him, so I don't know anything about his family. I think I remember something about him talking about his dad, but not for sure."

"Okay, well, you might want to call the prison tomorrow and find out what you can. I think that it might be a good thing if we go to it—that is, if they are having one."

"Really?" she asked, in shock that he felt this strongly about it. "You really want me to do that then, huh?"

"Honey, we both have forgiven him for everything that he had done, and I feel it's our Christian duty to see this all the way. I want to show others that we have forgiven him, and this is one way that we can do this, by going to his funeral."

"That is, if he is even going to have one, but I will call tomorrow and see what they are going to do."

Samuel and Katie sat down to eat, not saying much to each other, but their eyes did all the talking that needed to be done at this time as they looked across the table at each other. Before they were to talk about Robert any further, it was time to put Michael to bed for the night.

"Honey, I know that I have not been home for very long tonight. Would you mind if I turned in early tonight? I feel so tired I'm having a hard time keeping my eyes open."

Katie cleaned up their plates and, taking her husband by the hand, began to lead him toward the bedroom. "Come on, honey. I too will turn in with you. I feel like I can sleep the whole night through."

"Get closer to me, honey," Samuel asked, pulling her closer to him while they lay in bed. "This is so much better. I love to feel you snuggle close to me."

Katie lay next to her husband, feeling the warmth of his breath on her neck as he cuddled her close to him.

I will have to make phone calls come morning about Robert, she thought as she tried hard to fall asleep. No matter how hard she tried to sleep, her mind was rolling with so many thoughts. *Why did Samuel really not want to talk about the death of Robert? Why was he so quick to go straight to bed after eating? Why can't I fall asleep now that I am lying next to my husband in bed, when the thoughts of sleeping sounds like something I could do?*

After lying there for what seemed like hours and still not falling asleep, she decided to crawl out of bed and go pray for a while in another room. Slowly picking up the covers from her side and carefully laying it aside her, she began to bring her foot out to the side of the bed when, all of sudden, she felt her husband's arm grip her and pull her in close to him again. Pulling the covers over her again, she decided to stay right where she was and prayed silently, *Lord, I'm not sure of what to do about the passing of Robert—please help me. I know that I have forgiven him, and I do believe that Samuel has too, but I really don't want to hurt Samuel in any way by pursuing this thing about a funeral for Robert when it might make Samuel feel uncomfortable. Show me what to do, and I will follow.*

"Good morning, honey," Samuel spoke, still holding Katie close to him. "Wow, I must have been very tired. I slept the whole night through. How bout you, honey? How was your sleep?"

"It took me a little longer than you to fall asleep, but once it was there, it was a nice, sound sleep. I never heard Michael wake, not once crying in the night."

"Maybe we should go check on him?" he said as he swung the covers off them. It sounded like fear coming from Samuel as he wondered why Michael never cried during then night.

"Calm down, honey. He is fine, and he is healed. We can't think that God will take back the healing that he has already given to Michael."

"I know that you're right, but just the same, I will check in on him." With that, he was out the door, heading to Michael's bedroom to see him. All of a sudden, through the baby monitor, she heard him say, "You were right, honey. He is sleeping like a little baby."

Katie, still lying in bed, smiled to herself when she heard him say that. She knew in her heart that he was okay and thought it to be kind of funny to hear Samuel reassure her of something she already knew.

Samuel agreed with Katie about finding out what she could about Robert's funeral. He knew that it was the right thing to do. After all, Samuel felt like he got to know the man that Robert had become after accepting Jesus as his Lord and Savior. He could no longer feel bitter toward him for what he had done to both him and Katie. It was Samuel himself who wanted her to make the calls to the prison in the first place.

"Thank you, Samuel. I know that this must make you feel awkward in some way, allowing your wife to make plans for his funeral." She looked at him as she talked to him, and seeing that in his eyes there was no regret in giving her permission to go ahead with her plans, she continued on, "You are truly an amazing man, and I am very blessed to have you as my husband." She walked up to him and wrapped her arms around his waist. "Oh, wait a minute. I don't know what I was even thinking. I now remember it was you who asked me to call to the prison and find out what I can about him. I guess with what has been going on with everything, I just must have forgotten that you had asked me to."

"I feel that I am the blessed one to have you as my wife. God has seen us through some tough times. Now we will see your folks coming around from time to time to see us and their grandson. That in itself is amazing, don't you think?"

"My ma and my da coming around to see us is nothing but amazing. God has answered my prayers in so many ways. I could never do enough to repay what he has done for me. Healing our marriage, our son, and the way my folks showed up here the way that they did after everything that has happened. God is so good to us. We owe him everything."

"Yes, we do, and like you said, there is no way to ever repay him for what he has done. All we can do is love and serve him with all of our heart."

"And share the love of Jesus with others whom we come in contact with. We are here to show others what God has done for us and let them want him as well."

"Yes, that is true, honey. I think that I will get dressed and go out to the fields and let you do what it is that needs to be done about Robert. Is that all right with you that I leave that for you to take care of?"

"Yes, honey, that is fine, but would you care for something to eat before heading out for the day?"

"Sure, a bite might be fitting. I hate to bother you when I know that you have things to do that is important."

"Honey, you are what is important to me. I will care for you first then do my other duties."

Katie got out of the bed and dressed for the day. Making breakfast for her husband was something she had always enjoyed since the first day they married. Her ma had taught her how to love and respect her husband as it was fitting to God. And as long as she had a husband, she would do what she needed to do to be a godly woman to him.

"Here, honey. I made you some oatmeal with a slice of toast. I wanted you to have something hot to start out your day."

Samuel sat down, waiting for her to take her seat at the table, unaware that she was going to wake the baby so he could come join them to eat. Looking around and not seeing her, he decided that he better start to eat before his food got cold. Seeing from the corner of his eye that she walked back into the room, he said, "I was wondering where you ran off to. So how is my little man this morning?"

"I can't believe that he slept for so long without crying to get out of bed. But he's a good and happy baby, full of smiles," she said as she pulled out her chair to feed the baby.

The day seemed to be going fast with Samuel out in the fields working and Michael taking a nap after he ate, rocked and sang to by his ma. Now Katie was making the calls needed to find out more about Robert. She was very disappointed talking with the warden at the prison about Robert and a funeral for him. She found out that Robert's dad had him cremated the day of his passing. No one knew anything about her and Robert's past besides her husband, so there was no way anyone would have considered her and Samuel to be part of Robert's life.

Katie knew that Robert was in a better place, and one day they would see each other again. It seemed almost funny thinking about how she felt about him after the letters that were written between them, talking about Jesus at first then sharing the love for him in the same manner. She knew that she had forgiven him for what he had done after the letters came in, talking about how he truly regretted his actions toward her and Samuel. It was almost like a friendship between them had developed, and she was very saddened when she heard of his death. Now she must share with Samuel what had taken place, and there was no more need to worry about where Robert would be laid. She new that it was time to let the old things go and move on with what she held deeply in her heart.

After Samuel came in for the night, she shared with him her findings of what took place with Robert. Even to Samuel, it was disappointing that they could not participate in anything for Robert. Samuel had also felt some kind of a friendship with just the couple of letters that he had written, but he had read the ones that she and Robert had written to each other. In those letters, Samuel could tell that the man had made a big change in his life and had some deep regrets for the things that he did that had wronged so many people.

Time went on to where the Katie and Samuel never talked about Robert anymore. It was like they never knew him in the first place. As they saw the baby growing, it was like he was their baby alone, and no other parent was part of him but them.

14

The Birthday Party

"Can you believe that Michael is going to be five years old already?" Katie said to Samuel while watching their son play with a toy tractor on the living-room floor.

"What are we planning for his birthday, might I ask?"

"I thought about having Ma and Da come over and celebrate it with us on Saturday. What do you think?"

"I think it would be nice if we invited a few of his friends from church and school over to celebrate it with us. Something a little bigger for him might be nice—that is, if it's not too much trouble."

"I don't think that it will be too much trouble at all. I will call some of the parents from the church and give Michael a couple of notes to take to school tomorrow to give to the ones he wants to invite. This is Tuesday, so I still have time to plan."

"Sound's good. I will take work off for the day and help you out on Saturday if you'd like."

"Yes, I'd like that very much. I can always use some extra hands to help out. What do you think that we should have to eat on that day?"

"How about some sloppy joes? That always is good, don't you think?"

"Well, I would say yes, but with a whole bunch of kids eating them in the house, not sure if I like that. They are called sloppy for the same reason of being sloppy. How about hot dogs instead? Those aren't near as messy."

"You're right. We will go with the hot dogs instead."

"I think he will be very happy having friends come over to play with. Should we keep this between us and not let him know about it?"

"I'd say yes, except the fact of you giving him some notes to invite some of his friends." He looked at her and started to chuckle lightly.

"Oh yeah, what was I thinking? I guess I wasn't. Ha-ha, and you laughed at me." She grabbed ahold of his shirt and pulled him close to her. "I love you, you know."

"Yeah, I know." He looked down at her with a smile that brought warmth all through her. She had always loved the smiles that he would give her.

"Are you leaving for work in a minute?"

"Yes, I need to get things done so I can afford to take Saturday off. But If you don't mind, I'd like to come in for lunch today."

"Oh, you know that I won't mind. I always enjoy having you for lunch. Is there something special that I can make for you?"

"Just some of the roast beef we had last night would be fine with me. I really liked what you did with it to make it taste so good."

Hmm, she thought to herself, *what I did? Nothing different that I remember doing.* "Okay, I will have some of that ready for you." She tilted her head up for a kiss good-bye as he put on his hat.

"I'll see you in a few hours." He was out the door and headed toward the barn.

"What to do first?" she spoke out loud. Looking around the kitchen she was still standing in as she saw Samuel disappear within the barn door, she saw that she could tidy up the kitchen a tad after there seemed to be a slight mess caused by Michael eating pancakes before leaving for school and Samuel having his hotcakes too. Katie loved to listen to her music as she cleaned up the house. Turning on the radio to the Christian station that she oftentimes listened to, she began to clean the entire house before Samuel was to come home for lunch.

"I better make some calls to some of the mothers to see if they could come and join us for celebrating Michael's birthday," she talked out loud while looking in the phone book for some of the numbers. After making calls and finding that just about all who was invited could come out to join them on Saturday, she decided it was time for her to make a house call to her folks.

Katie drove up the long road to go see her folks. She was sure her da would be out in the fields like most of the Amish at this time of the year. She remembered the years that she would walk down the long path to get to wherever it was that she was going to. Passing by the old mill that carried a dark hidden secret from most of the world brought back all the chills from that one night racing through her mind. Quickly shaking off the thoughts of Robert, she determined to focus on getting her folks to join them with many others over to their home.

Katie knocked on the door.

"Oh, Katie girl," her mother said as she opened the door. She looked around and saw it was just Katie there. "Come in, dear. So what do I owe this visit to?"

"Ma, Saturday will be Michael's fifth birthday Well, we decided to throw him a nice little gathering of some friends. Now, I know how you and Da don't usually like to come over when we have others over, but I thought that since it's for Michael, maybe the two of you will come and join us."

"I can't answer that, Katie. Your da is the one you need to talk to about that. Just maybe he will say that we can come, yah."

"Maybe, Ma. You guys haven't come over lately, and I've been wondering why not."

"There's been some talk with the leaders about some of us going places that we ought not to be going. Your da feels that we should stay more to home is all. But I will talk with him. I know he loves you, Katie girl, and that boy too. I will let you know what he says soon, okay?"

Katie was getting the feeling that she was being rushed to leave, and knowing how the Amish were, she wasn't going to stick around until asked to leave. "Okay, Ma. I love you and Da, and I miss you not coming over lately." She stood up to walk toward the door.

"I will talk with your da when he comes in tonight. I will let you know, yah?"

"Okay, Ma. I hope that you will come. I know Michael always enjoys seeing you."

Katie closed the door behind her, feeling sad about her short visit with her ma, not knowing why they could come over and visit for quite sometime without worrying about their beliefs but then when they heard from the leaders, they soon forgot all about their daughter and grandson again.

"Why can't they just get out of that dead religion where they won't forgive their own people but think nothing on turning their back on those sins that have been committed against them by the English?" she spoke out loud to herself. "God, please speak to my da and my ma about what they are doing. I want them in my life, Jesus. I love them and want my son to know his grandparents. Those are the only ones that he has." After saying that, she thought of Robert's family. *No way do I want my son to know those people. Who knows what they are really like. From what I hear from others, his dad is not a good person at all. I have to protect Michael from them. Fact is, I have never heard Robert mention a mother to me. He only talked about his father.* She was getting upset at thinking about Robert's dad and the rumors she had heard.

Pulling into the driveway at her home, she sat in the truck looking at her home and remembering the day she came here before getting married. She felt so scared at that time in her life, not knowing what would become of it, so unsure of what would happen with her and Samuel—not knowing that he was not the one who fathered her son. She had learned so much since that time in her life, and she was sure to learn so much more. One thing she was sure of, she had a man who loved her and her son as his very own. She was sure that even if her folks were never to come over again, she still had the love of a man in the way that God had ordained it to be, not one that was so caught up with a religion that didn't allow one to forgive others or to love others as Christ had loved them.

Katie made out all the invitations for Michael's birthday party come Saturday. It was unclear if her folks would be coming, but she wasn't going to allow herself to get upset over something that she was unable to help. However, she could pray and ask God to speak to her folks' heart about coming over and joining them on the day of celebrating.

Samuel told her that if she wanted him to go speak to her folks, then he would. But she wanted to let it alone and leave the speaking to them from God.

She gave some invitations to Michael to pass out to his friends at school, telling him to make sure to give them to his close friends. He promised to give them to three of his very closest friends.

After coming home from school, Michael seemed to be lost in tears.

"Mama," cried Michael.

"What is the matter with you, honey?" Katie asked the crying child.

"I did what you asked me to do—you know, give my very closest friends the letter you gave me for my party," he spoke with sobs, and tears were coming down his cheeks.

"Then what is wrong?"

"I had too many closest friends. Now I have no closest friends."

"What do you mean, you have no friend now?" she asked.

"I did what you asked. Then Mark and Tommy got real mad at me and started to call me names," he said as he wiped his tears away.

"Why would they do that? I don't think that is being a very good friend."

"That's why I never gave them one in the first place. I gave it to my other friends instead. Now Mark and Tommy got my other real good friends mad at me."

"Michael, I don't understand why they got your other friends mad at you. How did that happen?"

"When I didn't give them a letter, they got mad at me and started to tell my really good friends that my place was for Amish people, not people like them. They said that we have horns under our hair and that we hurt people. Now no one wants to be my friend anymore." Sobs began to pour out once again.

"Now, now, stop your crying, honey. Mama's gonna make it okay." She looked at him, wiping the tears away again. "Now give me the names of who you gave those invitations to, and I will have a talk with them tomorrow, okay?"

"Okay, Mama. So will I still have a party?"

"Yes, you will, and a very good one too," she promised him, swiping his hair on top of his head with her hand.

Katie went to the school and had a talk with the teacher and then to some of Michael's friends. After she was done, she had the word of three little five-year-olds that they would come to the party.

Saturday came, and folks were showing up with their young children, but still no sign of Katie's parents coming into the home. Katie was busy dishing up plates of hotdogs and potato chips to all the people who were standing in line. Every once in a while, she would look out the bay window, then toward the kitchen door, in hopes of seeing her folks show up, but still no show.

The party went well, with all of Michael's closest friends from school and from church. Games were played, and prizes won. Laughter and joy filled those who joined the games and the watchers. Katie was pleased that everyone seemed to be enjoying themselves. She couldn't help but laugh at the children blindfolded and trying to hit the piñata, missing it as they swung the bat. After everyone had left and Katie was cleaning up, Michael came in the kitchen to talk to her.

"Mama, I had the best of time today. Can I have another one tomorrow?"

Katie started to laugh, and Samuel walked in, carrying some plates and cups to the kitchen when he overheard what Michael had to say.

Samuel knelt down to Michael's level. "Michael, this was a birthday party for you that your mama and I wanted to give to you. But your birthday only comes around one time a year, not as many that you want," he said, snickering.

"Okay, Pa, but I had the best of time," he said as he ran into the other room to play with some of the new toys he had just gotten.

15

The Pregnancy

Katie woke up in the early morning hours feeling sick to her stomach. Running to the bathroom to relieve herself, she thought that this feeling was something she had felt once before. *Oh my gosh, I can't be…* She felt excitement swell up on the insides of her. She and Samuel had wanted a baby for a few years now, but she had never conceived. And now, if her feelings were right, she was going to be a mama again and Samuel a daddy. Oh, how pleased she was, even though she was being held over the toilet. She wanted so much to tell Samuel right now that they were going to be parents again, but he was nowhere around. She knew that he must be out on the fields, working again.

Well, I guess I will just have to wait until he gets in here, she thought out loud. Then the thought came to her—what if she was just getting the flu, and she wasn't going to be having a baby after all? She would never want to get

Samuel all excited for nothing. Maybe she would go to the store and buy a pregnancy test and see what it says before saying anything to him.

She showered and dressed, all excited to run down to the store to buy an early pregnancy test. Jumping into her little white escort car, which Samuel bought for her a few months back, she couldn't get started down the road fast enough. She felt all excited just at the very thought of her possibly having another baby. She knew there was no doubt with this baby being Samuel's, although she knew that his love for Michael was just as genuine as if he had fathered him.

She picked up one box and read it then laid it down to pick up another. She read box after box in its entirety to see which one was the best. Having never bought anything like that before, she was unsure which one was the best on the market. After much reading, she took the box that said, "Know if you're pregnant within three days of conception." Hurrying home and going to the bathroom to take the test, she watched closely to see how many lines on the stick would show up. Seeing the first line coming through, she waited to see if there would be a second. All of a sudden, there it was—the second line coming through next to the first. She placed her hands on her chest. "Thank you, dear Lord," she said out loud as she looked again at the test results.

She walked out of the bathroom, knowing that what she first thought when getting sick earlier in the day was right. "Now I will make something very special for supper tonight so I can surprise Samuel with the news," she spoke to herself out loud.

Going into the kitchen to find what it was that she was going to make to eat, she went looking in the freezer, then in the fridge, then in the cupboards, until she had it all laid out on the counter. Before she knew it, she was putting stuffed cheese shells into the oven and turning it on to a low temperate because it would be a while before Michael was even due home from school, and that's not saying how long before Samuel was to get home.

Michael came home at his usual time as every day. Katie was still filled with much excitement about the baby that she almost gave the surprise away to Michael before Samuel came home. She quickly began to talk to Michael about how he was doing in school.

"I'm doing really well in school, Mama," he told her when she asked how he was doing.

"I'm glad that you are doing so well, honey. I know that you are a very smart little boy."

"Mama?"

"Yes, Michael."

"Will you come to see my play?"

"Sure, I will come, but this is the first I have heard anything about a play. What kind of play is it? And when is it?"

"The name of the play is *Leaders*, and I think it's in two weeks. Here, Mama. I have this for you to look at," he told her, handing her a piece of paper from his backpack.

She took the paper from him and began to read it. "Oh, this sounds very nice, Michael. What part are you playing?"

"I am playing Abraham Lincoln. I will need a big beard like Papa's beard. My teacher told me that he had a big beard."

Katie started to laugh at the thought of Samuel's beard being compared to Abraham Lincoln's beard. "I will talk with your papa tonight and see what we can come up with." She was thinking about what Michael said about Samuel's beard being big. She laughed to herself at the thought of it. *What can I do for him about a beard for the play?* she asked herself.

"I'm home," came a deep voice as Samuel walked through the kitchen doorway. "What smells good? It smells like you have been very busy cooking a great meal," he said as he gave her a big hug after taking his boots off.

"Well, thank you very much. It's stuffed shells, and I know how you told me the other day that you wanted some again."

"That's nice that you remembered. So how has your day been today? You look very chipper for someone who's been in the kitchen cooking."

"Why don't you go get washed up, and I will set the table." She didn't answer his question about how her day had been, and Samuel found that strange, but he did what she asked him to do.

"Where is Michael?" he asked, coming out of the bathroom.

"Michael," she raised her voice a little so Michael could hear her call for him while he was playing in his bedroom.

"Yes, Mama," he yelled remove so she could hear him.

"It's time to eat now, and come say hi to your pa."

Michael came running out of his room full of talking about his play he was to have at school.

"Really? So you will need a big beard then, huh?" Samuel asked, chuckling at his son.

"Yes, Papa. My teacher said a big one like your beard." He jumped up on his dad's lap then gave his beard a little tug. "When I get big like you, Papa, I want a big beard just like yours."

"Oh, you do now, do you? Well then, I'm sure when you are older, you will grow one out like me."

"Okay, Michael, take your seat so we can eat," his ma told him.

"Okay, Ma," the boy said as he jumped down and got in his own seat.

"It smells very good, honey. I am so hungry," Samuel commented.

"Let's say grace and eat," she said as she looked at him with an ear-to-ear smile.

"You seem to be pretty chipper tonight, more than usual. Is there something that I should know?" he asked, giving her a strange look.

"I was going to wait for after we eat," she said, all excited. "But I just can't hold it in any longer."

"Hold what in?" Samuel asked. "Come on, tell me what's going on in that silly head of yours."

"Samuel, we are going to be having a baby."

He sat there without saying a word, just looking at her, then at Michael, then back at her again.

"I thought that this would please you, Samuel." Her heart felt sick. "I waited all day for you to come home just so I could tell you." She didn't know if she should act out what she was feeling at the very minute—which, by the way, would not be good—or just wait to see what he had to say, if he was going to say anything. "What is wrong? Don't you want us to have a baby?" Her voice began to fade away as she thought for a moment that Samuel was unhappy with her being pregnant.

Samuel finally found his voice. "Is it really true? Are we really going to be having a baby?" He knew this time around, it would be his baby.

Not responding to what he asked right away and just looking at him for a moment, she then held out her hand to him. "Yes, it's really true. So you are pleased?"

"Yes, very pleased. I just thought at first you were teasing me."

"Teasing you? Really, Samuel, about something that is as important as this? No, Samuel, I could never tease you in this kind of matter. I have been bubbling with joy all day, just waiting to have you come in so I could share this with you."

"How far do you expect to be?"

"I think about two months, or about near that. What are you hoping for, a boy like his da or a little girl like me?" she said in a teasing manner.

Samuel got out of his chair and knelt down by Katie. Taking her hand in his, he held it up to his face. "Katie, I pray that we have a beautiful little girl just like her ma. We already have a son. We need a daughter who will help you when she is older." He kissed her hand as a tear ran down his cheeks.

"Oh, Samuel," Katie said as she turned to the side of her chair and laid her head on his broad shoulder. "That is one of the nicest things that you have ever said to me. I love you so very much."

"Mama, am I going to be a big brother?" Michael asked.

Turning her attention to Michael so he didn't feel left out, she answered, "Yes, honey, and you are going to be the best big brother anyone could ever ask for."

"Your ma is right. You are going to be a wonderful big brother, one that any brother or sister can look up to. What do you want, a brother or a sister?"

"I want a baby brother," he said as he looked at the expression on his ma's face.

"As long as the baby is healthy and has all its parts, that is all I care about. I want to get in touch with my ma and my da to see if they are willing to come out for a visit." She looked at Samuel to see if there was anything he wanted to add.

"Katie, I want them to come out too," he said as he sat back in his chair to finish eating what now is a cold supper. "I know that you miss your folks often, and now that we are going to have a wee little one again, it would be nice to have them come for a visit. I'll pray tonight before I lay my head and ask Jesus to commune with them."

"I too will pray that God softens their heart toward us. They have missed so much of Michael's life. I hate for them to miss this child's too. When they came out the few times that they did, I took it for granted that it was going to continue," Katie added.

"Ma, why do Granddad and Grandma never come over?"

Katie looked at Samuel in hopes that he would give the answer to Michael's question, but as she looked at her husband, he was busy eating his food so fast in hopes of it not getting any colder than it had already gotten.

"You see, son," she went on, "my ma and my da…" She was trying to find the right way to give him the answer in hopes that he could understand. "Well, you see, they have their own beliefs, and they are different from the way your pa and I have raised you."

"Like what, Ma?"

His words left Katie unsure of how to answer him in a way that a five-year-old might be able to understand. "They are Amish, and the Amish do not have indoor plumbing or electricity. Many don't have a car, or truck, or even a tractor to drive or ride in." She was hoping what she said was enough for him.

"Why are they like that, and we aren't?" Michael went on with the questions.

"Michael, your pa and I were both raised Amish, but after we married, we both decided that we wanted a better way of living. We left the teachings of the Amish and began going to the church that we go to now. We have lived their way all our life until we were having you. Then we left. I never wanted to raise you to be Amish. Their way is very hard in many ways, but the biggest reason we left was that we found out that God forgives us and we must forgive others as he forgives us."

"Do they not forgive others, Ma?"

"In some cases, they do not feel that they can, and that is not what the Bible tells us. Now, honey, enough questions about the Amish for tonight. I have to get these dishes cleaned up." She didn't want to go into any more of what had always put a sore spot in her stomach.

"Okay, Ma."

Katie started to clean up the table of all the dishes, all the while thinking about the way she was raised. In some sense, she liked the way of the Amish. They were hard workers, rising up so early in the morning, which her Samuel had grown accustomed to since he was a young boy, and he stayed that way, rising early every morning. She began to think of her ma and her da, how at times she really missed them, her ma more than the other. She wanted to tell her folks about the baby that will be coming some eight months away. Will she ever really connect with them again? Her heart felt sick at the thought that she may never be truly welcomed by them again.

Lord, please speak to my ma and my da. I miss them, Jesus, and I want them to be a part of my life and my family's lives. She ran the water in the sink, thinking about how, at home with her folks, she would go to the side of the house and fill up buckets of water from the pump to do dishes. *Yeah, this is so much easier than the old way of doing things*, she thought. Her thoughts were interrupted by Samuel when he walked up behind her and gave her a light squeeze and a rub on her belly.

"It don't really matter to me, honey, what we have as long as she is healthy. That's all that matters."

Katie turned around to face him, with a smile that lit up her face. She then giggled softly. "*She*—what makes you think that the baby is going to be a girl?"

"Because," he said as he put his hands on her hip and gave her a little sway, "that's what I prayed for, and I believe that God not only heard my prayer, but he will answer it also."

Katie returned his playfulness and put her hands around his neck. "If that's what you really want, a daughter, then I pray too that we will have a little girl to love."

"Oh, I know that Michael said that he hopes he has a baby brother, but I think that he will love a girl even more," commented Samuel.

"What makes you feel that way?" she asked.

"Because boys are different from girls in a sense that they feel it's their job to look after their sister to make sure that nothing happens to her. Whereas if it's a boy we have, then Michael may feel that he is equal to him and think that he don't have to watch out for him as he would a girl."

"Okay, I guess that it's a guy thing. I don't really understand it myself, but as long as you do, then I know it will be all right. Now, shoo out of here while I finish up with my work."

"Okay," he said as he walked into the other room to talk with Michael.

"Pa"

"Yuh Mike"

"Pa, I was wondering if you would know how Ma can get me a big beard like yours so I can wear it in my play at school?"

"Like mine, huh? I'll have to think on that and let you know."

"Okay, Pa, but I need one soon for my play, okay?"

"Okay, son."

Samuel knew that it was important for Michael to have a beard for the play he was going to be in at school. Samuel thought about how he might get hair or fur for a beard for Mike. Then the thought came to him about using his own beard if there was a way for either Katie or himself to make a beard of it. He would talk with Katie come bedtime to see how she felt about it.

That night came to where Katie felt like lying down earlier than usual, and Samuel thought that it might be a good thing for him to get some sleep too. He had worked several long hours and was quite exhausted.

She announced, "Come, Michael, it's time for rest now. We are going to bed, and morning comes early."

"Okay, I'm going," the boy said reluctantly but, nonetheless, he got up from the chair he was sitting on and walked to his bedroom.

'Good night, Michael," Katie said as she tucked him under the covers.

"Night, Ma."

"Have a good night's rest, son," Samuel commented.

"Katie, how would you feel about me cutting off my beard for us to make Mike a beard for his play at school?"

"Really?" she looked at him, surprised by his question.

"I still have an Amish beard after all this time. I was thinking about cutting it off for Mike to get a beard for his play."

"I think if that is what you want to do, then maybe you should do as yo feel. It might seem different for you to be without it after all the years of you growing it out. I might not recognize you with it off," she said, giving him the smile that he always liked.

The next day, Samuel did just what he talked about doing. He went into the bathroom with a long beard and came out looking like a new man. Turning the corner of the kitchen and hallway, Katie jumped when she looked at him, not knowing that he was going to cut it off. She knew that there was talk of it, but never had he told her that it was a sure thing.

"Wow, Samuel, you surprised me. I didn't know that you decided to go through with the cutting of your beard. So now what do we do to get it to be a beard for his play, might I ask?"

"You have not said if you like it, or maybe not, yuh?"

"It makes you look much younger, Samuel, but I do like it. It will take some time to get used to seeing you like this. Do you like how it looks?"

"Yuh, I think that I do."

The two put their minds together on how to make a beard for Mike. After it was all done with the gluing, they tried it on Mike to see. It was a nice fit, and the boy was very happy to have his pa's beard for the play.

The night of the play went really good, until Mike was to make his speech, and he began to sneeze so hard that the beard fell down from his chin. Picking it up as fast as he could and putting it back where it belonged, he continued with his part. Katie and Samuel were so proud of their little boy that after the play was over, Samuel treated them out for an ice-cream cone.

16

A Blessing

Katie could feel that her time for having her baby was coming soon. She was feeling contractions on and off all morning long. She would look out the window toward the fields in hopes of seeing Samuel coming up to the house. But when he was nowhere in sight, she would go sit for a while longer to where she would feel scared that the baby might come and she would be all alone in the home to deliver it all on her own. As she could feel them start to come more often and harder, she cried out to God, "Oh God, please help me to not have this baby all by myself. Please send Samuel up here to the house." She got up and waddled her way to the window once again, but still no Samuel in sight.

She began to talk to herself out loud out of fear, "Okay, if he won't come to me, I will write him a note and leave it on the table. I will just have to drive myself to the hospital and hope that this baby will not come until I am there safe and sound."

She grabbed a paper and pencil and started to jot down a note, telling him that she was having the baby and to meet her at the hospital after Michael got home from school. She picked up her purse and her diaper bag. She was all made up and ready to walk out of the house when, lo and behold, Samuel came walking up on the porch.

Seeing her with the diaper bag in one hand and her purse in the other, he knew that the time was now to get her to the hospital. "I see I got here just at the right time. Come on, honey, let's get you to the hospital right now."

Katie walked out to the car with the help of Samuel, who held her things and her arm. "We better hurry. I feel like the baby is ready to come right now," Katie told him.

"I'll hurry, honey, just as soon as you can put your feet in the door so I close it." With those words, her feet were inside the car, and they were headed down the road. He did just what he said he would do. Speeding down the road and hoping that no cops were anywhere in view of him, he was at the hospital before the baby came. He ran up to ring the bell at the emergency door so someone could come for Katie.

"Hello, can I help you?"

"Please hurry. My wife is having a baby right now," he shouted back into the speaker on the wall.

"Coming right now," a voice spoke back.

"They're coming right now, honey. How are you feeling?"

"I feel like I'm about to have our baby." She gave him a slight grin while having another contraction. "I sure hope that they hurry."

"Come on, honey. Let me help you get on this table," a lady spoke as she and Samuel helped Katie up on the table. "How far are your contractions apart?"

"They're getting closer by the minute. I just had one, and now I am having another one. I know that I am ready to have the baby any time now."

"Let me get you over into the delivery room. I think we might be having a baby here very soon," the nurse commented as she pushed the bed down the hallway. "I remember the day I had my little ones. In fact, it was just four months ago when I was the one being wheeled down these hallways."

Katie noticed that she said *little ones*, as in plural. "Did you have twins by any chance?"

"Yes, I did, but how did you know that?" she said, forgetting that she used the term *little ones*.

Through her pain of having a hard contraction, Katie answered her question, "I noticed that you said *little ones*, so I just assumed you had more than one."

"Oh yeah, that was silly of me. I had two boys that are identical twins. It's hard for me to tell them apart."

"Ouch," Katie tilted her head back, and her body moved with the pain she was having. "I feel the baby coming. Where is the doctor?" she yelled, but not for anything that the nurse was doing or not doing. It was just that her pain was getting more intense.

"I'm here right now. Let's see how far you are with the wee one." He bent down and took a look at her. "I see the baby is right there now. Let's get this baby born."

While the nurse talked with Katie about having her twins, she was putting an IV into Katie's arm.

"I see it coming, honey," Samuel said as he looked for his baby to be born. "Push, honey."

"I'm trying. I'm just so tired."

"Let's see if you can give one big push on the count of three," Dr. Hills said as he lightly tugged on the baby's head. "One, two, three—pushhh!"

Katie bore down with a big push till her face was red as a cherry. Then she took in a deep breath to push again. This time was a charm. Right before Samuel's eyes came the most beautiful baby girl he had ever laid eyes on before.

Before the doctor could say anything to Katie, Samuel spoke with great excitement that they had a beautiful daughter.

"Is she all right, Doctor? Does she have all her parts?" Katie asked, trying to see what the nurse was doing by cleaning up the baby.

"She appears to be perfect."

"You have a beautiful baby girl at twenty-one inches, and her weight is six pounds and seven ounces. Would you like to hold her?" the doctor offered.

"Yes," Katie she said as she held out her hands for her baby girl. "Samuel, would you like to name our daughter?" she asked as she looked all over her little baby.

"We had the name *Leah* picked out for a girl. Were we still going to call her that?"

"Yes." Then she focused her attention on her baby. "You are so beautiful, my little Leah. I am so glad to have you here with us." Then she remembered Michael. "Samuel, what about Michael?"

Samuel checked his watch on his wrist. "If I leave right now, I'll get there about the same time that the bus will."

"Hurry, and bring him back to see his little sister."

With those words falling from his wife's lips, he gave her a light squeeze and was out the door to pick up his son. In the meantime, Katie watched the nurse as she cleaned the baby to perfection so she could hold her again—but this time, for longer—and see if she wanted something to eat.

Samuel was pulling into the driveway just as the bus was pulling in. He was very relieved that his son wasn't already at home before he got there. He watched as Michael stepped off the bus and was ready to run up to the house. "Hey, wait a minute!"

Michael turned his head to see who was yelling out to him. Samuel could tell by the way he stopped and looked around that he was unsure who was calling.

"Yeah, Pa? Did you yell for me?" he asked, walking up to his car.

"Yes, son, I did. Your ma had the baby today. She wants you to come down and meet your baby sister."

"Really? Ma had me a baby sister. Where are they?"

"Down at the hospital, so hop on in here so we can go see them."

Samuel watched as Michael ran around to get in the passenger side of the car. Samuel had a smile of excitement on his face from having a baby girl. It was hard for him to drive back to the hospital following the speed limit. He wanted to go much faster than what the law allowed.

"So I have a baby sister, huh? What's her name?" Michael asked with a tone just a little under a shout. "And now that I'm a big brother, Pa, do you think that you and Ma can start to call me Mike instead of Michael?" He looked at his pa. "My friends at school already call me Mike."

Samuel looked over at Michael as he talked about being a big brother. Samuel knew that the reason the boy was talking so loud was because he was excited that he now was a proud big brother.

"To answer your first question, her name is Leah, and as for the second one, we'll talk to your ma about that one," Samuel said as he reached over and rubbed the top of Michael's head.

"Leah—well, that's a nice name, Pa. Who named her? You or Ma?" Michael asked, forgetting for the time being about him being called Mike now since he was a big brother.

"We both liked the name, so I'd say it was the both of us together. She looks like your ma, I think. But your ma is a modest woman and thinks she looks like me."

"Who do I look like, Pa? You or Ma?"

Samuel knew that there was no way for Michael to take after him, being that he was not the boy's birth father. But to Michael, Samuel was his only father, as was with Samuel.

"Oh, I think you look a lot like your ma's side of the family. You look like your grandfather, your ma's pa."

"I don't remember him that much, just a little bit of him."

Samuel laughed at the way he talked about remembering his grandfather. "Yeah, they don't come around much at all, and I'm hoping that will change real soon. Well, come on, we are here. Let's go see your ma and Leah."

Samuel and Michael started walking up the sidewalk toward the hospital doors. Michael was skipping alongside his pa.

"Pa."

"Yes, son."

"Do you think that Leah will like me being her big brother?"

"Oh, I'm sure she will, but you have to understand. Right now she is just a very tiny, little baby. She will be very unsure of just about everything unless it's eating."

"Okay, Pa, I'll remember."

The two walked down the hallway into Katie's room. Samuel could hardly keep himself from just bursting out.

He was so full of joy. He knew that his first wife was going to be having a child, but she died during childbirth.

"How is my lovely wife and my beautiful daughter doing?" Samuel said in greeting.

"Hi, Michael. Come see your little sister," Katie said as she turned the baby to face Michael. "And as for you, husband, we are doing great. She is quite a big eater already."

"Can I hold her, Ma?"

"Well, I don't think right now, honey. But when we get her home, I will let you."

"Okay, Ma. I think she is a nice baby sister," Michael said while rubbing her fingers.

"Oh, you do, do ya?" Katie said, laughing. "I think that she is too."

"Did the doctor say when you will be able to come home?" Samuel asked, lifting an eyebrow.

"No, I'm sure that they will want to keep me here for at least a day."

"I didn't think that you would be able to come home today, honey. I was just wondering."

"I'd like to see if my ma and my da want to come and see the baby?" She looked at Michael when she said what she did. Seeing the look on his face, she then had to mention him too. "I'd like for them to come see both of their grandchildren."

"When I leave here, I'll make it a point to stop around their place and let them know that you had a beautiful daughter by the name of Leah. And yes, they need to come and see Michael also."

Samuel and Michael stayed at the hospital until nightfall. Then they knew it was time for them to go home. It was hard for Samuel to leave the two at the hospital. He so wanted to take them home with him. But he also knew that in all reality right now, they needed to stay at least one night to be looked after and to make sure that everything was okay with both of them. He knew that after having a baby and with a few men and women from the church coming to visit throughout the day, Katie needed much sleep. He just didn't know how he was going to get any sleep with them not being home with him.

Samuel was true to his word. Even though the time was getting late, he still stopped by Katie's folks' home. Looking up at the house before approaching it, he saw that there were no lit candles or lamps. He decided to come back in the morning before going to see Katie at the hospital.

"Pa."

"Yeah, son?"

"Did you decide not to go and talk to them tonight?"

"Yeah, well, I didn't see any lights on, and I hate to wake them."

"What about Ma?"

"I will stop by there again come morning before I go see your ma." He looked over at Michael without saying anything else. He figured that he would have something else to add.

"Pa."

"Yeah, son?"

"You forgot something, Pa."

"I did? And what was that?"

"Well, Pa, I wanted you to ask Ma about calling me Mike now."

"Yes, you did, and I just plumb forgot too. Well, let me ask you something, Mike."

"See, you just called me Mike. Now isn't that a lot easier than the long name *Michael*?"

Samuel started to laugh at the thought of how Michael was confusing spelling the longer name than just saying it. "Why didn't you ask your ma?"

"Well, Pa, it's like you said. I just plumb forgot it."

"We will ask her tomorrow, but you might have to remind me, okay?"

"Okay, Pa, I will. Well, I will try. I might forget it again after seeing Ma and Leah. I love Leah, Pa, and I can hardly wait until Ma lets me hold her."

"I think you will be a good big brother for her, one who will watch over her when your ma and I are busy doing other things, like me being out on the fields and your ma cooking us a nice meal."

"Oh, I will, Pa. I want to help take care of her when you an' Ma have to run into town an' pick something up. I can watch her then."

Samuel looked at the seriousness of his son talking about caring for his little sister. Not having one of his own to care for when he was young, Samuel was getting a kick out of listening to Michael. "I'm sure that when Leah is a little older and you too, buddy, your ma and I will let you watch her so we can go places at times."

Morning came, and Samuel wanted to get to the hospital and see the rest of his family, but first, he knew that he needed to stop by his in-laws to see if they would like to come over for a visit once Katie and Leah were home. He prayed before going over to talk to them, in hopes that they would come without bringing up their religion. He so wanted to have them be part of all their lives, especially Katie's and the children. His folks were gone, and that left them being the only grandparents that his children had. He wasn't all too sure how his own folks would have reacted to him and Katie leaving the way of the Amish. He would like to think they would have never disowned him, but in all reality, he had no way of knowing just what they would have done. One thing he did know for sure was that he was going to do everything he could to get Katie's parents to come around as much as possible without holding anything against them.

"Pa, are we going to see Ma and Leah now? I'm all dressed to go now."

"Yup, just as soon as we stop by to see your grandparents."

"I was hoping that you'd remember that Ma wanted to see them," Michael said as he jumped into his ma's car.

"I know how important it is for your ma to see her folks, and I'd do just about anything for your ma."

"I know you would, Pa."

"How'd you like to walk up to their door with me?" Samuel asked as they pulled into the driveway.

"I'd like that, Pa," he said as he opened the passenger door and jumped out. Running around to the other side of the car, he walked up the steps with his Pa like he was a big man.

"Relax, son. These are your grandparents. No need to act tough," Samuel said as he chuckled, looking down at his boy. "I hope they're home," he spoke just above a whisper.

"What, Pa?"

"Oh, nothin'. I was just talkin' to myself is all." Samuel knocked on the door, feeling his heart begin to beat faster and faster to where he put his hand on his heart to feel the beats. It was as though it was about to beat right out of his chest.

"Maybe they're not home, Pa," Micheal said as he placed his face against the glass on the door.

"I'm sure that your grandma is. Your grandpa is more than likely working the fields right now."

All of a sudden, the door opened. Samuel saw his mother-in-law standing there, looking at them.

"Is Katie all right?" she asked.

"Yes, she is fine." Samuel answered her, trying to find more words. "The reason for us stopping over at this time in the morning is because Katie had a baby girl yesterday, and she was"—he paused for a moment—"we were hoping that the two of you would like to come over and meet your granddaughter?"

"Katie had a baby girl? Oh, that is nice, but I will talk with her da when he comes in for the evening." Mary looked down at Michael. "Hello, do you know who I am?" She smiled at him.

Michael never answered her with his voice; however, he did nod his head up and down.

"I have to go see Katie and the baby at the hospital. I will be bringing them home today. I hope to see both of you come evening time." With that, he and Michael turned and walked back to his car.

"Pa."

"Yuh."

"You think that they will come see Ma and the baby?"

"I can't answer that for sure. They have their ways that are not our ways anymore. I pray that they come see everyone tonight."

"Me too, Pa."

17

Coming Home

Katie walked in the house carrying the baby, so proud to be a new mama again. As she walked through the door, she noticed just how clean the house looked and smelled. "Wow, does this place look great, and that smell is so nice. I can see that you went all-out for me and Leah," she spoke to Samuel.

"It wasn't just me. You must thank Michael as well. He might have done more than I did." He gave Michael a wink.

"Michael, you helped your pa do all of this for me? Thank you so much. You don't know how much I love that you helped your pa."

"We wanted to surprise you, Ma," he said with an ear-to-ear smile. "You really are surprised, aren't you, Ma?"

"I sure am, honey. I was not expecting such a warm welcome home. I, at times, forget that we are no longer Amish and no longer conform to their beliefs. Thank you both so much. I really do mean that." She sat down on a rocking chair that Samuel bought her when she had Michael.

"Samuel, you care if I rest just for a while before I make our meal for the night?"

"You don't have to fix any meal. I have called in an order at Pasta's Inn. I know how much you like that place, and I knew that you would still need to rest up before getting back to your everyday duties."

"Oh, I do love their pastas. Thank you so much. It don't look like my ma an' my da are going to come see us, yuh?"

"Yuh, maybe yet. You know when the fields are ready, we work long, hard hours, and you know that your da won't come in until sundown. Maybe your ma will tell him that I stopped by and asked for them to come tonight."

"Well, I thought while I lay in bed at the hospital…"

"Yuh, what was that?"

"I thought about my upbringing with my ma and my da. It was very hard how we had to do everything. I am so happy that I married you, Samuel. I have two beautiful children that I would never change. I love my life now. I can do so much that I never thought as a child I would ever be able to do. I am a very blessed woman, and I just want to take time to thank you for wanting me and taking me out of that lifestyle. Thank you for our children." Katie began to get all choked up and started to cry.

"I love you, Mama. Why are you crying? Are you sad, Mama, 'cause your ma and pa never come over?"

"Oh, honey, I'm not sad, quite the contrary. I am so happy for you, your sister, and your pa. I would not change a thing." She looked at Samuel with tears still lingering in her eyes. "I love you, Samuel."

"I'm glad that you do, 'cause I sure love you. I want nothing more than to love God with all our hearts, tell others of him, and to love and care for my family."

Michael looked at his folks like he was so unsure of what was going on. In his mind, when he saw his ma cry, he thought she should be sad. Yet she told him that she was happy. He just plainly didn't understand adults.

"Ma, can I hold Leah? You said that I could when we come home."

"Yes, but you will have to sit down, and all the way back. I wouldn't want you to drop her, honey."

"I won't drop her, Ma. Remember that I am her big brother, and she is my little sister. Silly, Mama, I think you forgot that I am her big brother." He laughed at his ma thinking that he would drop his baby sister. He ran over to the couch and sat down, scooting himself all the way to the back until he felt his back touching. "Okay, Ma, I'm all the way back," he said as he held out his hands for Leah.

"Katie placed her in his hands, slowly until she could feel that he was not going to drop her head down. She then placed a couch pillow under his arm to help hold her head up. "How does it feel to be a big brother and hold your little sister?"

"I love her, Mama. I want to hold her all the time."

She watched the way he held Leah with such compassion and caring. She knew that he really believed in his heart that he was big enough to watch her all on his own. It was cute to watch his tenderness toward her, the way he told her that he was her big brother and that it was his job as a big brother to watch that no one would ever hurt her.

Samuel stood close by, watching him as well. He smiled seeing the way Michael cared for Leah. "Hey, Michael, maybe now would be the time to tell your ma what you had asked me."

"Oh, and what would that be, Michael?" Katie asked.

"What, Pa?" he said, forgetting what he had talked to his pa about.

"Your name, son."

"Oh yeah, my name, Ma."

"Your name? What is wrong with your name?"

"I was wondering…now that I am a big brother…well, I was wondering if you and Pa would start calling me Mike instead of Michael?"

"Oh," Katie said, surprised by what he was asking at such a young age.

"All my friends at school call me Mike, Ma."

"I guess, if that is what you really want. It may take me sometime to get used to calling you just Mike instead of Michael. How do you feel about that, Samuel?"

"This is something that he wants. I see no harm in it. It's still his name, just shortened down a little."

211

"Okay, Mike," his ma said, bringing a smile on his face, but she felt sad in the sense that her son was getting to the age where he wanted a big boy's name. "I think that I will take a little nap. I feel very tired."

"You go ahead, honey. I know that you must be tired. Mike and I will go out to the fields for a while and work. Would that be all right by you?"

"But, Pa, I was going to see if I could watch Leah for Ma so she could get some sleep."

"Oh, thank you, Michael—Mike, I mean. But I'm sure that your pa would like your help today, and I believe that Leah is tired too."

"Okay, I'll go in the fields," he reluctantly replied.

Katie was feeding the baby when she heard what sounded like a light tap on the door. Unsure of where the sound was coming from, she continued to feed the baby while lying on her bed. Then she heard it tap louder. *Where might that be coming from? I better go see*, she spoke to herself. She went to the kitchen to look out her door when she noticed a buggy sitting in her driveway.

Pulling back the curtain on the window, she saw her ma standing there. "Ma, is everything all right? Where is Da? Did you come over here all by yourself?" She looked around in hopes of seeing her da.

"Katie girl, your da…" She stopped for a moment then continued, "It's your da, Katie girl. He took ill."

"What do you mean he took ill? What is wrong with him, Ma?"

"Not for sure, he's been talking about you, and now he can't talk at all. I think that you might want to come by to see him."

"But what will people say, Ma, if they see me stop over?" Right after those words fell from her lips, she regretted them.

"If they do, I will deal with that then, but for now, I need for you to come see your da," Mary said as she looked around in her kitchen from where she was standing on the porch.

"I will get myself together and my baby. Samuel and Mike are out in the fields and won't be back for a while. I will write him a note letting him know where I am."

"Fine, Katie," she said as she turned to walk back to the buggy. "I will see you there." With that, she climbed up into the wagon.

Katie worked fast at getting what she needed for the baby, and then she was out the door and riding down the road. *Please, dear God, whatever is wrong with my da, please don't let him die. Help him feel better and help my folks know you in a better way than they do. Help them find the truth and know that it's what will set them free from the bondage that they are in. In Jesus's mighty name, amen.*

Pulling up into the driveway and getting to the house before she could even see the buggy that held her ma, Katie took the baby from her car and went into the home that she, just a few short years ago, was kicked out of. Now memories of her childhood filled her mind, and she laid the baby down on her seat to find which room her da was in. Walking through the home as she quietly called out for her da and not hearing anything, she continued to go into other rooms. Without being given information by her ma which room her da was in, she decided to search all of them until finding him.

"Da!" she shouted as she saw him lying on the floor in a crumpled-up position. "Da, what is wrong? It's me, Katie girl, Da." She looked down at him then knelt next to him. After seeing no movement from him, she began to shout and shake him lightly. "Da, please answer me."

She heard her ma come into the room.

"Oh, Katie girl, what is wrong with him?" She too joined the two of them on the floor. Tears flooded Mary's face now, fear building up inside her.

Katie laid hands on her da and began to pray in the spirit, her ma not knowing what she was doing and giving her a weird look.

"Stop that, Katie. What are you doing?"

"I was praying for Da, Ma."

"I don't know that kind of prayer, Katie girl. It don't look like he is breathing." She put her ear on his chest.

"Da, Da!" Katie shouted again. "Please da get up." She too put her ear to his chest. She sat back, and she too had a tearstained face. "Ma, I think that Da is gone. I'm not hearing his heartbeat. We need to take him to the hospital." Right after she made that statement, she heard her da make a weak noise, which sounded to her like a cough. "Da, are you okay?" she asked, bending back down to hear what he was trying to say to her.

"I love you, Katie, and I want you to know that I am sorry for how I was to you."

She heard him, but it was a strain for her to make out what he was saying. "I love you too, Da, and I'm sorry that I hurt you and Ma."

"Katie, take care of your ma for me." Then looking toward his wife, he asked her to care for Katie.

"What do you mean? You're not going anywhere, Da. You're going to be fine."

He grabbed ahold of her hand and gave it a light squeeze. "Pray for my soul, Katie."

Katie looked at her ma. Then she did what he had asked from her to do. "Da, I'm going to pray now. Father God, right now, I ask you to please touch my da. Make him know who you are right now in the name of Jesus. Speak to his heart and never let him die without knowing you." Then she took this time to talk to him. "Da, talk to Jesus, Da. Make that peace now."

"I have it now, Katie." He looked at his wife. "Please let Katie teach you what is right and true. I love you." With that, his eyes closed, and his hand went limp.

"Issac!" his wife cried out, leaning down and crying on his chest.

Katie began to cry again. She took ahold of her ma and put her arms around her. "He's at peace now, Ma, no more pain. He held on long enough to tell us what he wanted us to know."

"I can't believe he's gone, Katie. My Issac is gone." The cries came harder than ever now at the thought that the man she was married to ever since she was sixteen years of age—and now she was thirty-seven—was gone from her. What would she do without him? He was all she had ever known as a man.

"Ma, I need to go call someone and let them know that Da is gone. Are you going to be all right for me to leave you for a short while?"

With her small-framed body sitting on the floor, still trembling over the loss of her husband, she said, "Go. I will be here with your da. I am trying to understand what happened to him."

"I have to go make a call, Ma," Katie said as she got up from the floor.

Looking down at her ma waving her hand at her to tell her to go do whatever it was that needed to be done, with a quick move, Katie picked up Leah, who was still asleep in her car seat, and headed out the door. She drove down the road as fast as she could, still trying to keep her car safe on the road. Tears began to stream down her face, mumbling out loud to herself, "I just can't believe it. My da is gone. Oh God, why? Why my da?"

She continued to cry, but now she found herself getting mad. She knew this was unlike her to be so mad. She knew that tragedy happens even to the best of them. She should be at peace knowing that her da made peace not only with her, asking for her forgiveness, but he also asked Jesus to forgive him. She knew in her heart that her da was now walking with Jesus in heaven, yet she was angry. She was angry with God.

"Why did you take him right when he asked me to forgive him? What is my ma going to do without him?" She noticed that she was yelling at God for something that was not of his doing. It was something caused by a man overworking in the heat—it was from his own doings, not God's. Crying harder now after putting blame on a God of love, who had healed her child when he was just a baby, she was now hurt by her own actions, not God's.

"Oh God, please forgive me for blaming you. I am so sorry for speaking to you with such anger. I really am so sorry, God. I know that was not your will for him to die. I trust you that you will be here for my ma and for me during this time." After asking God to forgive her from the bottom of her heart, by repenting. She felt the peace of God cover her. She knew then that God was not holding anything against her for her outburst.

Pulling into her driveway and taking the baby out of her car seat in the back, she went into her home to call up the hospital for help. She was unsure of whom to call, not having this happen before. But she was sure that the ambulance was at the hospital. Talking to someone at the nurses' desk and giving her her ma's address, she wasn't sure if she ought to go back there right away or wait for Samuel to come in so he could go back over there with her.

As Katie sat down and cried for her ma, Leah began to cry. Knowing that she must be hungry, Katie took the time to feed her and talk out loud while doing so. "Lord, I know that you know all things. There is nothing that is hidden from you. I just don't understand how a young man at the age of thirty-six can just die. I know that he is just too young to leave my mom all alone, and now what will she do?" While in the middle of trying to figure things out in her mind, Samuel and Mike walked in.

Noticing that she was crying, Samuel at the time, not knowing what was going on, seeing tears come from his wife's eyes, streaming down her cheeks, brought worry at first to his mind. Quickly going to her side to understand what was wrong, he asked, "Why the tears? Is there something wrong?"

"My da...he's dead."

"Dead! What you mean dead? How...what happened?"

"Ma came over to tell me to come quickly 'cause he was not feeling so good. When I got there, he was lying on the floor." She continued to tell him all that she knew. The more she talked, the more it all became real that her da was really gone—and the harder she began to cry.

"I am so sorry, Katie, for your da's passing. I believe we should be there for your ma. Did you call for help?"

"Yes, they should be there by now." She looked at the fear in Mike's eyes. Not wanting him to feel scared, she began to wipe her tears as she burped Leah. "Come over here, Mike. I have something to tell you." She stretched out her hand toward him.

"Yeah, Ma?"

"I want you to know that everything is going to be okay. My da is with Jesus now in heaven. We just need to be praying for your grandma. She is all alone at her home now." She gave Mike a hug.

"Okay, Ma, I'll pray for her not to be sad and that Jesus will bring her another husband."

Katie didn't know what to say after Mike's comment on another husband. She was taken by surprise. Another husband would be the last thing on her ma's mind, Katie was sure of that. Knowing that her da was the only man her ma had ever known, she was not sure if her ma would ever look for another.

After the burial was over with, Mary went back to stay with Katie and Samuel. She felt lost without the man she was with for the last twenty-two years. They had a big home, but now it was empty of not just her daughter but now her husband. Not knowing just what to expect staying at Katie's home, she felt that she was in a stranger's place. Having running water, electricity, an indoor plumbing were just few things that she herself had never had before. She knew that it was not her ways to have all these things now available for her. She also knew that it was Katie and Samuel's choice to have them, and there was nothing she could do about it. She would respect them for what they have. She just didn't want them trying to push anything on her.

18

The Move

It's been two weeks since the death of her dear husband, and Mary felt lost without him. "Katie girl, may I have a talk with you about something that's been on my mind?" Mary asked, drawing her attention away from watching television at the time.

"Sure, Ma. What would you like to talk about?" She turned off the TV, knowing that her ma felt that she was in sin if she was to sit and watch a bit.

"I have been wondering if I should be selling the home and moving elsewhere. It's been hard for me to go back there and stay, not just because your da's not there anymore but I have callers coming over and telling me who I am to marry."

"Ma, how do you feel about marrying again?" Surprised, by the callers already. "You know in the Amish faith you are to marry again." She looked at her ma, but what she was seeing was not one who wanted to marry, at least not yet, or could it be not to marry to another in the Amish faith?

"I really feel like selling the old home and buying a smaller place for myself. And I have been doing a lot of thinking about what you and Samuel have been talking to me about. The faith that the both of you have, I want that, and I believe that your da knew that is what I ought to do too. I don't believe that I will return to the Amish. Oh, I know that I will be shunned, and that is okay with me. I will miss some of my closest friends like Naomi and Edith. But I must do what I feel is right for me at this time. I am at a young age, and I'm not going to spend the rest of my days shunning my only child and her family anymore."

"I'm glad that you have made this choice, Ma, but where will you live?"

"I've been thinking about that ever since your da died. I think if I move into town, it will be close for me to get to all the stores there." She looked at her daughter for direction of some sort, knowing that her thoughts of moving into town might be a big mistake.

"What will you do with the horses and the buggy? Or are you planning of taking them into town with you?"

"Of course not, but I must sell them to move into town."

"Ma, are you sure this is where you want to go? You have never been into town to live before."

"I don't drive as you do, and it might be too late for me to be taught such as yourself."

"Ma, you are still very young, and either Samuel or myself can teach you to drive. It's not hard like one might think. I thought that I would never learn to drive, but it really was quite easy once you put your mind into it."

"Katie, right now, I am so unsure about everything in my life." Mary put her head down low and shook it back and forth. "I don't know what to do. Being Amish is all that I have ever known. This was the way I was taught all my life. Then your da turns in his last breath and changes all that for me. I don't know what came over him at his last moments here on earth. Why did he not do this change for him and me together? Maybe he would still be here for me."

Not knowing what to say to her own ma at the time, Katie bent down to comfort her the best that she knew how. "Stay here with Samuel and me for as long as you need to, Ma. There is no rush for you to leave now, is there?"

"I don't want to be a bother any further, Katie. A man and his family ought not to have to care for someone that is not family."

"Ma, what are you saying? You are family. You are my ma, and we want you to stay for as long as you want to stay." She looked at Samuel, who did not say a word until now.

"She is right, Mary. You must stay and put your mind to ease from worry. And furthermore, for all those men who have been wanting to get with you, forget them too. God will bring you a man on his timing, not anyone else's. Now I will hear no more about you leaving until you are good and ready. It's time that you get to know your grandchildren and for them to get to know you."

Mary smiled at the words that he spoke to her, making her feel welcome to stay longer. It brought comfort to know that she was not only welcomed in her daughter's home but also wanted. "If you are sure, then I will stay," she said quite sheepishly.

"Now we will hear no more talk of it, Mary. You are wanted, and we expect for you to make this your home for as long as you like. Katie and I will even put on the bedroom door "Mary's Room" if you like." He was teasing her now, trying to bring laughter to a woman who felt she had nothing to laugh about since losing her husband a few weeks ago.

"I don't know what I have done to deserve to be treated so kindly from both of you after what your da and I have done to the both of you not to mention never really coming around here to know our grandson." She put her head down in shame of what had taken place in the past. Tears now running down her cheeks, she said, "Oh, Katie, can you ever forgive me and your da?"

"I already have, Ma, a long time ago. Ma, where I go to church you have come before, they teach us about forgiveness and moving past from what has happened. We must look to the future now, Ma. I know that is what Da wanted when he asked us to care for each other. He didn't want anything to stand between us any longer.

"When I was unable to see you and Da, my heart cried for you both. I missed you so much and our talks. I know since you've been staying here, there are many things that you don't care for because of what you have always been taught and believed. But, Ma, I will never ask you to do anything that you are not comfortable in doing. I want you to do what you feel is right to do and please don't be upset with the way we do things around here."

"I'm not upset with the way things are done for you and your family. I know this is something that you have been doing for many years now, and that is okay with me. I will maybe try some things at times if you don't mind," she said, acting a little shy about inquiring about other things that she had never done before.

"Anything you feel, Ma." Katie looked at her, waiting to see if there was something that she felt that she wanted to try. "Is there something that you would like to try?"

"I have never had a cup of coffee in all my life, but every time I smell it come morning, well, it smells so good." She put her hand over her mouth, like maybe she shouldn't be asking of that.

"I must admit, it can become quite addicting. But it sure does taste good. It was the smell that got me too. Whenever Samuel and I went over to a friend's home, they would always put on a pot of coffee, and the very smell of it made me want some. I must admit, it did take me a while before I started to drink it. But once I got the taste of it with the sweet creamer they would put in it, I loved it. It was different than anything that I have ever had before."

"Will you think bad of me if I ask you to make some so I might try it?"

"No, not at all. Like I said, Ma, I love coffee now, so I don't mind putting some on right now, and I will have a cup with you." With those words, Katie was up walking into the kitchen to start her coffee.

While walking in the kitchen, Katie had her da running through her mind, wondering if this was all part of what he meant by taking care of her ma. She was sure that coffee did not run through his mind at all. In fact, he probably would be very much against it. "It will be just a minute, for it to be done," she said as she walked back into the living room. "Would you like to come out to the table in the kitchen to have our coffee?"

"Yuh." Mary got up from the chair she was sitting on and walked to the kitchen, leaving Sameul in the living room. "Do you think that your da would approve of me doing this thing?"

"Ma, to no disrespect in Da, I believe that when he asked us to care for each other, he wanted you to be happy. It is not sin to drink coffee, like we were always taught. There is no place in the Bible that tells us that we must not partake of coffee. It's just a hot drink such as tea."

"We don't drink that, either," Mary said, looking at her daughter's slim built with her long flowing brown hair as she poured two cups of coffee with sweet cream to add to the flavor of the coffee.

"I know, Ma. I remember never having either before. Here, try this and tell me what you think." She watched as her ma brought the hot cup up to her mouth very slowly, as if the cup was going to bite at her.

"I feel that it's very hot, but to say that there are some Amish folks who will drink coffee, I have known them."

"Yes, it's hot but ever so good. Just take a tiny sip at first to get the feel of the hotness. I have not ever seen any Amish who have before."

As Mary brought it to her lips, she took a very small sip then snapped her lips together, getting the taste of it. "Hmmm, this is good, Katie," she said, taking a bigger sip this time then quickly putting down the coffee cup on the table. "My, that's hot." She looked at Katie and lifted her eyebrows. "But it sure is good." She picked up her cup again to drink some more.

Katie watched her ma enjoying for the very first time ever having coffee. "I told you, Ma, it does taste very good." Looking into the other room to see if she could see Samuel and ask if he wanted to join them, she found that he had fallen asleep on his favorite chair. She knew that he must have worked hard in the fields, and he was just plain worn out. The last thing that she wanted was for him to die an early death like her da did.

"Katie girl, if it wouldn't be too much to ask of you…"

"What, Ma?"

"Would you mind if I have this coffee with you each morning?"

"Oh heavens, no, it wouldn't bother me at all. I'd love to share coffee with you in the morning. Samuel is gone so early every morning that we barely get a chance to have it together until evening. Ma, you don't feel ashamed drinking it, do you?"

"Before putting it to my mouth, I felt that my heart would come out of my chest, but now I am okay with it. I think it's just that I have never done this sort of thing before, and I guess I just thought it wrong to try."

"I am glad that you are okay with it. Since we did have this at evening time, it might keep you from sleeping for a while."

"Really?"

"Yeah, it has caffeine in it, which may keep you awake for a while. Samuel and I usually never drink it after seven because we need to get sleep for the upcoming day."

"Oh my, maybe you should have told me this beforehand, yuh?"

"I'm sorry, Ma. I guess I just wasn't thinking about that at the time, seeing how you wanted to try it. Maybe one cup won't keep you awake. Besides, we have a couple more hours to be up before bed anyway. By then, it should all be worn off us."

Mary laid down about an hour after having coffee. She thought about what Katie told her about maybe not being able to sleep. She waited, which she thought would be hours of lying there in silence; but before she knew it, morning had arrived, and the light was peeking through the curtains.

"I slept good, even after having coffee," she told herself.

Walking out into the kitchen to see if Katie was up yet then seeing the time was only 5:30 a.m., Mary knew that Samuel would be getting up at any time. She put a pot of coffee on for Samuel and Katie, hoping that she made it right by watching how Katie made it the night before. She knew just by the smell of it that she would be having a cup for herself. Although Katie told her that there was no sin in drinking it, the thought of her wanting some again made her feel guilty, but she knew that it was only because this was something she had never done, up until last night. She did know that some of the Amish weren't opposed to having a cup of black coffee from time to time, but her Issac never felt the need to have it in their home, so she never questioned the reason why. It was looked at as sin because it was not something you had to have; it was vanity.

"I thought I could smell some hot coffee brewing while I was lying down. Ma, you did this all by yourself?"

"I woke and thought to make some for everyone before Samuel leaves for work."

"Samuel has left already, but I would love to have a cup with you. It helps wake me up," she said as she grabbed two cups and put the creamer in them, then poured hot, steamy coffee over the creamer.

Taking a small sip to see if it was made to her liking, Katie said, "Yumm. Ma, you made this just like I like it, not too strong but strong enough to wake me before I get Mike up for school. And the baby needs feeding."

"Oh, honey, this is so good. I can't figure why your da was so against having coffee when it tastes so good," Mary stated, smiling.

"I'm sure if he would have given it a chance, he might have liked it too. Ma, we are having one of Samuel's and my friend over for dinner tonight."

"Oh."

"Yeah, he goes to the church that we go to, and he is a very nice man."

"Katie, why do you feel the need to inform me of your company?" she asked with a curious look.

"Well, the truth is, Samuel has been talking to him about coming over and meeting you. He told him that you are staying here with us and we'd like him to come and meet you."

"Katie, please don't put me in a place of having to marry as of yet."

"Ma, I would never do that, but you are young, and I don't want you thinking that it is wrong if you wanted to see or date someone."

"Date? I don't date."

"Ma, we are not Amish any longer, and you said that you were leaving their way too. Is this still your plan? You've been gone for quite sometime, and I'm sure that the Amish is well enough aware of where you've been staying ever since they were calling on you to marry another."

"You are right, but I know nothing about dating. And what about your da?"

"Ma, we are not setting you up to marry anyone. We are having a friend come over to meet you. If in time you two feel the attraction with each other, then we will go from there. But for now, it's just a single man coming to meet my ma."

"What is your friend's name?"

"Jim and he is a very nice man right around your age."

"What will we be having for dinner?"

"I thought that a roast and potatoes with carrots might be good. What do you think?"

"That does sound good. Honey, I'm not quite sure of how to act." Mary saw the strange look that her daughter was giving her. "What I mean is, was it easy for you to leave the Amish ways and become like the English?"

Not knowing how far she should go back with wanting to be like the English folks, she didn't want to offend her ma in any way. Now that her ma had made the choice to change from Amish to English, maybe it was the right time to tell her about her dream of being English ever since she was about thirteen years old.

"Ma, it wasn't that hard for me or for Samuel to be like the English. We both wanted the same thing, and that was to become like the English. Ever since I was about thirteen years of age, I would dream about what it would be like to wear pants, have running water, have electricity in your home." She looked at her ma beginning to squirm in her seat a little. "Ma, I've always wanted to be able to drive a car, watch TV. I'm sorry if this hurts you. It's not that I hated the way you and Da raised me. It's just that I wanted something different. Are you upset with me?"

"No, not really, not upset, just thinking about all those nights that you would sit outside on the porch swing. Was that when you did all your thinking about the English?"

"I did a lot of it then, but I also did when I was in the barn milking the cows, feeding the chickens, taking walks."

"Is that why you and Emily stopped being friends?"

"That is one reason why."

"Yuh, what's the other?"

"When I was told that I was to marry Samuel, I rebelled in my heart about it, and I shared that with Emily. She got very upset with me when I told her that I didn't want to marry Samuel, but what I wanted was to marry and Englishman."

"Then you still went and married him even after your feelings. Why was that?"

"Because we wanted the same thing. We wanted out and become English. I never gave him a chance before judging him too harsh. I just thought that he would never change and always stay Amish. And I, being a person who wanted different, just thought that I'd never get that from him."

"Are you truly happy with your life? Are you happy that you no longer live as the Amish do?"

"Ma, I love my life. I couldn't ask for more than I have. God has blessed me and Samuel's marriage greatly. I have the love and respect of a man. I have two beautiful children. I have a nice home, running water, and a bathroom in my home." She chuckled at that.

"All your da and I ever wanted for you was to really be happy. Yuh, we wanted you to be Amish, but even though we never came around much at all, we did believe that you were happy." She gave her daughter a big hug. "Oh, honey, I have many regrets on things that your da and I should have done."

"Ma, that is the past, and we don't live there. I want you to not worry about what should have been but think about what is now."

"Yuh, okay, I will put that in my mind, what you say about not living in the past."

The two women worked on preparing for the meal and their company. All the while, Mary was thinking about what she and Katie talked about forgetting the past. *Does she think that I will ever forget her da if and when I meet another man?* Mary thought to herself.

"Come, Ma, let's sit a spell," Katie told her while everything was on the stove and cooking. "I need to feed Leah, and Mike will be coming home any minute now. He gets so excited to get home to hold his little sister."

"I have seen that in him. He will make a wonderful da when that times comes."

"Yuh, like his pa." It seemed to Katie that every once in a while, the talk of the Amish would still come out when she spoke.

"Your da was a good man too, Katie. He might have been a little strict with ya, but that was just his ways."

Katie remembered who it was that allowed her and Samuel go for a walk. It was her da, not her ma, who did that. But she was not one to bring up the past hurts, so she decided not to mention what it was that she remembered. "Yuh, Ma, Da was a very good da to me, and a good husband to you."

"I think I hear the bus coming near, Katie. Do you want me to stand on the porch for Mike?"

"If you like, you may, but there really is no need to. I'm going to feed Leah right quick before Mike holds her."

Mary stood by the window, watching her grandson get off the bus. "He likes riding the bus?"

"Yuh, Ma, he does."

"Hi, Grandma," Mike said as he entered the door as if to own the world.

"Hi, Michael, how are you today? How was school, yeh?"

"It was good. Where is Leah?" He walked past his grandma to look for Leah.

"I'm just about done with her feeding. Then you may hold her."

"Okay, Ma." Mike sat down next to his ma while she finished up with the feeding.

"Mike, while I am feeding her, why don't you go and feed the chickens?" Katie suggested.

"Okay, Ma, I will."

After two hours had gone by, Samuel came in for the evening. "Hi, honey. How was your day today?"

"Good, and how was yours?"

"Busy, but I had a good day today. I got a lot done. I'm going to get my shower before Jim gets here, okay?"

"Okay, honey." Katie watched him walk toward the bathroom, looking at the smirk he gave her when he mentioned his friend Jim coming over. She knew what he was thinking when he said that. She knew that he had been talking to Jim about her ma, and that was why he decided it was time for him to come over to meet her.

19

First Sight

Katie watched Samuel as he kept walking over to the window looking for his friend to pull in the driveway. She knew that he was excited to see if there would be a match between her ma and Jim. She had never known Samuel to be a matchmaker, but ever since her ma had moved in and he met Jim, he knew that he was a good man and would make a good husband for her ma.

"He's here," he said with excitement in his voice and actions as he hurried out the door to welcome his friend. "Glad to have you here this evening. Come on in. I'll introduce you to my mother-in-law."

"Okay," Jim said, looking a little nervous at Samuel.

"Don't be nervous. I think that she is nervous enough for the both of you." Samuel laughed at what he said, knowing that Mary was nervous about the whole thing.

Mary tried not to look toward the door as they entered, but at the same time, she couldn't help but see what this man looked like that she was to meet tonight after all the talk about him. She was curious in her own way to see for herself. After all, she never looked at another besides her Isaac. She was with him since a young lady and had never thought to stray. But now that her Isaac was no longer here for her, she would either stay with her daughter or move out in town—or marry again, if and when she found the right man.

Mary watched this handsome tall, thin, yet built tanned, dark-haired man come into the house with a white shirt on that was all about showing off his muscles. Mary could see that everything Katie said about his built and his looks were true. He was clean-cut with no facial hair at all. This was not something that she was used to seeing, coming from the Amish background. Although different, it was to her liking. If she was going to be like the English, which her daughter was now, then she must also adapt to their ways. She knew that she never wanted to marry in the Amish faith again, but after seeing what Samuel's friend looked like, she wasn't opposed to possibly dating the Englishman.

"Jim, this is my mother-in-law, Mary. And, Mary, this is my good friend Jim Weller." Samuel looked at the way the two were looking at each other. He wasn't sure at first if it was good or not seeing the way Mary responded by turning her head away. "Mary, is there something wrong?" he asked.

"Nah, nothing, Samuel. It is nice to meet you, Jim," Mary said with a smile, trying to talk as much like the English as possible.

"Yes, likewise. I've heard a lot about you," Jim replied.

"Yuh, I hope not so bad, yuh?" She gave him a slight grin.

Jim looked at Samuel then back at her. "Oh no, not bad at all. I see where your daughter got her great looks. I think she looks a lot like you." Jim was hoping that he wasn't coming on too strong to where it would scare her off before it even started. He knew that she came from the Amish, and it was quite different from anything that he was used to. So being that, he was not sure if his talk just might seem strange to her.

"Oh, I see. I'm not sure how to take that, being we just met."

"I'm sorry if I offended you. I nearly was saying that you are a pretty woman is all." He looked toward Samuel in hopes of getting some kind of look, maybe a headshake saying no more or something that could help him with his talk to her, but Samuel just smiled at him.

"I think I should say thank-you. I am sorry, I am not used to this talk."

"That's okay. I need to be more careful when talking to someone whom I just met."

"Come on in, everyone. Dinner is all set on the table, and I don't want it to get cold."

"It sure smells good, Katie. Where would you like me to sit?" Jim asked.

"You can sit right here, and, Ma, you can right here." She pointed to the chairs that were next to each other.

First it was Jim who seemed to be coming on strong; now it was Katie. *What is really going on here? Are they trying to set me up with him or just trying to be friendly?* thought Mary

Everyone was eating and laughing at some jokes Jim was telling—well, everyone but the one he was trying to impress. Mary didn't know how to take the jokes, nor did she think they were funny. After it seemed to go on forever, the laughing and joke-telling seemed to come to an end, and Mary was happy that it did. She was feeling unsure about the English ways at this time. Some things were just not normal to her, coming from an Amish background. After everyone was done eating, the ladies cleaned up the dishes and talked among themselves. Then they joined the men in the living room.

"That was a great meal, ladies. Thank you very much for having me over tonight," Jim said.

"You're welcome, Jim. I'm glad that you enjoyed it," Katie said.

"So, Mary, what kind of plans do you have now that you have left the Amish community?" Jim asked.

"I was talking to my daughter and Samuel about me selling my home and moving into town where I can just walk to the stores that I will need to go to."

"Oh really? Well, are you serious about selling? Or is this just something that you're thinking about doing?"

"I'm thinking as of right now I'd like to, but I will see what happens."

"If you do decide to move, let me know, and I will help with your things."

"Okay, I will." She had a smile come across her face.

"Hey now, enough about moving. We have decided that Ma will live right here with us for as long as she wants to," stated Samuel.

"Yuh, you did decide. But what about you having your time alone? You don't need me staying here, yuh?"

"Ma, we like having you around. It's nice to be a family again," Katie said.

When Katie said *a family again*, Mary wished that she would have thought before speaking because now she had Jim looking at them strangely. "Oh, it's nothin really. It's an Amish thing." Mary gave a half smile.

"So what type of things do you enjoy doing, Mary, if you don't mind me asking?"

"As you know, I have been Amish all my life, and being Amish, there is just so much that one can't do. I have never watched TV until coming to stay with my daughter. I still feel different when seeing it on and playing movies for us to watch. I have never had a washtub like Katie's, or a dryer—I have always hung them out to dry. This is all so different in many ways, but I am trying to get used to it."

"What did you do for the winter months about drying your clothes? It would be much too cold for hanging them then, wouldn't it?"

"Yuh, way too cold, but we have nice hot stoves to heat our homes with, so we hang clothes by the stove." Mary looked over at Samuel and Katie, wondering how many questions Jim was going to ask.

Noticing how she looked at them, Jim decided to do something that took everyone by surprise.

"I'm sorry for asking you so many questions. If you don't mind me saying so, I find you to be a very delightful woman, and if it's not too forward, I wouldn't mind taking you out sometime."

"Oh my." Mary put her hand to her mouth. "My husband has not been gone for very long at all. Wouldn't it be wrong for me to consider such a thing?"

"Ma, no, I don't think so. You are young still and can't wait for others to tell you when it's time enough to stop grieving for da. No disrespect, Ma, but Da did ask for me to care for you, and I say if you would like to go out with Jim, then you have my blessing."

"Would you like to go out to a dinner and a movie with me?" Jim asked again.

"You hungry again already?"

"Oh no, not tonight. I was meaning another night. The way you ladies cook, I'd be lucky if I felt hungry tomorrow. I can't say when I have eaten so much food." Now it was his turn to give a big smile.

"Yuh, I think so. I'll try and go out."

"That is awesome. I am happy that you have accepted. Now I will be able to sleep good tonight." He smiled again, showing her that he was teasing with her now.

The night went good with them all talking and kidding with each other. The time was getting late, and they all needed to get some sleep, and Katie needed to feed the baby again before bedtime.

When morning came, Katie put on a pot of coffee for her ma and herself. She didn't mention anything to her ma about the night before. She was waiting to see if her ma would bring up anything about Jim or show any interest in him.

"Ma, would you like a cup of coffee?"

"Yah, that smells very good. I never thought that I would ever be thinking that about coffee—then to be drinking it."

It seemed to Katie after her ma made that statement, she went into deep thought. "Are you all right, Ma?"

"Yah, I'm just thinking about what your pa would be thinking of me drinking this here." She held up her cup of coffee.

"It's okay, Ma, to drink coffee. I have never seen anywhere in the Bible where it tells us to not drink it."

"Yah, I know. I have been studying God's word to see if I could find anything in there that would tell me it's sin. I have not found it, but I did find where it tells us drunkenness is sin, and wine is a mocker, and strong drink in raging."

"That's right, Ma. Samuel and I have both studied to see if we could find anyplace that mentioned not to drink coffee. We could not find anything there either."

The two women sat down to study together. They wanted to see everything that God spoke about drinking of any kind. After what seemed like hours later, they found nowhere in the Bible telling one not to drink coffee.

20

Finding Fault

Weeks had passed since Mary and Jim started dating each other. Katie seemed pleased seeing her ma moving on in life since the passing of her da and her ma never returning to the Amish faith again. She would watch things come out of her ma that she had never seen before, and she liked seeing that. It was like her ma had a whole new life. She would hear singing come from her ma when she knew that Jim was on his way to pick her up to take her out for the night.

"Where you kids going tonight?" Katie asked her ma in a teasing manner.

"Kids, ha-ha," her ma responded. "He wants to take me out to dinner then to the new movie *Noah*. I think that will be a good movie, at least I'm hoping that it will be."

"I hope so to. Remember, not all movies they call Christian movies are really godly movies. They change things that aren't even in the Bible and put their own junk in it."

"Yes, I know, and trust me, I will be watching for that," Mary said.

"Ma, I've just been wanting to tell you this for a while now. I am very proud of you for all the change that you have made to become more like the English. You really have come far with the way you're talking more and more like them. I have noticed that you are working hard to put the past behind you and moving on with your life."

"Oh, thank you, honey, for those kind words. There is something that I have to tell you also."

"Okay, what is that?" Katie looked at her almost in a frightened way, not knowing what her ma needed to say to her, sounding all mysterious.

"I have an offer on the farmhouse, and it's a good one. I think that I'm going to take it."

"Really? When did this all come about?"

"I got the offer two days ago, but the reason for me not saying anything until now is because I've been praying about it before accepting."

"Hmm, well then, if you feel peace in your heart, I say I'm happy for you," Katie said, looking at her ma then quickly away.

"Katie girl, why do I get the feeling there is something that you're not saying to me? It's like you are holding something back."

"Not really, Ma, it's just…" She stopped for a minute. Then a tear streamed down her cheek.

"What, honey, is it?" Mary begged to know.

"It's just silly really. I was just thinking that when it's sold, what we had with Pa will forever be gone."

"Katie, what we had with your pa is forever in our heart. It's not what we have here on earth that matters, honey. I know that you know that. It was you and Samuel who finally got me to understand the ways of the Lord. I'm letting the past of the Amish part go, but what I shared with your pa will never die. When I see you each day, I am reminded of him also."

Katie walked over to her ma and wrapped her arms around her, giving her a big hug. "I'm sorry, Ma, for being a silly girl. I don't know what came over me."

"Oh, I do. It must feel like you will not have the family you once had anymore, now that your da is gone then the house. Well, honey, I just think this is what I need to do then to get my own place."

Katie quickly swung around from cleaning off the countertop and looked straight at her ma. "You're leaving me too?"

"Katie, what has come over you today? I can't live with you and Samuel forever. You know how I feel about that, honey. I feel that it's time to move on, get my own place. Now, I want you to know what you and Samuel have done for me over these past few months have been more than I could have ever asked for."

"Then why are you in such a hurry to move out?"

"Honey"—Mary walked over to her—"this is not like you. Would you like to tell me what is really going on with you?"

"It's nothing, Ma. I am just being silly. Of course, you want your own place. I'm sorry for acting like a child again. It's just that Samuel is gone so much in the fields, Mike's in school, and Leah"—she paused for a moment—"Leah is so young. I can't drink coffee with her and have talks with her like I can you. I loved having you here to share my coffee with," she stated with a laugh.

"I'll tell you what."

"What, Ma?"

"When I do find the place that I want, you can come visit me one day. Then the next, I'll come visit you. That way, we can still have our talks and our coffee," Mary stated.

"That sounds like a great idea. Have you been looking for a place in town then?" asked Katie.

"Yes, there are two different places that Jim and I have been looking at."

"Jim?"

"Yes, Jim. Is there something wrong with him helping me find the right place?"

"No, not at all, Ma. I was just saying. I didn't really know the two of you have gotten that close to where you would feel comfortable with him helping you find a place."

"We have been seeing each other for quite sometime now, and we get along very well also. I see no harm in him helping me."

"Like I said, Ma, I have no problem if he helps you." Katie smiled a half smile at her ma. Her feelings at the time were what you would call a little mixed up, not knowing how she really felt about Jim helping her ma find a home. For some reason, she just thought that it would be her helping, not Jim.

Mary looked at Katie and wanted to reply, but she decided to keep quiet. Although she was not sure why Katie seemed to be acting different toward Jim. Up until now, Mary thought everything was going good with her seeing Jim, and Katie had always seemed pleased with them seeing each other. After all, it was her who introduced the two together. She thought for a moment, *Maybe it wasn't Katie after all who wanted me to move on in life. Maybe it was just Samuel who wanted to do all the fixing up with me and Jim.*

"Katie, if you would like to help me go out and find a place for me to move into, then I will tell Jim that if he doesn't mind, you and I will be going by ourselves."

"No, Ma, I am sorry for how I acted. It's not the fact that you are having Jim help you. It's just"—she paused for a minute—"well, Ma, it's just I have so enjoyed our time together here having coffee every morning, and I think that so much will be different when you move out and be on your own. Ma, you have never been on your own before. You went from living with your folks to being married to Da to being a single woman living with us here."

"Katie, I have to grow up sometime." Mary was now teasing, picking up some of Jim's humor.

"Ma."

"Now, Katie, I am not a child, honey. I have to learn to do some things on my own. I can't invade your home for the rest of my life."

"Invade my home? What made you ever think that you have been invading my home? Ma, you are family. You can live here for as long as you like."

"I know you mean well, honey, and I do appreciate all that you and Samuel have done for me. We will still have our talks and our coffee too. I will still come and visit my grandchildren and my daughter," she said as she put her arm around Katie's small-framed body.

"Okay, I know that I am just being silly, acting like a small child. I really do want you to be happy, Ma, and if spending time with Jim makes you happy, then spend time with him and be happy."

"Are you telling me how you really feel about Jim and me, honey?" She paused for a moment, then started to talk again. "There is something that I need to tell you about, that I did a couple nights ago."

"What is that?" Katie asked.

"Oh, never mine, honey."

"To answer our question, Ma, I was just being silly is all. I trust that God will work everything out for his glory. So if you really feel that it's time for you to move out, then I want you to find what suits you best."

"One of the houses I've been thinking about has three bedrooms and two baths. I really like it 'cause of its indoor bathrooms, and it has carpets in all the rooms except the kitchen and the bathrooms."

Katie watched the way her ma was telling her about the house she liked with so much excitement. Katie could see that her ma wanting to have her own place was something that needed to be done.

"I'm happy for you, Ma. I can see the way you get so excited about the house by just talking about it. It must be very nice. I will have to say I sure am going to miss you. I am just kind of wondering something."

"Like what, honey?"

"If it's only going to be you living there, then why get such a big place? I mean, why do you need a three-bedroom place for one person?"

"Well, one can just never tell what might happen in life. I may need those three rooms at some time."

"Hold on a minute. I hear Leah crying."

Katie walked out of the room to go get Leah out of her bed. In the meantime, she was wondering just what her ma meant by making that statement about her sometime maybe needing three bedrooms. Was she up to something?

Was she planning on something that she was not telling her daughter about? Did Samuel know what was going on? Did Jim have anything to do with her decision? She had so many thoughts entering her mind at this time that she felt sick to her stomach. She knew at that point that she needed to stop worrying about what her ma was up to and allow God to take care of it all. The last thing she needed was to be getting sick with worry to where she would not be caring for her family the way that she ought to.

"Oh, there's my little angel baby," Mary said as she held out her hands to hold Leah.

"I need to get her something to eat. I am surprised she slept in for so long. She usually is up by now, eating somthing," Katie told her ma.

"Hand her over to me. I'll hold her while you make her something to eat," Mary said, still holding her hands out.

Katie was looking for the bread when she noticed that they were all out. "Ma, would you mind watching Leah just for a minute while I run down to the store and pick up some bread? I had no idea that we were out."

"Sure, honey, you go ahead. My little Leah and I will have some fun while you are gone."

Katie got dressed to go to the store, but what she didn't know was that she would be a witness to something and would not know the right thing to do. As she drove to the store, she was about to take a turn to the right into the parking lot of the little store, but right at that time, her eyes

251

caught sight of Jim, the man whom her ma had been seeing for the past few months. She stopped right there halfway into the parking lot, the other half still on the road. She wanted to see if what she first thought when she saw Jim was really what she thought or if her eyes were deceiving her. She knew that she couldnt'keep her car halfway on the road, but if she was to pull all the way up into the parking space, she would not be able to see what she thought she was seeing. In a hurry and in hopes of not being seen, she pulled her car up and got out and hid behind a wall by the gas pumps so she could have a perfect view of what she was seeing.

She stood very still and peeked around the wall to look across the road. *Who is he with?* She was very curious with what she was witnessing. *How can it be? Who is that woman he is with? Did he and my ma break it off? No, of course not, she was just telling me that he was helping her find a home.*

Katie could not believe what she was seeing. How could he do this to her ma? What should she do? Should she yell a cross the road, "Hi, Jim"? She stood there like a peeping Tom, watching and waiting to see what came next, which seemed to be forever. What she was watching now was making her heart sick. Should she tell her ma what she had just witinessed? She had no idea what she was to do next. She stood there watching Jim with this black widow, this Englishwoman who was stealing Jim from her ma. They were playing like children, laughing and carrying on outside of a house. *That must be where she lives.* Well, she was just not going to stand for it. She must do something. Right when she was about to walk over to where they were, the two walked in the home they were standing in front of. Katie decided to go into the store to get what she came for in the first place.

"Well, hello, Miss Katie," Mr. Combs, the store clerk, said as she entered the store.

Katie looked at the man, who was wearing a huge smile. She knew him to be one of the sweetest men she had ever met. He was always so nice to her every time she came in the store. This time, with other things on her mind, she gave the man a smile, but no reply.

He knew that was not something Katie normally ever did. She was always very sweet back to him, but today was not that day. He would wait until she came up to the counter to carry on with talking. He watched as she seemed confused as to what it was she wanted. Then she finally picked up two loaves of bread and walked to the counter.

"Is everything all right, Miss Katie? Excuse me in saying so, but you seem to be having much trouble right now. Is there anything that I can do for you?"

"Oh." She looked at him. "I am very sorry, Mr. Combs. I just have a lot on my mind right now. How are you and the missus doing?" she asked, hoping to change the subject.

"Oh, ya know, when we get old, it just seems that things want to attach themselves to us. And it seems the older we get, the harder it is to get them off."

Although Katie knew to tell him that Jesus can remove them from him and his wife if they would ask of him, she was just going through her own thoughts at this time to bother. "I'm sorry. You will be in my prayers," she said as she gave the man her money, and she was out the door.

Mr. Combs knew that was not the Katie he always had little conversations with. Something was surely wrong with the young lady, he thought.

On the ride home, Katie had many thoughts going through her mind. *What am I to do? Do I tell my ma what I saw? Do I wait and tell Samuel? Do I say anything at all?* Too many thoughts were clouding her mind with so many questions. She had never faced this before, not even when it came time to what Robert had done to her and her never knowing it until her son got sick. Now she was seeing with her very own eyes a man who claimed to really like her ma but was seeing someone else on the side when he was not with her ma. Katie's heart ached for her ma. All the change she watched her ma do over a few months' time since losing her da was a big step for her. Watching a woman who was Amish all her life transform from the Amish faith and beliefs to an incredible Christian woman, Katie was in a place of thought she had never been before. *God, please give me the answer in what I ought to do about seeing Jim with another woman. I don't want to see my ma hurt. She has already been through so much. Help me to be there for her and help her not to hurt. And I thank you for it, Jesus, amen.*

Katie walked into the house, trying to act as if everything was fine. But the moment she looked at her ma standing with her little Leah in her arms, playing with her and swinging her gently in the air, Katie began to cry.

"Katie girl, what seems to be the matter?" Her ma rushed to her side. "What is it, honey?"

"Oh, Mama." Katie fell at her feet and wept very hard.

Mary knelt down to where her daughter was on the floor. "Is Samuel all right, honey?"

"Ma." Katie looked up with a tearstained face. "Mama, I just saw Jim with another woman." She put her head back down in shame that she and Samuel ever introduced him to her ma in the first place. She could not believe what her own ears were hearing, how she just spilled out about Jim at the moment as she looked at her ma.

"Katie, what are you saying, dear?" Mary asked with a look of shock written all over her face.

"I'm so sorry, Mama. I always thought that he was a good Christian man. I'm just so sorry, Ma. Please forgive me for ever bringing him here to meet you."

"First of all, Katie, I'd like for you to start from the beginning. What did you hear or see?"

"I drove to the party store for bread, and as I was pulling into the parking lot, I just happened to see Jim and this woman standing there. I stopped right there to see if I knew who she was."

"Did you know her?" Mary asked.

"No, I have never seen her before."

"Okay, so what did you see?"

"I saw the two of them laughing and teasing with each other. Then I saw…" She stopped right there before going on and looked at her ma again.

"Please continue, honey."

"I saw them kiss right there. I pulled up more and got out of my car and watched in shock of what I was witnessing. The two held hands as they walked into a house they were standing in front of." She watched as her ma's face turned a sheet of white.

Katie watched as her ma put Leah down and walk into her bedroom and close the door behind her. She knew that her ma's heart was broken for what she had just found out about a man she had been seeing for the past few months. She was not sure if she should go check in on her or let her alone for a while. Just as she was thinking about what to do, Samuel came in for midmorning coffee and break from the fields.

With a huge smile on his face at seeing Katie standing there holding his baby girl, he said, "Well, good morning, sunshine." Taking a closer look at Katie, he saw the look on her face was as though she had been crying. "Am I missing something?" He looked around for Mary. "Okay, now I know something is wrong. Did you and your ma have a disagreement?"

"No, it's not like that at all. The truth is, Jim—well, I caught him with another woman today. I told my ma what I saw, and she went into the bedroom now."

"You what?" he asked with his eyes wide open.

"I saw Jim with another woman today, some Englishwoman down by the store."

"What do you mean by some Englishwoman? I thought that's what we are too."

"Yes, I'm sorry. I went to get some bread at the store, and there the two were right across the street, carrying on with each other."

"This does come as quite a surprise. I thought that just the way he talked about your ma and acted, he was really hung up on her. I am so sorry for ever bringing him here in the first place."

Samuel wanted to have it out with Jim and find out why he did this to Mary after he was the first person she went out with since her husband passed away. He thought that the two were making a good match together.

Samuel acted as if he was going back to the fields after having breakfast and his coffee with Katie, but what he really had in mind was make a call to Jim and meet him somewhere in town and have it out with him.

"Hello?" Jim answered his cell phone.

Acting as if he was not aware of anything about him and another woman, Samuel said, "Hey, buddy, what's going on? How would you like for us to meet at Sparky's and have coffee?"

"That old coffee shop?"

"Yeah?"

"Sure. When?"

"Right now if you can."

"I'll be there in five."

Samuel drove to the coffee shop, trying to think of how to bring this up to Jim. He knew that Katie would never make something up like that, but somehow, he was just wondering if there could be some kind of misunderstanding. He was about to find out just what was going on.

"Hey, Samuel. You sound like there is something of importantce you wish to talk with me about in the morning hours. I would have thought that you would be in the fields."

"I should be, but they can wait. I need to understand something that my wife told me that she saw today, and it has left all of us at my home wondering what is going on."

Jim stood there. Then taking a seat at a table in the little coffee shop, he said, "I think I know what you are talking about. Would this have anything to do with Mary breaking things off with me?"

"Mary breaking things off with you?" Samuel was shocked at what he was hearing.

"Oh, this isn't anything to do with that? Then what is it?"

"Are you telling me that Mary called things off with you? When did that happen?"

"A couple nights ago when I took her to the movies. She told me how she felt that she was rushing into things and she needed to slow down some and think about what she really wanted in life."

"Wow." Samuel leaned back in his seat with a light smirk across his face. "I am sorry, but at the same time, I am glad I can go home and explain to Katie why she saw what she saw."

"I think you lost me. What does this have anything to do with Katie?"

"Katie saw you with some other woman today. It left her devastated. I was hoping that there was a reason why she saw you with another woman."

"I thought that Mary would have told the two of you about it. Maybe she just wanted to think about things, like she told me."

"I'm sorry, Jim, to have called you about this."

"The only reason I was with Lona in the first place was because I was trying to get my mind off Mary. I really liked her very much"—he corrected himself—"*like* her. I was hurt when she told me that she wanted us to stop seeing each other." He stopped talking like he was in thought. Then he went on, "You know what, Samuel?"

"What, Jim?"

"I was going to ask Mary to be my wife. I had a beautiful ring I bought for her. I'm just glad to know that she really only wanted to be friends now instead of me asking her and her saying no. That just might have really hurt me even more than I feel now." Jim chuckled about it, trying to make things light about being dumped and hurt by Mary.

The two talked for a while more. Then Samuel headed back home to let Katie know what was really going on.

"I just can't believe it. Why, when I told Ma, she looked so hurt about it, if that is the truth?"

"Maybe because she didn't want to hear about him out with another woman so fast. Maybe she liked him more than she was willing to allow herself to feel."

"I bet that's just what it is, Samuel. You might as well go back to the fields, honey, and I will talk with my ma. Thank you, honey, for talking with Jim and getting this all figured out."

21

Changed Mind

After Katie talked with her ma about what she heard from Samuel, Mary admitted that she was the one who broke it off with Jim. She told Katie that after hearing Jim was out with another woman so soon after their breakup, it felt as though she had been betrayed. She had never known that feeling from a man before until now since she had only ever been with Katie's da.

"Ma, was that what you wanted to tell me, when you decided not too?"

"Yes, that's what I wanted to let you know, then I changed my mine."

How does it feel that you were the one betrayed when you were the one who broke it off with Jim?" Katie could not understand what Mary was feeling, and it made her feel frustrated that she couldn't be more of a help to her ma.

"I know that sounds strange, but I guess I never knew just how much I really cared for him until you told me that you saw him with another."

"So what do you plan on doing about it?"

"I don't really know what I can do about it. He is already seeing someone else now. I feel that I messed up on what could have been the best thing I had going for me."

"I'm sure he feels the same way about you, Ma. It's just from what I gather, the English don't like to wait for long periods of time and dwell on being hurt. He wanted to get you off his mind, so he went out with another woman."

"Do you really think that's what it is? He was just trying to stop thinking about me?"

"I do, and I believe Samuel does too."

"This is all new to me, Katie girl. I just got scared. I wonder if I talked with Jim and explained myself to him, he would be willing to give me another chance?"

"Ma, according to Samuel, Jim told him today that he was just trying not to think of you, so he went out with this other woman. I don't believe that he already has feelings for her like he did you. If you really are having a changed mind, then I'd call him up and ask if he would be willing to have a talk with you."

"Okay, I will." Mary sat at the edge of her bed, looking up at Katie still standing there. "I really hope that I didn't mess things up with us. I just don't know what I was doing, breaking it off with him. After all, I find myself thinking about him all the time. I sound like a young schoolgirl now, don't I?"

"Not really, Mama. You sound like a woman who has just discovered that she really is in love."

Katie had a smile come on her face, although she felt a spear hit her heart when she spoke those words. Katie had a da who was faithful to her ma all the years they had been married, even though, at one time her, ma and her da told her that she was never to come back to their home after finding out about her having a baby before ever being married. All that was part of the past and forgiven at the time of her da's passing. She knew that he was a good husband and da when she was home. Now her ma was in love with a new man, and all Katie wanted was for her ma to find true happiness like she had when she was with her da.

"Katie, if you don't mind, honey, I think that I will make that call to Jim. I pray that he will give me another chance."

"I'm sure that he will, ma. If someone truly cares for you, they don't just forget you like that." She watched her ma as she walked over to the phone. Mary hesitated for a minute picking up the phone and put it back down. "It's okay, Ma. You need to call and have a talk with him. I can go into another room if you like?"

"No, please, Katie, don't." Mary held out her hand as if to say, *Come closer to me*.

Katie walked closer to her ma. "Okay, I'll stay here for as long as you need me to."

Mary picked the phone back up and began to dial some numbers. Placing the phone to her ear, she waited for an answer to come from the other end. "Hello, Jim, this is Mary. Do you have a minute where we can talk?"

Katie stood there next to her ma, feeling Mary shake just a slight as she talked with Jim. Katie prayed silently for the two of them. *Dear Lord, I pray that you help both my ma and Jim. I ask that if they are to be together, then you bring them back together. Take away all fear from my ma, for this is not of you that she should fear and tremble. Thank you, Jesus, amen.*

"Okay, thank you, Jim." Mary hung up the phone and looked at Katie with a huge smile. "He told me that he loves me. He really loves me, Katie."

"And why shouldn't he? You are an amazing, beautiful woman, Mama. You are funny, sweet, not to mention the best cook that I have ever known. A man would be crazy not to love you."

"Aww, you are only saying that because I am your ma and you feel that you need to."

"Ma, that is not true at all. I said that only because it is true. So what did he say?" she asked, very eager to hear all about it.

"He said he was sorry for being with that other woman but that he has no feelings for her at all. It was like you said. He was with her to get his mind off me—which, by the way, he admitted was wrong in the first place. But he also said it didn't help take his mind off me. I just can't believe that handsome man loves me." She pointed at her chest as she said that. She was very excited to know that he loved her.

"Like I said, Ma, you are a very beautiful woman. Any man would truly be blessed to have you part of their life. Is he coming over so the two of you can talk?"

"Yes, he is. Do you think that I'm doing the right thing?"

"Of course, Ma. If it feels right in your heart, then I'm sure it's okay."

"I just hope that I'm not getting into something that I shouldn't be doing. I would never want to get so involved with him or any man and have them hurt me. Your da was a good man all the years we were together. I'm not saying that we never had our disagreements with each other because every couple does at some point in life. I just know that he was always there for you and me while you were growing up, and he was a faithful, hardworking man."

"Mama, I really think that Jim is a good man. I have always thought that about him—well, until earlier today, when I seen him with that other lady, I began to think differently."

"He's coming over here so he and I can talk. Honey, if you wouldn't mind very much as to when he gets here, can we talk in the living room by ourselves?"

"Oh, sure, Ma. That is not a problem at all. In fact, I was thinking it's really turning out to be a beautiful day, and I'd like to take Leah for a walk. So when he gets here, Leah and I will go for our walk."

"Oh, honey, I don't want to push you out of your own home like that. I just need to let him know how sorry I am for what I did the other day by breaking things off with him."

"Mama, really, you aren't pushing me at all. I love the warm, fresh air, and it's a perfect time to go for a nice, long walk. You remember how I always went for long walks when I was still at home, don't you?"

Her ma looked at her like she was thinking about where Katie was getting at. "Sure, I remember that. Every chance you had, you were going for walks. I used to think that you were trying to get out of doing your chores, but I can see now that was not the case. You keep a beautiful home, and you still want to go for walks. Okay, honey, just as long as it's not me pushing you out the door."

"No way, not me. I love the great outside, and I love the smell of all the wildflowers that are in all the fields I pass by on my walks. God sure knew what he was doing when he made everything, even down to the trees."

"Does Leah like to go for walks as well?"

"She sure does. All the while I'm pushing the stroller, she is kicking and smiling. I can tell how much she loves it."

As the two were talking, Jim pulled up in the driveway.

"I'm going to get Leah now for our walk. I'll be back a little later. Now, Ma, don't be nervous. Just speak from your heart."

"Okay, honey. I'll try not to be nervous and just explain how I really feel."

"Hello, Jim," Mary said as she opened the door. "Come on in."

"Hi, Mary. I am so glad that you called me to ask me to come over. God answers prayers."

"You prayed that I'd call you up?"

"I prayed and asked God to speak to your heart. I asked him that whatever I did wrong, he would give me another chance to make it right."

Just when Mary was ready to comment, Katie walked out of Leah's room. "Hello, how are you?" She felt a little awkward as she was the one who saw Jim with the other woman.

"I'm good. Glad that your ma called me, that's for sure."

"Ma, I'll be back soon. Bye, Jim."

"You leaving?"

"Yes, I'm taking Leah out for a walk. I want to give you two some time to sort all this out." She gave a half smile and was headed to the door, not saying another word.

"That was nice of her," Jim stated as he watched Katie walk out the door.

"I think she feels like all this was her fault, but it had nothing to do with me telling you that we needed to stop seeing each other. If anything, it got me thinking that just maybe"—she stopped talking and took ahold of his hand—"what she told me is part of the reason that I called you."

"I wondered if it was."

"Jim, first I have to say that I never meant to hurt you at all. This is all so new to me. I have never dated anyone before you. I was chosen to marry Katie's da, and I just did what I was told. He was the only man I have ever been with, and as you and I began to get closer, I started to get very scared of what might happen."

"I can understand that. I just wish that you would have talked to me about it."

"I'm sorry, Jim. I am asking you for another chance, if you are willing to give me that?"

"Another chance—what does this mean to you that you are asking?""

"I'm asking that you give me another chance at showing you how much I really do care for you. Even when I told you that I thought it best that we stop seeing each other, I hurt deep in my heart because I really did care for you. All the while in those two days of not seeing you, I missed you so much and wanted to call you up and ask you to come over."

"You really care for me like that?"

"Yes, Jim, I do. And if you will give me another chance to show you, I promise to be the best that I can be to you."

Jim sat there, squeezing her hand lightly. Then after looking at her for a minute and not saying anything, he let go of her hand and got down on his knees right there in front of where she was sitting. Putting his hand in his pocket, he pulled out a shiny little blue box and opened it up.

"Mary, I love you with all that I am, with all that I have. Will you be my wife I don't want to live without?"

Mary began to cry and placed her hands over her mouth. "Really? You want me to be your wife?"

"Please be my wife, Mary. I loved you since the very first time that I laid eyes on you. You are a beautiful woman, Mary, and I love you."

"Yes," she spoke out in a quiet voice.

"Was that a yes, Mary?" he asked with pleading eyes.

"That is a great big yes. Yes, I will marry you, Jim. I love you, and I don't want to live without you either."

This time, she was not quiet at all. In fact, she was so overjoyed that she was yelling louder than she herself thought she could. Wrapping her arms around his neck, she kissed him like she had never done before, with a passion she never knew that she had, and what Jim himself had never felt before.

"Mary, I want us to get married just as soon as we can. After the way you just kissed me, I think it's best we marry very soon. How do you feel about that?"

"Yes, Jim, I agree. I want nothing more than having God first place in our lives and you as my husband." She blushed after the comment he made about her kissing.

"It's settled then. We will talk with Katie and Samuel and let them know that we will be man and wife. Do you think that they will be pleased?"

"I think so. I know that Samuel has never spoken a bad word about you, and the only time that Katie has was when she saw what she later told me."

"We need to talk with Pastor Mike and let him know that we would like to be married just as soon as possible. What kind of a wedding would you like?" he asked.

"I don't care really about having a big wedding. It can be small, just a few friends. What kind do you want?"

"I agree with you. Just a small one is nice. If we plan a big one, that could take months, and I really don't want to wait that long. But, Mary, it's not about just what I want. If you would like to have a big one, then by all means, I want you to have what you want."

"No, I don't want to wait either," she said with a smile.

"Then let's plan a wedding." He took ahold of her hand and kissed it very gently.

"I'm back," Katie spoke as she entered the kitchen door, trying to give a warning to her ma and Jim. She came around the corner of the divider between the kitchen and the living room. "My, is it ever pouring like cats and dogs out there." She peeked into the living room.

"Raining?" replied her ma.

"Yes, Ma, raining. Do you mean to tell me that you haven't noticed that it was pouring outside?" Katie said as she took the wet clothes off Leah and wiped her down.

"I'm so sorry, honey, that you were caught out in the rain. Jim and I have been making plans, and I just never noticed."

"I am sorry also, Katie. Had I noticed that it was raining, I would have come to pick you and Leah up. The truth is, I just asked your mother to marry me—"

Before he was able to finish his sentence, Katie yelled, "Married!" She had a look of shock on her face.

Not knowing if the look meant good or bad, Jim asked, "Do you not approve of us wanting to get married?"

"Oh no, it's not that at all. I guess I'm just a little surprised after all," Katie replied.

"After what, Katie girl?" Mary commented.

"Mama, all I want is for you to be happy. I am happy for the both of you." She sat down in her wet clothes. "What does Samuel say about this?"

"I haven't had a chance to discuss this with him as of yet, but I will, just as soon as the opportunity arises. Do you think that he may disagree with me marrying your ma?"

"No, not at all. Neither do I disagree with your marriage. It just came as a shock to me is all. But truly, Mama, I am very happy for the both of you. It was Samuel and I who introduced the two of you together. We must have thought that something good can happen between you." Katie looked at both her ma and Jim sitting on the couch, holding hands like two young children looking for her approval. "Ma, Jim, you have my blessings. Congratulations to both of you." She smiled just as big as she could. The last thing she wanted was for them to feel that she didn't care about them getting married.

"Oh, honey, I am so glad that you are truly okay with this," stated Mary.

"Yes, I feel the same. I know that your approval is something that means a great deal to your mother, and to me as well. I have loved and cared for you and Samuel for a very long time, and now for your mother, more than ever."

"Ma, what kind of a wedding are you two planning? And when is the big day?"

Mary looked at Jim with an ear-to-ear smile. "We have been talking about having just a small wedding, and soon. Neither of us want a big wedding. We just want to be married and happy."

"Are you planning on Pastor Mike performing the wedding?"

"Yes, we would like him to, but we have yet not called him. Jim is planning on calling him today to see when it would be a good time for a quick wedding."

"So who is going to stand up for the two of you, Ma?"

Mary was uncertain of what her daughter was talking about, coming from the Amish background, where there was no need for someone to stand up for them. "What are you talking about, Katie? Someone standing up for us?"

"Mama, when the English get married, they have what is called a best man standing in for the man and a woman called the maid of honor standing in for the woman. It's just usually the best friends of the couple getting married."

"Oh, I've never heard of such a thing. Jim, have you heard of this before?"

"Oh yes, she is right. It is usually the best friends who stand up for them. With Samuel being my best friend, I'd like to ask him if he would for me."

"I'm sure he would love to," Katie spoke, knowing that Samuel cared for Jim just the same.

"Katie, you are the closest person to me outside of Jim. I'd love for you to be there for me as well. I know that you are my daughter, but if you are able to with the law of the English, I would like it to be you."

"Mary, I am a lawyer, and there is no law saying just because someone is their child that they could not stand up for their parent."

"Then it's all settled. I know I can speak for Samuel when saying we accept."

The following morning, Jim called Mary to let her know that their pastor had agreed to marry them. She was so excited to hear that he had agreed. Even though there was really no doubt in her mind that he would, it was just hearing it was really going to happen was exciting to her.

"Did he say when he would?" she asked with excitement.

'He said, 'Name the time and day.' So I guess it's up to us to decide when we want it to happen."

"Okay, well then, when are you thinking would be a good time?" she asked.

"Mary, I'd marry you right now if it were up to me, but I'd like you to talk with Katie today and the two of you come up with a date."

"Okay, I will. Then I will call you and let you know."

"That sounds like a plan. I will be waiting for your call."

After the two hung up on the phone, Mary started coffee for her and Kate to sit and talk about a good day. She waited for her to come out of her room. It seemed to Mary that her day was slipping away. She knew that she was still thinking back in the Amish ways when she rose up early in the morning. Mike was out of school for the summer, and baby Leah liked to sleep in till half the morning was over. She just kind of figured that Katie was taking sleeping in to the fullest now that she had no reason to get up early mornings 'cause Samuel was out the door by 5:30 a.m. Mary had her first cup of coffee while planning how she wanted the outside of Jim's house and yard to look like. Katie walked out while Mary was in deep thought of her wedding.

"Good morning, Ma. It looks like you were in deep thought."

"I was. I was just sitting here planning my wedding."

"Did you talk with Pastor Mike about it?"

"Jim did last night. He called me and said that Pastor said anytime we want to get married, he will make himself available."

"Wow, Ma, that is nice of him. So have you come up with a date yet?"

"I've been waiting for you to get up so, together, we could come up with a time and date," Mary said with a big smile across her face.

"What are you thinking? Like having it on a Saturday or a Friday evening?"

"A Saturday."

"Well, let's just look at what sounds good to you, Ma. I know that you and Jim seem to be in a hurry," Katie said with a grin. Then she walked over to the calender she had hanging by the fireplace. "I am looking at the second week in June. That falls on the fifteenth. That will give us a couple of weeks to make sure that everything is just the way you and Jim want it. Does that sound like a good date, or do you want something different?"

"Oh no, that sounds perfect."

Katie watched the look on her mother's face as she talked to her. Katie was seeing, for the first time that she could remember, her mother beyond excited for something. "I can see just how much this marriage means to you, Ma, and I am so happy for you. I want you to have the best wedding ever. Samuel and I got married in a little chapel by a nice man. We wanted to do what was right, and we got married right after I was asked to leave the farmhouse."

When Katie said as polite as she could about leaving the farm, Mary knew what the real story was back then. She put her head down in shame at the very thought of how she and her husband had treated their own daughter at the time.

275

22

The Wedding

Pastor Mike agreed to meet with Jim and Mary about their upcoming marriage. He wanted to make sure that with the background of the Amish, there wouldn't be any trouble coming from them. Not that he wouldn't marry them, but he wanted to make sure they knew just what they were getting into. After their talk together, it was planned for the fifteenth of July, which was in four days. Jim and Mary told the pastor they wanted nothing fancy, just a quick wedding with Katie and Samuel standing up for them. After if was all said and done, there would be a wedding held in the comfort of the backyard of Jim's home.

The first time Mary laid her eyes on Jim's home, she felt as though she would melt. Never seeing such beauty in all her life, she fell in love with his home before ever having feelings for him. Although she was married to Katie's da for a number of years—as he provided well for her and Katie—she lived from day to day working hard to keep a plain home, and the way she had to fetch water for bathing, cooking, and feeding the animals was something she thought she would do all her life, never expecting to lose her husband at such a young age, leaving her all alone. She was so thankful for Katie and Samuel when that time came. Even though she knew that the Amish care for their own, it was not the same.

After seeing how happy her Katie truly was and still being a good girl not living among the Amish faith anymore, Mary knew that she wanted the same, especially after her husband's last breath, asking Katie to care for her. Katie was good to her word. She took her in, even though at one time Katie herself was disowned by her and her husband. Katie and Samuel showed her a whole new way of life, and the longer she watched their way of living, the more she wanted to be part of it.

As Katie and Samuel made the change to become like the English, Mary herself took the same approach and studied the way they lived. Now she was going to become Jim's wife in just a few short days and live in the most beautiful home she had ever seen. Her wedding would be in the back of her very own yard, something that she never thought would happen. She only hoped and prayed that the fifteenth of July would be a bright and sunny day, with all the warmth added on to a glorious day of celebration.

Jim drove Mary back to Katie's while sitting in his seat with a huge smile across his face. "I can hardly wait until the fifteenth. You will be mine for the taking." He looked at Mary and noticed that she turned all red in the face at what he said out loud. He was not sure if that was something he should have spoken out loud. "I'm very sorry, Mary. I should not have said that out loud. I am just so excited to hold you in my arms and call you my wife, not to mention wake up with you every morning."

"I feel the same. I never thought that after losing my husband just a few short months ago, I would even think of another man. But after meeting you, and all that charm…" She giggled a little.

"So that was it then, huh? All my charm did you in?"

"It sure helped." She gave a light laugh. "Truly, I love you, Jim, and I am so grateful to God that I have met you, and so grateful that God saw fit for me to marry again and not have to be alone for the rest of my life."

"My dear Mary, you would not have been alone for long, that I am sure of. With all your beauty and your charm, men would have walked a thousand miles to be with you. I am so thankful that Samuel told me about you and it got me wanting to meet you. And yes, God is good to bring the two of us together. Do you think that Katie and Samuel will think that we have lost our minds wanting to marry in just a few days?"

"It's not about what they think or want. It is how we feel and what we want now. But I am sure they will be very happy for us. I know Katie told me that she is very happy for me that I have found a good man who loves me and wants to care for me."

"I'm glad to hear that. Then I am sure that Samuel will feel the same about it."

They turned onto the driveway to Katie's place, still glowing with excitement of their upcoming wedding. Not waiting for Jim to open her door to the car, Mary flung it open with so much excitement and was out the door before Jim even got around to her side of the car.

"I see that you are in a hurry to get inside the house," he said as he closed the door for her.

"I'm sorry, Jim. I just can't wait to tell Katie all about the wedding. We will have to get things started right away for planning on getting the backyard with some flowers to dress it up. Oh, not saying that it's not already beautiful."

"I know, honey, and that is fine. You gals do whatever you want to add to it and order all the flowers that you want and anything else that you want for our wedding, and I will pay for it."

She stopped dead in her tracks as she was ready to step up on the porch. "Thank you, Jim, for everything. I don't need much for it. Just a few flowers should do it."

"Talk it over with Katie. She may have some nice ideas of her own to add to it also. I don't want you to worry about the cost of anything. Once we are married, what is mine is yours as well. I will be adding you on my bank account too. So if there is ever anything that you would like to get, the money will be there for you."

She could not believe what a catch she got when she got Jim. He was such a good man, very handsome and a hard worker too. He had been a lawyer for quite a few years, and with that, he had more money than she had ever known to have. At one time during their many conversations, he told her that he had made some every wise investments, and it helped him to get his beautiful big home and many more things, plus a sizable bank account. Although she was never interested in him for the money he had, having a nice home with all the indoor plumbing was a plus. She knew all her days of having to fetch water from outside her home was done. She felt so blessed to have him choose her over anyone else. She knew that Jim could have the pick of the crop when it came time for other women if he wanted to. But for reasons not known to her, he chose her, and she was just fine with that.

"Katie, I have some very great news," Mary spoke with such excitement.

"Oh, Mother, you are beaming with excitement. What have you done? Did you and Jim get married?"

"Of course not, what without my best lady next to me."

Katie began to giggle a bit. "Ma, it's called your maid of honor."

"Well then, my maid of honor, but to me, you are the best lady. We have a date set to be married."

"When is the big day?" She was excited for her ma, just knowing that Jim made her ma very happy.

"We are getting married in four days, on July 15. I will become Mrs. James Taylor. I have so much to do in four short days, and I was wondering if you would mind helping me pick out some flowers for Jim's backyard?"

"His backyard?" Katie asked in shock that it was going to be outside. She had never heard of too many outdoor weddings before. She could not believe that it was her who had picked the day out for her ma, and her ma forgot all about it. But Katie would not mention that to her seeing how happy that she was.

"Yes, honey, we want to have it in the backyard, hoping that it will be beautiful and sunny out on that day. His yard is so beautiful, and it will be my home as well as his. We both want it there. Are you okay with that? After all, he has the prettiest lilac trees that I have ever seen, and you know more than anyone how much I love those trees. They smell so good."

"Sure, Ma, whatever you want. I am very happy for you, and Samuel is too."

Katie could tell by the look of her ma that she was very excited about the wedding. She was happy for her as well and wanted her ma to have a wonderful marriage as she and Samuel had. And on top of that, to have lilac trees there was a plus. She knew how often her mother went outside when they were in full bloom, just to walk up to them and take a branch and bring it down to her level and smell them.

Katie and her ma went to work on getting everything needed to make a perfect wedding. Her ma had ideas of her own, and Katie had some of her own. Together, both of them bought what was needed from four different stores. Mary took everything bought over to Jim's house. She figured that it was better there than to make several trips of carrying them from place to place.

When getting home, Samuel asked the ladies if they had everything needed for the wedding. Remembering how he and Katie married without all the flowers and friends, he wanted to add anything needed for his mother-in-law and Jim's wedding day to make it a perfect day for them both.

The following day, Mary and Katie set up Jim's backyard the way Mary wanted it done. It was so pretty the way it looked, so summery looking. It brought tears to Mary's eyes as she stood there looking at all that was done. She could hardly wait until the three days got here. The excitement was almost too overwhelming to her. She stood there looking toward Katie.

"Can you come over here for a minute, honey?"

"Mama, what's the matter? This should be a good time for you, not sad."

"It is good, honey. It's just I am so happy all I can do right now is cry. I just can't believe that Jim chose me to be his wife."

"Mama, now, don't be silly. Why would he not choose you? Mama, you are the kindest, most thoughtful person I know. You are a person who loves and cares for others more than anyone else. It is he who is blessed to have found you, Ma. So how do you like the way the yard looks for the wedding?"

"It is just beautiful, honey. I only hope that Jim will like it as much as I do."

"What's there not to like? Anyone will think that this has to be the best-looking backyard ever."

After Mary looked around at all that she and Katie did, she agreed with her daughter. She could hardly wait for Jim to come home from work to see all that was done. She very much wanted to please him in every way. She was always thinking what she could do to please him.

"Mama, are you ready to go back home now? Leah is getting hungry, and I can tell she is getting very tired. She can use a nap about now."

"Sure, honey. I am getting a little hungry myself. I think that we should check on Michael too and see what he is up to," Mary said.

"Michael is helping his dad on the farm. I'm not too worried about that."

The two women got into Katie's car and drove back to the house. Leah had fallen fast asleep before getting to their destination.

"I knew she was sleepy. I wonder if I should just wait until she wakes up on her own before feeding her? I hate to wake her when she is so tired," Katie questioned.

Mary didn't comment on anything that Katie was talking about. She had other things on her mind. Right now, Mary felt like she was in cloud nine, and all she could do was picture what married life would be like with Jim. Although she loved Katie's father with all her heart, she knew that if she was ever going to make a good wife for Jim, then all the past of how she was with him should not be lived out the same way with her new husband. She really did believe that God brought her and Jim together, so she would do everything she could to be a good and honorable wife to him. It felt like her heart would just melt as she thought of the ways that would make him happy. And why wouldn't they make him a happy man? After all, just the thought of it alone made her happy. She had heard somewhere after leaving the Amish faith that if the woman of the house was happy, then all the house was happy. She chuckled silently to herself as she thought about that phrase.

Katie stood there watching the look on her mother's face as she carried in some bags from the car. Although she didn't talk at the time, Katie knew deep in her heart that Mary must have been thinking about her wedding day coming in just a few days. Katie felt a sharp pain hit her insides real fast at the thought of her da. Then she quickly erased those thoughts. After all, it was her da who asked her to care for her ma when he was gone. Her da knew that she was no longer in the Amish faith, and he still asked for her to care for her ma. So if she was really going to give her ma a chance to be happy with another besides her da, then she would have to stop thinking about her mother's marriage to her da. After all, Katie knew that he would want what was best for her ma too.

Three days had gone, and Mary was beside herself getting dressed for her wedding. She was trying to look out the window at what, in just a couple of hours, would be considered her home as well as Jim's. Katie was trying to put the last touches of flowers in her mother's hair and her own hair, but Mary kept walking to the window to see if all who were invited to the small wedding had shown up yet.

"Mother, please stop moving. I am trying all I can to make your hair just as beautiful as you are, but it is really hard when every two seconds, you are looking out the window. Now hold still for a few minutes please," Katie entreated.

Mary could tell that Katie was feeling overwhelmed at her bouncing all around like she was some small child. "I am sorry, honey. I guess am just so excited for this day to have finally come that I'm not sure how to act. This is so different from the way I was first married. I just want everything to go well today." She looked at her daughter with tears forming in her eyes.

"I know, Mama, and it will. You and Jim are going to have a wonderful life together. I believe that with all of my heart. If I truly didn't believe that, then I would do everything that I could to stop this wedding."

Mary turned around to look at her daughter. "Thank you, honey, for those encouraging words. I think I needed to hear that one last time before I say I do."

"Ma, I believe that we are ready to get out there. At least I have to be standing in front while everyone awaits the beautiful bride to walk down the carpet."

Katie was the one looking out the window now. She was admiring all the work that she and her ma had done to the backyard in just a few short days. They bought a beautiful white piece of long remnant carpet to go from the back of the chairs, which were set out for everyone invited, to reach all the way to the front to where the bride and groom would stand before Pastor Mike. There were flowers everywhere to bring out a sweet-smelling scent as Mary walked down the aisle to be united in marriage.

"I'll see you out there in a minute, Ma. They are waiting for me."

"Okay, honey, I'll be right there."

Mary was looking out at the guests now, and seeing that it looked like everyone had shown, she walked to the door to make the big entrance. Then all of a sudden, all the heads turned, looking toward the back. Yep, they were looking right at her. Mary could feel her heart begin to pound as if to jump right out of her chest. She looked to the front and saw Jim standing next to Samuel with the biggest smile she had ever seen before. She tried not to look at anyone other than Jim. She was afraid to take her eyes off him 'cause if she did, she just might lose her thought of what she was doing and take off and run down the carpet.

Mary was now standing next to Jim as their pastor began to talk to them about their vows. As the pastor was talking, her mind drifted off to what Katie teased her about the day before while getting the backyard ready for the wedding. "Ma," Katie had said, "wouldn't it be funny if when Pastor Mike goes to marry you and Jim, he would say, 'I pronounce you rooster and hen,' instead of man and wife?" At the thought of what Katie said, Mary began to chuckle, and it was right at the point where Pastor Mike was saying "loving the husband."

At this point, every eye was on her, wondering why she thought it was funny when vows were to be taken very seriously. After noticing how Jim and her pastor were looking at her, she realized what she was doing. "I am so sorry. Can you please repeat that? I was thinking about something else." Right after she said those words, she realized just how terrible that must have sounded. But nonetheless, Pastor Mike repeated what he first stated about taking Jim as her husband and to love and honor him all the days of her life.

"I do." She looked at Jim with tears forming in her eyes.

She was not sure if it was because she was utterly embarrassed from what just happened with her laughing, or was it because she was just about to become the bride of Jim?

Pastor Mike focused his attention on Jim now, and Jim took what was being said to him very seriously. He had no other thoughts that would make him chuckle at this time. "I do," was his reply.

Pastor Mike had the couple face their friends and family. "Let me introduce you to Mr. and Mrs. James Taylor."

Mary watched as everyone stood and began to clap for them. This was something that she had never seen before at a wedding. But she didn't mind. She was very happy to be married to the best man alive.

The wedding had now come and was over. Now Mary was looking toward the honeymoon. Jim told her that it was a surprise where he was taking her. He didn't even tell Samuel in fear of him telling Katie, then Katie telling her ma. Jim wanted two weeks alone with his bride at the best place that she could ever ask for—the Grand Canyon. After listening to her talk about what she had never seen and the things he would like to see, he thought it would be the perfect place to go.

Jim looked around at all that his wife and Katie had done to make his backyard look amazing. After the thought his wife entered his mind, he had a huge smile come across his face. "Honey," he said as he took Mary into his arms, "I am so happy that you agreed to marry me. I love you, Mrs. Taylor." He pulled her in closer to where there was no breathing room. "Sorry, my love," he said as he realized how hard he had her up against him. "I am just so happy, and I cannot wait until we leave for our two-week honeymoon."

"Are you going to tell me now where we are going?"

"No, not yet."

"Okay, I will be patient and wait for my surprise. When are we leaving?" she asked.

"First thing tomorrow morning. I thought that we would have fun with our guests tonight. Then after they leave, we can have more fun with just us." He looked at Mary when he said that, waiting to see what kind of expression he was going to get back.

She smiled at him when he said that to her. She was still shy for any kind of talk like that. She was never raised to have open conversations of invites quite like that, not even when it came time to it being with her husband. This was going to take her some time to get used to, but she was married to the man who was saying these things to her. She knew in the eyes of God, it was not sin.

Mary took Jim's hand and pulled him toward the dance floor. She was trying to overcome being shy in some ways, and dancing would be one way. Jim told her that he wanted to dance at their wedding, so she and Katie had a company in town bring out a dance floor, as well as music to play. Mary was now moving to music she, at one time, could never listen to, it being wrong in the Amish faith to listen to music. She was in heaven on earth with her new husband.

He kept her out on the dance floor for most of the night, so it seemed.

After the guests were gone—and Samuel and Katie stayed to help clean up everything—and all the music and dance floor and chairs and tables were all gone, Mary and Jim started heading inside. Without paying attention to what was about to take place, Mary was swept up into Jim's strong arms and carried into the house.

Slowly and gently, he lowered her down to the floor. Bending over to kiss his wife, he took his time in a way she had never experienced before. Chills began to form all over her body as she was being kissed in a way she had never been kissed before by her husband or any man. He picked her up in such a way that she didn't care where he was about to carry her. She allowed him to take her as his wife and do whatever pleased him.

She lay next to this incredible man whom she had just made love to with the thoughts running in the back of her mind that she had been touched for the very first time. At least, that was how she felt. This was true love, one that she had never known before, not like this. She could hardly wait until they were to rise in the morning and leave for their honeymoon. She wondered if she would always be loved like this, or was this just a onetime thing? She was sure to find out when they would get to wherever it was Jim was taking her.

"Rise and shine, you beautiful, wonderful woman. I am so blessed to have you as my bride." He leaned over to her side of the bed and gave her a morning kiss.

"I am the one who is blessed to be married to such a wonderful man. I love you, Jim, and so thankful that God brought you into my life."

"How about we get our things together and I will take you out to eat before we leave town? Are you hungry enough to go eat at Ben's Breakfast?" He looked at her, knowing Ben's Breakfast was an all-you-can eat place that served anything and everything edible for morning food.

Mary began to stretch her arms as a huge smile came across her face. "Oh, I don't know if I am up to eating a whole lot right now. I think I am just a little too excited about going on my honeymoon than eating." She gave a look to say *I'm sorry.* "Are you real hungry? 'Cause if you are, then we will go there and get something."

"No, not really. I just want to make sure that you are okay with us grabbing something small on our way."

"Yes, by all means, something small is fine." She got out of bed, noticing how Jim watched her every move. It made her almost feel like she was doing something wrong. "Are you okay? I noticed that you keep watching me, and I am not sure why."

"Oh, I'm sorry, honey. I was just thanking God in my mind for such a beautiful wife. You are amazing, right down to the way you get out of the bed." He smiled at her when he finished talking.

Mary was not quite sure what to say at this time, so she just gave him a smile back. She could tell that he loved her by the way he was with her, and the way he was always looking out for her made her feel very safe. "I have everything that we will need for us to take. Is there anything else that I might be forgetting?"

"I think you have gotten everything." He looked around to see if he was forgetting anything, but it seemed to him that all was good and they were ready to head out.

"Wait," said Mary, "we did forget one thing, and it's a biggie."

"What's that?" he asked, looking around the room again.

"We forgot to pray for a safe trip before we leave," she said, with a smile that made Jim's heart skip a beat.

"Oh, honey, you are so right. We must always pray and ask for God's protection on us." They stood right there with baggages and all and bowed their heads in honor and reverence to God and began to pray and thank Him once again for uniting them together.

23

The Honeymoon

Morning was here, and the two had their things packed for their two-week getaway. Jim took ahold of his and Mary's baggages to carry them down to the car.

"Are you ready, my beautiful wife?"

"Yuh, my handsome man." She chucked as she said that. Although it had been several months since she walked away from the Amish faith, she was still trying to get used to talking like the English. Every once in a while, her old talk would come out and make Jim laugh slightly at her. Never did he make fun of it at all but found it cute in a way hearing *yuh* instead of *yeah* or *yes*.

They packed the car with what they had for their trip, and they were off for a good breakfast then on the road. Mary was excited to see where Jim planned on taking her for their honeymoon. Secretly she wished that he would just tell her where they were going or at least give her some kind of a hint so she could at least envision a place in her mind. But until she either arrived to where they were going or he caved in and tell her 'cause of his own excitement of what he had planned, she would just try and picture a beautiful place on her own.

He interrupted her thoughts with, "We're here at Ben's. Do you think that you are ready for something to eat now?"

"Yuh, I think that I have a little more appetite than I did when I first woke up."

Jim walked around to her side of the door and opened it for her, taking her by the arm and walking with her. "I want everyone to see that you belong to me," he said, chuckling.

Mary gave a smile when she heard him say that. Even though it was different coming from him, she knew that he loved her and thought that she was a pretty woman because he had never been shy telling her so. But this was something she never heard him say, not even when teasing her. She was not quite sure how to take it.

Jim noticed that she didn't say anything to what he said. He wondered if his sense of humor might have upset her. "You're not upset with me for what I said, are you, honey?"

"No, I have just never heard that before, not quite sure how it was meant."

"Honey, I was just teasing with you, even though I do want others to know that I married the prettiest woman alive. I am proud that you married me, and I am so glad that God brought us together."

"I will get used to all the talk that you say in teasing with me. Just be patient with me. I am really trying to be like the English."

"Honey, I want you to be like who you are. It was how you are now that I am attractive to, not someone or something like all others. I could have had all others, but I waited for the right woman. Honey"—he turned her toward him before walking in the restaurant—"I need for you to understand, I have never really been in love. You, I fell deeply in love with because of who you are, even right down to where I will hear you say *yuh* every once in a while. I even love that part of you, so please, honey, don't think that I want you to talk or act more like the English. Be yourself because that is who I love."

Mary felt so good after his kind words she wrapped her arms around him tightly. "Thank you, Jim, for those words of love. I love you so much and can't wait to see what God has in store for us to do together."

"I feel the same way, but I think we are drawing an audience." He noticed that there were people in the restaurant watching them.

Mary took him by his hand, and they walked in to get something to eat. As they walked in, to their surprise, some of their audience began to clap their hands. Jim and Mary's face turned a bright red. Mary really began to laugh out loud when she saw Jim begin to bow for them, all the while laughing himself.

The waitress smiled at the couple. "So whom do I owe this honor to?" she asked with a little chuckle. "I'm sorry, I am only teasing. Where would you like to sit? At a booth or a window?"

Jim looked at Mary for an answer.

"Window would be nice," Mary she said, taking the look on her husband's face to mean that it was up to her.

Jim, being the man that he was, liked to play around at times. He looked at Mary. "See? You are already reading my mind. You knew just by me looking at you that it was all up to you to choose where we would sit."

"I guess that was already formed into me. Remember, I was through this before." As soon as those words fell from her lips, she regretted what she said. "I was out of line saying that to you, and I am sorry."

"No, honey, it's quite all right. You have been married before, and I am sure that if he wouldn't have passed, you would still be married, am I right?"

Mary looked at him, not knowing how to answer now that she was married to Jim. Seeing how he was waiting, she knew she must give an answer. "Yes, I am sure, honey, that I would not be sitting here with you right now. As much as I am pleased to be married to you, I would never have divorced him to marry another."

"I would never have wanted that either. I love you very much, and I am so glad that it was me that Samuel wanted to hook you up with." He smiled at her. "I am the luckiest man alive."

Mary didn't correct him saying that he was the luckiest man, but she did feel in her heart that she was very blessed.

The two ate breakfast then were on the road again, headed to a place unknown to Mary. She could not believe that Jim could keep it a secret for this long. All the time, she wanted to know where they were going so badly. But it didn't make a difference to him when she would look at him with pleading in her eyes. He was going to make sure that she would be completely surprised. He was so excited with the very thought of surprising her.

"Can you at least tell me how long of a ride it will be?"

"Well, I guess I should have asked you if you like boat rides."

Mary's eyes opened wide real quick at the thought of going on a boat. She had never been on one before, and what if it were to sink when they would be way out in the water? "No, you never did ask me that," was all she could muster out of her mouth in fear that his surprise would be with them on a boat.

"Oh, Mary, you don't think that you would like to go on a boat, I take it?"

"What if it sinks and we are way out in the water?"

Jim smiled without saying a word. He really didn't have it planned for them to go out on a boat. He was just watching to see what kind of reaction he would get from her if he were to plan a boat ride. But after seeing fear grip her at the very thought of it, he knew not to plan a boat ride.

"Jim, can I ask you a question, honey?" She looked at him with a scared look.

"Sure, honey, you can ask me anything."

"Are you being serious about us gong on a boat?"

He looked at her, not wanting to give her any idea of where he was taking her, but he also knew that he needed to let her know that they would not be going out into the water. "No, honey, I do not have a boat ride planned for us. I just wanted to know if that would be something you might want to do in the near future."

"Oh, thank you, honey. I would not care to do that. I have never been in a boat before, and I don't believe that I would like it."

"Honey, I would never have you do something that I was not sure you would want to do. What I have planned for us, I am sure you are going to love. I have talked with you about many things before we married, and I think I have a pretty good idea what you would like."

"I'm sure I would. It's not going way out into the water, so I am sure I will like it."

The car ride got quiet. The two were in deep thought of what would come next. They drove for a few hours only having small talk. After many hours of driving, Jim decided to stop for them to eat and get a motel for the night.

"Are we there now?" Mary asked.

"Oh no, honey, not at all. I figured that this would be a good place to eat. Then we can get a place to stay the night then start out again after breakfast in the morning."

She looked at the place that he stopped at, and seeing that it was a well-known place, she didn't mind stopping in and getting a bite to eat.

"Honey, what time is it now?" she asked him as she did not wear any kind of watch to see for herself.

"It's half past six. I thought that maybe we have spent enough time in the car today. Maybe we might want to get a nice place to sleep and get into a nice hot tub, what do you think?" he asked, raising his eyebrows.

"A hot tub, huh? Well, I think I know what that is, but maybe you might want to explain it to me just to make sure that I am thinking of the right thing."

Jim explained it to her and watched the expressions on her face as he talked. "So tell me, how does this sound to you?"

"I guess I can try it. I've never been in something like that before. But I'm sure with you next to me, everything will be all right."

After they ate, Jim went about looking for a nice motel that had a hot tub for his wife and himself to relax in. He very much wanted to give her things that she had never had before and do things that she had never done before.

"Hey, look it right here," he said, looking at a sign all lit up. "Hot tub and indoor swimming pool with breakfast. Honey, I think this is about the best we are going to get around here. Does this sound okay to you?"

"It sounds wonderful. I think it's a good idea to get out of the car for a while. I didn't realize until we got out to eat how sore my bottom feels." She chuckled when she said that.

The two got their room for the night, and Jim could hardly wait to get Mary into the hot tub. He knew that with her coming from the Amish background, she would not have been into one before. He waited to see if she would undress to get into it, being that it was in their room at the motel and not out in the open for all who wanted to get into it. He stood there and motioned to her with his hand toward the tub, but she just stood there, smiling at him.

"Okay, I guess I will make the first move," he said as he undid his pants' buttons then his zipper.

Being the second time for the two to ever be alone together, she was still shy for her new husband to see her undress and then naked.

"Okay, now turn your head so I can undress," she asked, smiling but very shy.

"Come on, honey. We are married, and there is no shame for me, your husband, to see you."

"But I'm shy."

"Honey, you are beautiful and amazing. I love you as you are. I will turn my head for you for now," he said as he did turn his head for her to undress then get into the tub.

"Okay, I'm in now. You can turn back around." She went as far under the water as she could without her head going under.

Jim came over to her and hugged her and began to kiss her all over. She responded better to him than he thought she would.

"Thank you, Jim, for loving me."

"Oh, honey, you don't have to thank me for loving you. I love to show you that I love you. I am so glad that you decided to marry me."

The two stayed in the hot tub until their skin began to shrivel. They laughed at how their hands looked so old. Then they decided to go to bed for an early rising and get back on the road again.

"Good morning, honey," Jim said, looking at Mary as she peeked her eyes open when the light came shinning through the opening of the curtain.

"Now, how long have you been lying there staring at me?" she asked with a slight grin, bringing the sheet up to cover half her face to where her eyes were the only ones showing.

"Not long. I just woke up a few minutes ago myself. I didn't want to wake you when you looked like you were sleeping so soundly."

"Oh, I was sleeping very well. This bed is very comfortable," she said as she began to push down on the mattress.

"I slept pretty good too. I thought that it was a nice mattress also. I wonder what kind it is," he said as he lifted the sheet to check out what kind it was.

"What's it say?" she asked out of curiosity.

301

"It says it's a foam mattress. For this to be a foam mattress, it must be very thick. I wonder where one would get one like this in out of town?"

"In the way of the Amish, we never had anything come close to being like this. Honey, I know that I only slept on your mattress just the one time at your home, but it was very comfortable to me as well."

"First of all, honey, it is our mattress and our home. There is no more mine and yours. We have things together now. But I do agree, it is comfortable. I paid a lot of money for that mattress, but I have to say, I think that I like this one more. I mean, if I could choose which I'd rather have, I'd say this one. I slept like a baby last night."

"I say a bed with you and I in it is all that I need." She got out and began to gather some clean clothes to get a shower before leaving the motel.

"How'd you like some company to come in there with you?" he asked, giving a huge smile.

"Really? I've never showered with anyone before. Well, I guess that is silly for me to say that. We never had showers all my life growing up. Until I came to stay with Katie, it was my first time having one." She looked at Jim as she was talking about never having showered until the last year. Then seeing his eyes get wide, she knew she must say something in her defense. "Oh, Jim, you look as if I had never washed until I stayed at my daughter's. Come on, we Amish do take baths."

"I'm sorry, Mary, it's just when I hear you say certain things, I guess it surprises me 'cause I forget so many times that you came from a different background from me. I really mean no disrespect when I give a certain look. I've taken showers all my life, so when you said that you have never showered until you came to live with Katie, it just seemed almost like you were teasing with me, although I do understand."

"I'm glad we have that cleared up. And as for you joining me in the shower, would you mind terrible if we wait on that for just a while longer? This whole thing seeing each other so soon after we married is still knew to me. Even though we did go in the hot tub together for a long time, I did try to keep myself hidden as much as possible."

"Mary, I will wait until you are ready, and when you feel that you are, then just let me know. I will not rush nor push you before you feel ready."

"Thank you, Jim. I know why I married you now. You are the sweetest, kindest man that I know. I love you."

"I love you too. Now, you go ahead and get one so I can get one before we leave too."

The two were headed back on the road again, going to a place that was unknown to Mary. Oh, how she wished that Jim would cave in and let her in on the big surprise. The waiting was more than she could take. She just had to know what to expect. She found herself ready to ask Jim again where they were going when she realized she was out of control with her thinking.

Come on, Mary, she told herself. *Just stop it. Get ahold of yourself. You are a grown woman. Stop acting like a young child wanting something that you just can't have.*

"I've been thinking, Mary," Jim interrupted her thoughts.

"Oh," she said, thinking that maybe now he was going to tell her where they were going. She was sitting on the edge of the seat. She was so sure that he was going to give it away.

"I was thinking about the mattress that we slept in last night. How would you feel about us getting one just like it when we get back home?"

"Oh, Jim, there is no need to do that for me at all. I love the one that we have at home." Although she was not telling him a lie when she said that, she still felt deep within herself that she did sleep like a baby on the mattress—or should she say *foam*—last night.

"I can put the one we have in our room in the spare bedroom so we can have just what we really want. Mary, I have to say that whatever ya call it, it was so nice and comfortable. I would really like to pick one up just like that." He looked toward her, waiting for an answer.

"It's your money, Jim. You may buy what you like."

"Mary, it's not like that anymore, honey. What's mine is yours now. We are married, honey."

"I'm sorry, Jim, I really am. This way is so different to me. I never had much say about things like this before."

"I know, and it's okay. I am just letting you know that I want you to make decisions with me about things that pertain to the house."

"Okay, I will try to remember that. Yes, Jim, I would love to have a foam like the one we slept on last night. It really was a good sleep."

Jim looked at her with a smile. "There, now that wasn't so hard now, was it?"

"No, I guess not. Who knows, maybe I just might really like this way of living." She smiled back with a wink.

The two talked for a long time, making plans together where they would go on their next vacation. Mary was unsure where they were going now. She knew that he really wanted this to be a nice surprise to her, and she was sure that it would be. After all, she never went anywhere for a vacation before. Deep in her heart, she was hoping that she would like where they were going. She didn't want to disappoint him in any way at all. *Oh God, please help me to love whatever Jim has planned for us to do.*

"We don't have much farther to go, honey," he said with excitement in his voice.

Up until she heard those words come from him, she did not pay to much attention to where they were driving toward and what it looked like outside. Now her eyes were wide open, and she was looking at everything they drove by past.

"It sure is pretty around here."

"Yes, it is a nice place. That is why I wanted to bring you here. Do you know where we are?"

"No," she said as she looked for signs that might give it away. Then driving by a sign that said "Strawberry Festival," she said, "Are we at Strawberry Festival?"

He chuckled at what she said. That was not the name of the place but the name of something that happened every year in Traverse City, Michigan. He knew that Mary loved strawberries and had planted some at Katie and Samuel's home, so he wanted to take her where everything was all about them for a week. Although at first his plans were to take her to the Grand Canyon, he changed his mind, knowing how much she loved strawberries.

"No, honey, this is a place that, for one full week, is all about strawberries. They have this every year, and people come from all over the nation for this. I really wanted to surprise you with something that you have never done before, and that is seeing everything done in strawberries, all the ways of making things and dressing up dishes with them. What do you think?" he asked her, all excited.

"I think there are a lot of people here, that is for sure, and I see there are even Amish buggie s here parked at different places."

When she saw them, something inside her belly felt like it was turning with excitement, almost like she knew if they would be here, then it must be an okay place to be. Even though she knew in her heart that Jim would not be part of the sinful things of the world, seeing the Amish walking about just confirmed it that much more.

"Now, honey, I know that we have driven for quite sometime. Do you want us to go to the hotel first to drop off our things or stop at a couple places before going there?"

She was excited about what she was seeing with all the banners hanging all over showing strawberries in ever which way manageable. "Can we stop first and see what all this is?" She was looking at where some of the Amish were walking.

He noticed as he drove by them that she turned her head to look toward them. "How about us stopping right here, honey? Maybe you can talk with them."

"Really?"

He heard excitement in her voice. Then all of a sudden, that excitment he heard went down to a, "Nuh, I better not."

"Why?"

"Well, the Amish have nothing to do with us when we leave the faith."

"But these Amish don't know that you were ever Amish, honey," he tried to explain it the best that he knew how. "So my guess is that they may talk with you. What do you think?"

"I never thought of it that way. Yes, they should talk with me then, not knowing that I was once Amish." That excitment she felt at first was swelling up again inside her. "Yes, Jim, I would like for us to stop. I just want to see all these delicious strawberries. After all, this is why we came here, right?"

Jim listened to her talk as she stared at everyone walking, looking at all the booths set up as far as he could see on the sides of the road. He heard every word she spoke and was wondering if she really was telling the truth about stopping for the strawberries—or was it because of all the Amish who was walking around? His guess was probably a little of both, but he was leaning more toward talking with the Amish.

"I am trying to find a parking spot." Just as he spoke those words and before he was done, he noticed someone backing out of a spot that was close to all the booths. "Hey, well, look it here," he said as he stopped. "I have a close spot for us right here."

"Oh, good, I'm glad. I was almost getting to wonder if we would find a place at all. I have never seen, in all my life, a place that was so crowded. One for strawberries is very surprising to me."

"Are you pleased, honey? I really wanted to make this something that you will never forget. I know how you love strawberries, and I wanted you to see this place."

"Yes, of course, I am very pleased. Thank you so much for bringing me here. May we go and begin to do some sightseeing?"

"As you wish, my dear," he said in a teasing manner as he held out his arm for her to take. "Let's go and get us some strawberries."

"Let's," she said in a tone almost unrecognizable to him.

The two walked around, looking at everything that was on display—well, all the things that had something to do with strawberries. Mary had never seen so many ways of making something with them in all her life, and she came up with a few recipes on her own, back in the days of living on the farm.

"Jim," Mary called to him. He was at a table just down from where she was.

"Yeah?" he shouted back, trying to get above everyone who was talking around them.

"Can you come here for a minute?" she asked.

"Sure, honey." Worry hit him by the way she asked for him.

"Would you mind if we were to go find our hotel? I am so tired of walking, and I think that the sun is getting to me."

"Sure, let me pay for what I was getting over here, and we will get going." Although he never said another word to her, he had his own questions inside him. The sun getting to her he felt that alone was strange, for he knew that the Amish were ones that stayed outside in the heat for hours. But nonetheless he would go if that is what she wanted.

She walked back with him to his table not saying anything, although she was hoping they would find a close hotel to go to. She felt troubled inside watching all the Amish walking around, and not one of them could tell that she was part of them at one time. She couldn't understand why this was bothering her so much. She thought that was what she wanted, until she purposely made it a point to stop and talk to several of them just to see what would happen. But after some talked back with her, even if it was just in small words, and some just smiled, she felt as though she was never part of the Amish at one time. This left her feeling sad deep inside, and she did not know how to tell Jim what was really going on with her. Why the sudden desire of leaving something so wonderful—strawberries in every way possible? Yet she needed to find a hotel to escape to in a hurry.

"Are you okay, my love?" Jim asked in a curious tone as to why they were leaving. He had hoped to give her the very best of a honeymoon that he could think of.

"I'm sorry, Jim. I am feeling a little overwhelmed. I hope you don't mind. I think it could be the long ride here and seeing all the Amish and not one of them could tell that I came from the Amish lifestyle. Please forgive me, honey. I will feel better after a bit of rest."

"Not a problem. I aim to please my beautiful wife," he said as he gave her a big smile then a wink.

Finding a nice place to stay for the next several days, Jim and Mary had a wonderful time at the Strawberry Festival and going to an amusement park. The two decided to head back home.

24

A Surprise to Be Told

Following their homecoming, Jim and Mary were surprised that Katie and Samuel had a homecoming party for their return.

"Oh, Mama!" Katie said as she hugged Mary as soon as she walked through the door. "I sure missed you. So tell me, how was the honeymoon?"

"Oh, honey, it was wonderful. Did Jim tell you where he was taking me?"

"No."

"He took me to Traverse City to the Strawberry Festival. I just couldn't believe it when we got there. There were so many ways to use strawberries. I thought that I knew them all." She started to laugh.

"I guess you had a good time then, huh?"

"More than I ever thought possible. He took me to a fair. Can you believe it—a fair? I have never been to one of them in all my life. I was kind of scared at first to get on a ride, but he assured me that it would be okay."

"I am so glad that you two enjoyed yourselves. Come on in, Mama. We have a surprise for you."

As Mary walked all the way in, she saw different people from the church she had been attending for several months now clapping their hands.

"Congratulations to you and Jim," a woman from the children's ministry said as she hugged Mary. "I always knew right from the beginning that the two of you would wind up getting married."

"Oh, thank you, Tami. I'm sorry that we didn't have a big wedding for everyone to come too."

"Oh, don't worry about that any at all, sweetie. That was your big day, and I understand wanting something small and quiant."

"It was small but very lovely. We had a grand honeymoon too. Although it was wonderful, I found myself getting lonesome for home. And I sure missed my grandchildren."

"Hey, I understand that too. Troy and I went for a trip a few months ago. We're supposed to be gone for a month, but it ended up being two weeks. I got lonesome for home too." She chuckled when it came time to say about her also getting homesick.

The night was filled with fun and laughter. Mary enjoyed the time with her friends and family. Then it was time for her and Jim to go back home. Jim was pleased to see that

Mary enjoyed her time with everyone, but he too wanted to have his wife at home with him, relaxing after a nice trip and from the surprise from Katie and Samuel.

It was a new beginning for Jim and Mary. The two were excited to see what plans God had for them to do together. They knew that what they did want, before Jim was to leave for the office, was to read the Bible together each morning while having their morning cups of coffee.

"Mary, would you like to start off reading today? Or should I?"

"I'd like you to if that's all right."

"Okay, I will read from Galatians 3." He began to read it. Then they talked about the meaning while drinking their coffee.

"I am really going to love being married to you, honey," Mary stated after they read and talked about what they read.

"I'm glad to hear that," he said as he pulled her close, giving her a gentle kiss. "I know I am going to enjoy every day being married to you too. I thank God He brought the two of us together. I am going to enjoy the journey getting to know everything there is to know about you, my dear."

"Oh, now you have got to be the sweetest man alive. I feel the same way, honey. I want to know everything about you too."

Katie and Samuel were also having their morning cups of coffee at their home, talking about her mom and Jim.

"I believe my mother has got to be one of the happiest women I have ever seen before."

"I think you're right. I was watching her whenever she talked about her and Jim last night. She glowed at the thought of being married to him. I am so glad they found each other."

"Found each other?" Katie laughed. "Yeah, at the hand of you bringing the two together."

"Are you saying that I didn't know what I was doing?"

"No, of course not. I am very happy that you did think they would be a good couple."

"A great couple." He laughed, getting the last words in before heading outside to go into the fields. "Love ya. Have a good day, honey."

"You too. Don't stay too long if it gets real hot out. Make sure you drink lots of water," she reminded him. As she closed the door behind her, Katie knew she wanted to call her mother up.

"Hello," a voice from the other end of the phone rang out.

"Mama, it's me, Katie."

"Good morning, honey. I was just thinking about calling you up to see what you and the children's plans are for today."

"That's what I was calling you about. I was wondering what you were doing today."

"Well, do ya want to get together and maybe take the children down to the water park? I think it would be nice before the men come home for the evening."

"Yeah, Mama, that does sound good. I will have to wake them and get them something to eat. Then I will come pick you up."

"While you are doing all that, I will pack us up some lunch in a basket. How does that sound?"

"That sounds great. I will be there within the hour."

The two ladies hung up the phone, knowing that they were going to spend the entire day together. Katie was really looking forward to it. She had missed spending time with her mother. She went some months after she and Samuel got married without seeing or talking to her mother, just to have her da die and then her mama moving in with her and Samuel to her mama getting married and moving out. Now Katie was going to be with her again without the men being there. She loved having the husbands around at times, but she also liked it when she and her mama could talk among themselves.

Katie had the children all fed and ready to head out the door when Samuel called her from his cell phone. "Hello," she answered.

"Katie."

"Yuh, Samuel? Is everything all right?"

He noticed at first how she sounded like they were still of the Amish faith, but he never said anything to her about that. He had other things on his mind. "Katie, I have some terrible news to hand to you."

"What terrible news, Samuel?" She wondered what it could be, knowing that he and her mother and the children were all right. "What news, Samuel?" she repeated herself, not hearing him say anything more.

"Katie, Emily is gone."

"Emily? What do you mean, Samuel? Emily is gone? Gone where?" she asked.

"Katie, Emily was traveling at night last night while we were celebrating at home with Jim and your ma. A man driving a big truck didn't see her buggy and hit her from the back, killing her." He became silent. Then he got worried not hearing anything come from Katie. "Katie, honey, are you there?" he talked louder.

"How can that be? She always hated to go out after dark. Hit by a truck? How could he not see her if she was in front of him?" she got louder, as if she was screaming at him.

Samuel could tell by the tone in her voice that she was not taking the news of Emily very good at all. "Honey, I am coming home right now."

Katie never made it past the door when she turned around to go sit down at the table and the tears began to flow.

"What's wrong, Mama?" asked Mike.

She looked at the fear that was in his eyes; and seeing him and Leah both standing there, all ready to leave, she knew that she had to tell them something. "Honey, your pa just called and told me some very sad news. I don't think that we will be going after all, guys, I'm sorry. Mike, will you take Leah into the living room and find something for her to watch on TV?"

"Yes, Mama. Come on, Leah, I don't think that we are going with Grandma now to the water park. Mama said something sad happened, and she is crying now." Mike took Leah by the hand, and they walked into the other room.

Katie sat there in shock, knowing that the last time she spoke with Emily was not in the best of terms. How she hurt for the loss of her friend now more than ever. Over the years of not talking with Emily, she had thought about her many times and wondered if she married and had a family of her own. She even thought of how she would have loved to be able to be friends with her again, if that would have been possible.

But now Emily was gone. *But gone where?* Katie asked herself. Did Emily really have Jesus living inside her? Did she really know who He is? Was she now with Jesus in His kingdom, or was she lost forever in hell for all eternity? The thought of there being a chance of her not making it to heaven was just too much. Katie began to cry out loud to where her whole little-framed body shook as she sobbed. "Oh, Em," Katie cried out, "I'm so sorry for everything." Katie remembered how she would talk about not wanting to marry an Amish man, and her dear friend would tell her that was blaspheming and that she needed to stop.

Samuel walked in the house and saw her slumped over her chair at the table, crying her eyes out. "I'm so sorry about Emily, honey," he said as he embraced her.

She leaned on him as she cried until the phone rang. She just knew that it was going to be her mama, wondering what was taking her so long.

"Hello," Samuel answered.

"Samuel.?" Mary was shocked hearing him answer the phone, knowing that he was usually out in the fields at this time. "Is Katie right there?" she asked, wondering why he was home but didn't ask him.

"Mama," Katie said as she took the phone from Samuel.

"Katie, what is wrong? Why are you crying?"

"Mama," she cried, "Emily is dead." More tears ran down her face.

Mary could hardly believe what she was hearing. "Dead? But how? When?"

"Samuel said a big truck hit her buggy last night, killing my Emily." Katie's heart felt like it was being torn into pieces.

"How does Samuel know, honey? Who told him about it?" Mary was wondering if something got all mixed up. She knew that Emily never wanted to be out riding in her buggy after dark.

"I don't know how. I hurt so bad for her, Mama." Katie turned to look at Samuel. "Who told you of this, Samuel?"

"Mark Peters did, just today as I went to the feeding stables. He was there and said he saw the buggy get hit last night, and some of the Amish came running to the buggy, saying who it was in it."

"Mama, a man Samuel knows told him that he saw it happen last night, and others who were there knew it was Em in the buggy."

"Honey, I am coming right over. I will be there in a few minutes."

"Wait, Mama, how are you getting here?"

"I am going to drive."

"Mama, you can't do that. You have no driver's license."

"Jim has been teaching me to drive, and you have taught me too."

"Mama, I don't want you to get into any trouble."

Samuel heard what was going on, and he knew that he needed to help. "Tell her no need to drive. I will come get her."

"I heard him, honey. Tell him I will be waiting," replied Mary.

"She will be waiting for you, honey," Katie told Samuel with more sobs, tears filling her eyes again.

"Mama," called Mike, coming into the kitchen from the living room, "are you going to be okay?"

Wiping her tears from her eyes, she looked at the fear that was in her son's eyes. "Yes, buddy, I will be fine. I just heard something bad happened to a friend of mine, and it's made me very sad."

"Do you need me to help you, Mama, with anything?"

"Oh, honey, that is so sweet for you to offer, but I really need you to keep a close eye on Leah to make sure she is not getting into anything. Little one-year-olds can put things in their mouth, which is not good for them to do."

"Okay, Mama. But right now she is watching a cartoon."

"Will you go into the other room with her then, honey?"

He never replied anything to her and just turned and walked away, heading into the living room.

Katie watched as Mike walked away, feeling so sad about the loss of an old friend, then also of her son's look on his face when she told him that she wanted him to go into the other room. But right now, she needed to know what the Amish were going to do about laying her friend to rest. She hoped they would put aside the way they felt about outsiders because that was what she was considered now, an outsider. Now she wanted to somehow be able to attend the small gathering they more than likely would be having with friends and family for Emily.

"Honey," spoke Mary as she entered the house to be there for her daughter at this time. "I just can't believe this to be true. She has never liked going out after dark. What can this all mean?"

Katie looked at her mama, not knowing what she was talking about. "What are you saying, Mama?"

"What I mean, honey, is she went out after dark, and this sort of thing happened to her. Why her? Why now? After all this time, she never goes out, and then she finally does after dark, and she gets hit by a truck driver and gets killed. I'm sorry, honey, it just isn't adding up to me how that person driving the truck could not see her. She would have been better off not ever going out after dark like it had always been before."

Katie's tears didn't seem to dry up yet. The sobs for the loss of her friend were just too much. After all, she hadn't seen nor heard from Emily in several years, and those years had always, in some sense, been empty without her best friend.

"She never got to meet my children, Mama. She never got to see that I found God in a real way, one that I never have before. I just hurt so bad right now, and for her mother also," Katie cried.

"I know, honey. There is nothing that we can do about the loss of Emily, but we can be praying for her mama. This has got to be so hard on her right now, Emily being her only child after all."

The day came for the funeral for Emily, and Katie decided that she was going to attend even though she may not be welcomed. She would stand away from everyone else so as not to cause a scene. She watched as the bishop began to speak about Emily. Katie tried to listen to every word that he was saying, but she could only hear parts of what was being said. She noticed that some had noticed her standing under a tree nearby, but she was far enough away so as not to see the looks on their faces. After it was over, she left quickly so no one would come to her and tell her she was not welcomed. Returning to her home, where her mama stayed watching her children so she could go to her friend's funeral, Katie noticed while pulling into the driveway that her mama had the children outside, playing with them.

"How was it, Katie?" Mary asked.

"I noticed that I got some looks, but no one came to me saying anything. I stayed at a distance so as not to cause a problem. I hurt for all of them and prayed silently as the bishop was talking about her. Thanks, Mama, for watching the children for me so I could go."

"What are grannies for?" Mary said as she poked Leah in her belly, playing with her.

"Thank you just the same, Mama."

"Honey, I need to get home. I will need to start cooking the meal before Jim gets home." Mary gave Katie a hug and told her to hang in there. "There will be brighter days again soon, Katie girl."

"Mike, let's go, buddy. We need to take Granny home now," Katie spoke in a louder voice so he could hear as he was on the other side of the yard, playing on a swing set.

"Okay, Mama, I'm coming."

On their way home from dropping off Mary, Mike decided to ask some questions, "Mama?"

"Yes, son?" responded Katie.

"Are you all done crying over your friend now?"

"I think so, honey." Katie wondered if all the crying she had been doing since hearing about Emily's death had been hard on her son, seeing her crying all this time.

"I'm glad that you are all done, Mama. I didn't like seeing you sad all the time. I love to see you play with Leah and me. I sure hope no one else dies, Mama. I never want to see you be sad again."

She smiled while driving and listening to him speak what was on his mind and heart. "Thank you son for making me feel better. I love to play with you and your sister, and I know that I have been hurting over the loss of my friend."

Weeks seemed to fly by after her mother getting married and her friend passing away before Katie got a phone call from her ma that was so shocking to her that it left her speechless for a while.

"Hello."

"Katie, this is Mama. Are you and Samuel going to be home tonight? Jim and I really need to talk with you."

"Yes, we will be home, but what is this about? I mean, Mama, you sound so different right now. Your tone of voice is different. What's going on? Why do you sound so mysterious?"

"Like I said, honey, we need to come and see you face-to-face. I don't want to say anything over the phone. Is that all right with you?"

"Sure, Mama. Why don't the both of you come over for supper?" Katie offered.

"Okay, that is good. What time?" she asked.

"How does six o'clock sound?"

"That is good for us, honey. We will see you then."

The two women hung up the phone, leaving Katie so unsure of what was going on. "Why is she acting so strange right now?" she asked herself. "I just can't imagine what this can be about," she continued to question herself as to why and what for. "Oh well, whatever it can be, I better get supper started, or we all will be going hungry tonight."

Mike sat in the other room, watching his mama begin to take things out of the refrigerator then the cupboards, all the while talking to herself. He wondered what she was doing that she would be talking to no one but herself. Maybe he should go and see if she needed his help with anything.

"Can I help you, Mama?"

"Oh no, thank you, honey, I got it. Your granny is coming for supper tonight, and I was just getting it started is all."

"Okay." Mike turned to walk away when he heard her start talking low again to herself. Turning his head to look back at her, he saw her pay no mind to what he was doing and continued to make supper. *I have never seen her talk to herself like this before*, he thought to himself, but he left it alone and went into the room where Leah was watching cartoons.

"Hello, honey," spoke Samuel as he came into the house from working all day.

"Mama and Jim are coming for supper. They will be here any minute."

"Oh, that's nice. What are we having to eat?"

"Chicken and dumplings—does that sound okay?" she asked, hoping that it did.

"Hmm, it sure does. I love the way you make that dish. You make the best like no other does, that's for sure."

"Aww, honey, that is so sweet of you to say. Mama called, asking if we were going to be home tonight 'cause she and Jim have something to talk with us about."

"Oh, really? She didn't say what it's about?"

"No, I even asked her, but she said she wanted to talk to us face-to-face."

"You don't think that they are having problems with each other, do you?"

"Oh heavens, no, Samuel. Mama would have talked to me about that before now. We Amish—" she stopped herself. "Well, Mama would never go that far as to have problems in her marriage then still come over with Jim."

"Yeah, I guess you're right. I better get cleaned up real quick before they get here then."

"Yeah, make it quick. They will be pulling in at anytime now," Katie commented.

Samuel wasn't gone but for a minute when Jim and Mary pulled in the driveway. Katie took the food off the stove while it was good and hot, setting it on some pot holders then onto the table. She could hardly wait for them to come into the house. She wanted to know what was so important that her mother couldn't tell her over the phone.

"Samuel, hurry. Mama and Jim are here now," Katie raised her voice just a little in hopes that Samuel would hear her.

"Is that quick enough?" he asked as he entered the room. "I have never washed up so fast in all my life," he said as he walked over to the door to open it for their company. "Welcome, welcome. This is a nice surprise. Come on in. I believe that Katie has just finished up with supper."

"Thank you for having us here for supper tonight," Jim commented.

"I will dish up the children some food then let them sit in the kitchen so we can talk while eating in the dining room." Katie started to get the food for Leah and Mike.

"Let me help you, honey," Mary offered.

"I got this, Mama. You and Jim go ahead and sit down at the table with Samuel. It will only take a minute." She hurried along so she could hear what was going on with her mother. "Okay, Mama, I am done with the children for now. Can you tell me what is going on?"

Mary had just sat down next to Jim at the table when she was immediately put on the spot. Taking ahold of Jim's hand then looking at her daughter, she said, "Katie, we have something that we feel would be best said in person."

"Mama, what is it? Please tell me. I have just about gone crazy all day thinking about it."

"Katie, you are going to be a big sister."

"Big sister?" Katie repeated with complete shock. "You have got to be kidding me, Mama. Really? You're going to be having a baby?"

"Honey, it came as a big surprise to us too. But we are very excited about this."

Katie sat there looking at Samuel. She just could not believe what she had just heard. She noticed how her mother was looking at her, and then she knew she must speak up. "Mama, I am happy for you and Jim, I really am. I guess I just never thought that you would ever have another child is all. I'm just surprised is all."

"Are you really happy, Katie girl? I know that this has got to be a huge shock to you. It is to Jim and me both also. I really never thought about having another baby after all this time."

"Well, buddy," Samuel said, looking at Jim, "what do you have to say about this? You know, with you going to be a da—I mean, a dad?" He chuckled.

"Well, I am pleased, of course, but like Mary said, this was not planned. We never talked about us having a child together, so this is what I believe, and it don't mean that you have to agree with me. I think this was all of God's plan for whatever reason. Look, your mom and I, Katie, are in our higher thirties. I have no children of my own, and when I married your mom, I thought that I never would. Well, we are going to be great parents to this little one and dedicate this child to the Lord."

"I couldn't have said that any better myself, buddy. I say to the both of you, congratulations on having this baby." Samuel looked at Katie after making his speech, wondering if she would have something to say afterward.

"I am happy for you, Mama, and for you too, Jim. I do believe that you both will be great parents. Hey, you have to look at it this way. I turned out to be a pretty good person." Katie smiled after her comment.

"You turned out to be a great person, honey. I am proud to call you my wife," Samuel told her.

"Samuel is right, Katie girl. You are the sweetest soul I know. You are funny, loving, and the gentlest person. I am proud to have you as a daughter."

They talked about family and many other things before calling it a night. Katie went to bed that night feeling like a part of her was going to be closed off after her mom would have her baby.

25

A New Member

Days and weeks then months seemed to fly by so quickly. Mary seemed to be getting bigger in her belly every day. Katie watched as her ma made plans for the baby, wondering if she ever did the same when she was carrying her some twenty-two years ago. As Katie was deep in her thoughts on the what-ifs, she heard a loud scream. Turning around, she began to run toward the back room where her mother was last. She saw the look of horror all over her mother's face as she entered the room.

"Call Jim. My water just broke." Mary was bent over as if the baby was ready to come now. "Hurry, honey. If this baby is anything like you, he will be coming anytime."

Katie helped her mother to the bed then called Jim. "Jim, it's Mama. Her water just broke. I will rush her to the hospital. Why don't you meet us there?"

"I'm on my way. Is she doing okay?"

"She…she…I need to hurry 'cause he could come anytime."

"Okay, tell her I love her, bye."

Katie knew that he was ready to leave his office before she even had Leah and her mother in the car. "Let's go bye-bye, Lele," she said to Leah, using the little pet name she gave her. "Mama, can you get up so I can get you to the hospital? I called Jim, and he is going to meet us there."

"Help me up, will you, honey?" Mary held her hand out for Katie to grab.

"Ready?" Katie said as she grabbed her hand. "One, two, threeee." She pulled a little hard in hopes of her ma getting up with the first pull. "Okay, now can you walk out to the car, Mama?" she asked after the first time was a success.

"I think so. I know this is what I must do if I want to see my baby born in a hospital this time."

When she heard her mother say that, Katie then thought about how she was never born in a hospital. So this would be the first time for her mama to do something like this. "It's going to be great, Mama. They take very good care of you and the baby. When I had my two babies, I was well taken care of by them."

As her mother was walking very slowly to the car, Katie could hear her talking just above a whisper. Then a louder voice came from her, "Katie, did you hear me, honey?"

"What, Mama?"

"I don't think that I am going to make it to the hospital. I feel the baby wanting to come now, honey."

"Hold on, Mama. I will drive fast. You will be okay. I'll never let anything happen to you, Mama," Katie tried to reassure her, but she herself was not quite sure what to do if her mother was to start having the baby before getting to the hospital. "Okay, Mama, I got Leah in her seat now. I will hurry as fast as I can."

"Honey, please be careful. If all else fails, you can deliver the baby." Mary seemed to be trying to encourage Katie, in hopes of her not thinking she couldn't deliver the baby.

Katie looked at her mother in horror. "Mama, please hold on. I am almost there. It's only a few miles away." She knew that her mother had already gotten to the point of her pushing. "Hold on, Mama, just a couple more minutes."

Katie pushed the pedal down even more, now driving faster than ever before. She was praying quietly, asking God to help her not wreck her car. "We're here, Mama. There is Jim standing there with some nurses and a gurney to put you on. Jim, please help her!" Katie yelled out, barely stopping the car. "She is already pushing. The baby is ready."

Katie watched as they put her mother on the gurney and quickly pushed her toward the open door of the hospital. "Dear Lord Jesus," Katie pleaded as she stood there watching her mama became lost behind the doors now, "please help my mama and my little brother she is about to have. Help everything be okay for them, in Jesus's name, amen."

Katie parked her car then took Leah out. They walked up to the hospital's doors. "Well, Lele, let's go see if you have a baby uncle yet." Katie chuckled to herself at the mention of her baby having a baby uncle. Then she went on to say more, "Let's see if Mama has a baby brother yet."

Walking down the aisle that pointed directions to the delivery room, the two headed straight there. Katie happened to see a nurse come out of the room within a few minutes of her sitting down.

"Can you tell me if a lady named Mary just had her baby?" Katie asked the nurse.

"And who are you?" the nurse asked, not giving out any answers until she got some.

"I am her daughter, Katie. I just brought my mama in here."

"Then to answer your question, you have a beautiful, handsome little brother," she said with a smile.

"And, nurse," Katie called out before she left the room, "how is my mama doing? Is she all right?"

"Your mother is a strong woman. She and the baby are doing fine. Your dad—well, I think he is just beside himself with excitement."

"Oh, thank you, Jesus," Katie cried out. Then she looked at the nurse still standing there. "Thank you, nurse."

"You're welcome. Have a great day. You will be able to see her in a few minutes. I'm sure your dad will come and get you when they are ready for visitors."

Katie noticed how the nurse used the term *dad* for Jim. That was the first time someone said that to her, but she understood it and never told her any different. "Thank you."

"How would you like to see your baby brother?" a voice came from behind a door that just opened up.

Katie quickly stood to her feet, taking Leah by the hand. "I'd love to," she spoke with a huge smile at Jim. "Congratulations, Daddy."

"Well, thank you. He is the cutest little guy. Come on in." He held the door open for her and Leah. "Look who I found sitting out in the waiting room," he said to Mary.

"Oh, Mama, I am so happy for you and Jim. He is so beautiful. Can I hold him?"

"Yes, you sure can," Mary said as she handed the baby over to Katie.

"What's his name?"

"Levi James."

"Oh, Mama, that is a very nice name. Look, Leah, this is your Uncle Levi."

Katie and Leah stayed at the hospital for a couple of hours holding the baby and talking with her mother and Jim. Then Katie knew it was time to go home before Mike was to get home.

"I have to go now, Mama. Mike will be home, and I need to get supper started. But I want you to know, I am so happy to have been blessed with this beautiful little baby boy as my brother." She chuckled. "I never thought that the day would come that I would ever have a sibling."

"Come back tomorrow, honey, if you're not doing anything, will you?" Mary asked.

"Yes, of course, I will, Mama. After I get Mike off to school, I will come back."

Katie was glowing on her way home, talking to herself just above a whisper, "I can hardly believe it. I am a big sister. He is just so cute, and I think that he looks some like me. I wonder if they will get any pictures of him." With that thought, she then realized that she had none of herself when she was small, knowing that the Amish never took pictures. "Well, I sure hope that Mama will get some of Levi. After all, she's not Amish anymore."

Samuel was happy for Jim and Mary. He was excited to see his best friend become a dad for the first time. "When your mother and the baby get out of the hospital, I think that we should have them over for supper. What do you think?"

"Well, Mama might not want to come over so soon, but I will go over to their place and make a nice meal for them and us. That way, she don't have to take Levi out so soon after leaving the hospital. And this way, she don't have to start cooking so soon either."

"I guess you're right. I wasn't thinking of that."

"Mama?" Mike asked.

"Yes, honey, what is it?"

"You have a brother now, huh?"

"Yes, honey, I do, and you will be meeting him very soon."

"Is he coming here today?" he asked.

"No, he's not, but we are going to go over to Grandma's in a day or so. I will find out tomorrow. Then you will be able to meet him."

Mary was able to leave the hospital after two days of stay. She was so excited to be able to come home to her husband with their son. She was still in shock that she was a new mama for a little baby boy. She had been a grandma for several years now. Then for her to be a mama again was just more than she ever thought could or would happen to her in this lifetime, so to speak. She wanted Katie and her family to come over so the grandchildren could meet their uncle.

"Jim," she asked, "will you please call Katie and Samuel and ask them if they would like to come over tonight after I get home?"

"Yes, honey, I will call. I'm sure they will want to come and see the baby, and also the baby's beautiful mom."

She laughed at the words of her husband being silly in his talk. "Yes, I am quite sure they will be coming to see me. You know good and well that they will come to see Levi Jim."

"Yes, they will, but I know that it is more important for Katie to see that you are doing okay after having the baby."

"She had come to see me every day since I had the baby. She knows that I am just fine. But I'm sure she will want to bring the children to see their uncle."

"Yes, dear," Jim said as he bent over and gave her a kiss on top of the head. "I know you are quite right. Are you ready to leave this place and go home now?"

"Yes, honey, we are ready," she said as she looked down at the baby in her arms, all snuggled up resting. "Please call them, honey."

"Yep, I will. Just as soon as we get in the car, I will call," he promised her.

When they arrived home, Mary noticed that Samuel's car was in their driveway. She just didn't see anyone in their car. "That's the children's car, but no one is in it by the looks of it."

"They must already be inside then." He stopped short before going on.

"It seems to be, but how is the question. I wasn't aware of anyone else having a key." She had a puzzled look written on her face.

"Well, let's get inside for little Levi to meet the rest of the family," Jim said as he opened up her car door.

As they were walking up the beautiful sidewalk that Jim put in himself with limestone, they were greeted at the door.

"Hello, Mama and Jim," Katie's voice seemed to echo as she talked.

"Hi, honey, what is that smell?" Mary asked with a huge smile coming from her, letting Katie know whatever she was cooking sure smelled inviting.

"Oh, I made a little something for you and Jim. I wanted you to be able to come home to a nice home-cooked meal," stated Katie.

"Now I know how you got in the house," Mary said, looking at Jim with a big smile. "You little sneak. But thank you for thinking of me, honey."

"Grandma, Grandma," yelled Mike as he came into the living room where everyone else was gathered. "You have a baby?"

"Yes, honey, I do. This is your Uncle Levi," Mary said as she brought the baby down to Mike's level.

"Yep, that's a baby for sure. Will he stay a baby for a long time?" He was very curious.

"Not too long. Look at you how much you have grown. It seems just like yesterday you were a baby. Now you are so big."

The family ate the meal that Katie prepared for them and stayed to visit for a while longer. On their way home, Samuel and Katie talked about her having a little brother now and how, when he would be older, Levi could come over and play with Leah. Katie knew that being shunned was not something that would ever take place in her life again, nor her children's. All and all, it was a good time watching their lives being transformed into more of the way the Lord would ask for them to be. Life was good, and they were excited to see what more God had in store for them.

|LIVE

listen|imagine|view|experience

AUDIO BOOK DOWNLOAD INCLUDED WITH THIS BOOK!

In your hands you hold a complete digital entertainment package. In addition to the paper version, you receive a free download of the audio version of this book. Simply use the code listed below when visiting our website. Once downloaded to your computer, you can listen to the book through your computer's speakers, burn it to an audio CD or save the file to your portable music device (such as Apple's popular iPod) and listen on the go!

How to get your free audio book digital download:

1. Visit www.tatepublishing.com and click on the e|LIVE logo on the home page.
2. Enter the following coupon code:
   d276-fd6b-6eee-b198-7e76-d038-8d81-3b9f
3. Download the audio book from your e|LIVE digital locker and begin enjoying your new digital entertainment package today!

CPSIA information can be obtained at www.ICGtesting.com
Printed in the USA
LVOW10s0353140716

495511LV00010B/90/P